A thrilling superhero journey that remains smart and thoughtful.

- KIRKUS REVIEWS (STARRED REVIEW)

Single Best Read of 2018...Every page compels you to look at our world differently— planting seeds of change in each of us. Our planet needs many more Biomen and Biowomen.

- H. SHOENECK, CREATIVE DIRECTOR, OGILVY'S

The cyberpunk story is awesome! The sci-fi visual effects that come into a reader's imagination during this story are stunning.

- C. AMATO, DEEP BRAIN STIM., BOSTON SCIENTIFIC

THE BIOMAN CHRONICLES

#2084 (BOOK 1)

A.L.F.I.E.

ALIFE MEDIA

SF
A.L.F.I.

CONTENTS

PART 5

INTO THE HEART OF ROBO-DARKNESS

PART 6

THE IMPOSSIBLE BIOMAN

A.L.F.I.E. designed story world of #2084 and its themes to resonate with global audiences who are awakening to the realization that a detached technological society based on unsustainable consumption and "fake news" is leading, not only to ecological disaster, but also to crisis of the human spirit and the real possibility of big brother enslaving humanity for generations.

#2084 is the first book of The Bioman Chronicles. Its explorations of science, technology, and consciousness are for readers who long to deepen their connection with nature, with each other and gain the courage to take authentic action.

PART 1
BIOGENESIS, EARTH DAY 2074

1 / *INCORPORATION*

LOOMING over the southern end of Central Park, on the flooded island of Manhattan, a single monolithic skyscraper towered above all others. A scolding finger of dark stone jutting into the sky, casting its shadow over the toxic swamp.

In the tower's fortified penthouse was an advanced scientific laboratory. On a steel table, inside a glass temperature-controlled glove box, robotic hands manipulated a test tube. Inside, a delicate needle injected the empty nucleus of a single egg cell with DNA. The engineered cell split.

Continuing to divide, the cells flourished. After a few days, the zygote was transferred to an artificial womb. There the embryo developed into a creature resembling a tadpole, gilled and slippery, then something birdlike, fetal with giant eyes and curled limbs. A tail grew and retracted as the body morphed into its mammalian form, finally resembling an unborn human baby boy.

A sleek helmet encasing the fetus' maturing skull directed billions of nanobots to nudge the burgeoning brain cells to grow in patterns that precisely mirrored a prescribed blueprint. Any deviations were pruned away.

Suspended in a tank filled with clear gel, the developing body was fed through tubes with nutrients and growth accelerant. He progressed through infancy and childhood at a hyper-accelerated rate. Pricked with hundreds of needles, the unnamed, unnatural toddler twitched rhythmically, kicking and swimming, as he was artificially exercised.

His pod was emblazoned with the words:

Neuro-Clone #9

Blackstone Scientific

As the two-year-old body neared the biological age of 10, the freshly-minted mind inside became aware, from the memories woven into his brain, that nearly everything in the cavernous laboratory around him was claimed with the same Blackstone logo, a bold letter B imprinted with thousands of tiny ones and zeros in a dense digital design.

The incubating clone had the memories of Arthur Blackstone, the genius founder of Blackstone Labs, the trillionaire creator of the Lucid operating system. Arthur was now an old man, shaky with tremors inside a sleek exoskeleton suit melded to his spinal cord that allowed movement and eased his worsening physical pain. Even in his current state, Arthur still took pride in inspiring more fear than admiration.

The 10-year-old neuro-clone and the 65-year-old body that Arthur lived inside were more than kin. For the elder, *father* wasn't the right word, not exactly, but it wasn't incorrect, either. Their DNA was exactly identical, differing only in that Arthur's epigenetic propensity for the incurable disease plaguing his brain had been removed from the new body's helixes.

An insistent, bluish light from a tiny camera drone passed across Arthur's wrinkled features as the device hovered between himself and the waiting host body in the clone pod. The 10-year-old body in the tank twitched as he integrated Arthur's current thoughts and experiences, recorded in real time. The drone floated silently, a Blackstone B logo embossed on its underside. Arthur's Helmholtz cavity blade design kept the compact robot's flying quiet. Projected by the drone's waiting teleprompter, the words of a prepared speech reflected on Arthur's milky eyes.

"Are you ready, sir?" asked Gabriel Benicolustro from his position behind a stainless steel table in the lab. The handsome, bulky technician in the open white lab coat was a descendant of the Ecuadorian Achuar, with the thick thatch of black hair and high cheekbones common to his tribal ancestors. He had been raised in Queens, absorbing his grandfather's stories of the rainforest. Gabriel's grandfather always claimed to be part of a line of shamans specializing in botanical healing, who believed that plants could guide the human species through visionary experiences in a kind of organic virtual reality.

Arthur knew that Gabe had no way to check the authenticity of those claims. The Ecuadorian rainforest was transformed into a giant industrialized cattle farm and the record of cultural Achuar information and artifacts were sadly incomplete. If Gabe still had contacts in the rainforest, he was keeping them secret, although Arthur had his suspicions.

When Arthur had bought the mind-transfer technology startup, he'd also acquired the services of its inventor. Gabe had proven exceedingly useful in imaginative engineering. When questioned by Arthur on the source of his ingenious solutions, Gabe explained that he relied on ancient meditation techniques which gave him exquisite control of the submodalities of his imagination. Apparently, he was able to clearly visualize and create complex processes and structures in the laboratory of his mind, where he was able to test out ideas before spending resources on real world experiments. Supposedly, he also carefully managed his diet to ensure optimal nutrition for neuronal activity. Suspicious, perhaps a little jealous, and missing his own chemically accentuated past, Arthur had Gabe's urine tested, but the results had showed no sign of nootropic usage. The only spike was in dimethyltryptamine, a chemical naturally produced by the body, but also the active ingredient in psychoactive botanicals, which perhaps lent some credence to Gabe's claims.

Gabe's size and strength were also advantageous when Arthur had so many enemies and such an infirm body of his own. Together they had survived three assassination attempts on Arthur's life in the past two years.

"Sir?" Gabe repeated. "Are you ready to record?"

"Yes," Arthur croaked. "How much time do we have, precisely?"

Gabe checked the readouts, his fingers poking and prodding the air as he made adjustments to the virtual display only he could see, his irises flickering from the microscopic LCD pixels embedded in his Lucid contact lenses. "We've scheduled your death for fifty-eight minutes from now."

"Start recording," Arthur ordered.

Gabe tapped an unseen icon in the air, and the drone's light flickered with multiple colors as its recorder switched on. "Go ahead."

Arthur took a deep breath, which caused the gills of his exosuit to expand. To protect his empire from the constant political, financial, social, and cyber-attacks by his multitudinous enemies all jockeying for his unprecedented and lucrative control over the global consciousness, it was crucial that the legitimacy of his heir would not be questioned, which made this rare public global broadcast necessary. He nodded, readying himself, and stared directly into the hovering drone's tiny camera.

"A neurodegenerative disease is laying claim to my mind," Arthur recorded, his voice only slightly quavering with infirmity. The words of the drone's teleprompter scrolled up on his own Lucid display as he spoke. "I am choosing to leave this plane of existence with my dignity still intact. I wish to face whatever is beyond with courage and clarity. Therefore, it is my last will and testament that my neurological and biological clone—" He waved his glove at the pod beside him. "Adam becomes my sole heir and successor to the Blackstone empire. My memory, my way of thinking, my very being have now been transferred to Adam. Through him, I shall be able to continue my endeavors . . . and serve humanity for . . . another. . . ."

Arthur trailed off, his eyes blinking blankly, his spittle-flecked lips frowning and gasping as he struggled to grasp the meaning of the next word on the teleprompter. He could see the word floating in contrasting blue letters against the white background of the lab: *gener-*

ation. But it made no sense to him. It meant nothing. It was a terrifying blank sequence of alphabetic characters that had no connection to its symbolic conception. Arthur gaped at the word, aghast.

"Cut," said Gabe.

The illumination from the drone blinked off.

Arthur's pupils dilated in adjustment, tightening to pinpricks in rage. He had been prepared for the betrayal of his body, but the treachery, the disloyalty of his mind turning against him made him grind his teeth. Furious, he raised his titanium-sheathed, servo-powered exo-glove, tightened it to a fist, and smashed it down on the mahogany table in front of him.

With a resounding crack, the wood splintered in a raw, jagged rupture.

Feeling a bit ashamed of his outburst in its aftermath, Arthur sat breathing in shallow gulps, letting his tensions abate.

Gabe softly asked, "Sir?"

"I'm sorry," sighed Arthur, "I'm having difficulty. . . ."

"It's all right," Gabe assured him. He blinked twice and his contacts flickered as he reviewed the footage. "We have enough to broadcast."

Arthur shook his hand free of the bashed wood, then traced the edge of the splintered section with his gloved fingertip. "The degeneration is happening faster than we expected."

"This will be the final scan," Gabe said, not without sympathy. Since Arthur's brain was continuously gaining new memories, Gabe scanned his employer's hypothalamus, constantly filtering out the damaged neurons and uploading the new patterns to Adam's developing mind. Gabe tapped on his virtual display, and the hovering drone projected a floating hologram of a brain in 3D, rotating in higher-than-life definition. Green laser lights illuminated the sections of Arthur's brain currently being scanned.

"Thank you for this," said Arthur, tottering over to Gabe in his exo-suit. "I know it's not what you signed up for." He glanced back at the pod containing his clone. "But Adam will become greater than I could ever wish."

Gabe consulted the readouts on his monitor, pulling up the data for the clone's physical incubation progress. "Even though we've removed the damage, there are still . . . risks."

"A lifetime's worth of experience in a ten-year-old brain," Arthur agreed with a sigh. He wobbled in his clunky boots and Gabe stood up to take the older man by the arm. Gabe's hefty but strong upper body had no trouble supporting Arthur's wizened frame, even with the exosuit's added weight. He guided Arthur over to a high-tech rig that looked a little like a sleek, modern electric chair, with a padded throne of brushed steel and a chrome headset that lowered in place.

With Gabe's help, Arthur settled onto the throne, his exoskeletal suit joints whirring almost imperceptibly as they eased him down. But when Gabe reached for his gloved hand, Arthur jerked it away. The impertinence of the Achuar!

"Remember?" Gabe asked. "Your DNA is needed so the system can ID you."

Grumbling, Arthur returned his covered hand back to the end of the padded armrest.

Gabe slid his finger across the back of the exo-glove's wrist, and the experimental technological garment peeled open along an invisible seam.

Inside the exo-glove, Arthur's hand was spotted and shriveled, trembling in the open air.

Gently, Gabe took Arthur's birdlike hand in his own meaty mitt, and raised Arthur's thumb up to press it against a small, glossy black sensor of the DNA scanner.

Beside them, a monitor flashed and shimmered with DNA sequences being analyzed, compared, and identified with blurry speed. After a moment, all the pairs latched into place and the scanner beeped softly.

ARTHUR BLACKSTONE, the monitor read. CEO BLACKSTONE LABS. WELCOME.

Arthur shifted uncomfortably inside his suit. "I'd like to have one final talk with. . . ," he said, "what's its name. You know. Myself. The other one."

"The stored copy of your mental-self is called SINE, sir," Gabe replied. The way he forced himself to keep his voice calm grated on Arthur's nerves as patronizing. Of course he knew what his stored consciousness was called! He'd conceived of it!

Arthur calmed himself with the thought that even though the word *soul* had been vanquished from the scientific lexicon, the precise nature of cognizance and the individual self still remained a mystery. Despite the best efforts of his research into the finest theories of philosophers, theologians, and scientists who had studied the concepts since the first glimmers of consciousness in our primordial ancestors, he had found only factual uncertainty, and that chain of historical doubt reassured him with the consistent scope of its unknowability. If Arthur's existence was anything, he was sure it was contained in his genes, his memories, and his experiential learning from life housed in the billions of interconnected neurons. If that could be replicated, then he might achieve a certain eternal . . . reincarnation? Resurrection? Rebirth? Restoration? Re—?

The mental fuzziness had returned, and Arthur squeezed his eyes shut, trying to hold on to the existential concepts and decisions that had once seemed to shine with such clarity.

Gabe tapped an icon on his personal screen and the chrome brain scanner began to lower. They both watched it carefully until it covered the wispy white hair of Arthur's head and enveloped his skull, connecting with a click to the back of the exosuit above the neck.

"That's right," said Arthur. "SINE."

Gabe paused before starting the sequence that would open communication with an enhanced electronic copy of Arthur's consciousness.

Arthur grunted at the delay. On his internal Lucid display, the caption Super Intelligent Neural Ectype appeared.

"The last time you tried to communicate," Gabe began, peering down, "it—"

"Until I am gone—" Arthur interrupted. His eyes lost focus, gazing blankly into the middle distance. He was slipping away so fast, too fast. He flared his nostrils with a deep breath, and he glared up at Gabe. "You do what I say."

"Yes, sir," replied Gabe.

Arthur waited as Gabe began the checklist of procedures and protocols that allowed him to communicate with the unnervingly cold, expansive, and perhaps immortal version of his own mind.

2 / THE TOWER

SIMULTANEOUSLY, a Helix multi-terrain vehicle in its space-jet configuration cruised through the orange and purple stratosphere at sunset. It soared high above the frothing whitecaps of the flooded Earth, a contrail cottoning out in its wake.

The Helix was the latest in Blackstone Space's extra-planetary multi-terrain vehicles. Designed to adapt to various inhospitable environments across the solar system, souped-up, fully-loaded versions could keep passengers safe beside the frozen nitrogen seas of Neptune's moon Triton, and survive the 460-degree Celsius afternoons on Mercury.

The current pilot, Penelope Blackstone, had a sleek boutique model custom-built for her and only used it to hop at hypersonic speed between her expensive homes on Earth. Her teenaged daughter Olivia Blackstone thought that was entirely indicative of Pen's personality.

Liv sat in the co-pilot seat of the luxurious cockpit. Even though the Helix could safely fly with its own automatic navigation system, Pen almost always preferred to control it herself. The vehicle's interior was as lavish as Penelope's astounding wealth could afford, paneled in tasteful rare wood, the walls and surfaces were lined with flowering vegetation as a nod to her bohemian attitude, which Liv knew was mostly a façade, even if the purple verbena flowers wavering around the cockpit were lovely. They had just come from their semi-annual visit to New York Fashion Week, which was a full-on waste of time, in Liv's opinion. She was a firm believer that who you were inside was what really mattered. The gentle wispiness of Pen's faux Earth Mother flowing scarves were a case in point that fashion was a false front.

Liv was occupied elsewhere, anyway. She fought back the sadness that kept rising up inside her, the sudden sharp reminders that her beloved, scary grandfather was losing his mind. She'd also heard that Penelope's ex-husband, Warren Montmartre, had won his Senate bid, which was bad news for everyone who wanted to keep even a speck of the remaining personal freedoms from being trampled by the frightening, ultra-conservative party he championed. Most of Liv's memories of Warren were from recordings and press conferences, as Pen had divorced him in the months after Liv's adoption, won full custody, and never allowed her daughter to interact with her ex again. There were untold stories there that Liv had never managed to get Pen to admit, or even mention, but Warren still loomed as a volatile, villainous figure from the half-formed, hazy recollections of her childhood. Grandpa Arthur wouldn't discuss Pen and Warren's relationship, either, and had only referred to Warren as "the personification of narcissistic self-interest disguised as patriotism," and "that jackbooted Fascist," but then Warren supported government takeover of Blackstone's many industries, especially the Lucid platform. After the divorce, Grandpa had refused to support this political campaign, and was not surprised when Warren aligned with the hawks and campaigned for the breakup of Blackstone's Lucid monopoly.

Now, given her grandfather's rapidly fading cogency, it was probably too late to get the full truth.

To keep her thoughts from wallowing in dark places, Liv focused on her Advanced Biochemistry homework, returning to her customized homepage through the latest generation of Blackstone contact lens-accessed display. Her Lucid system featured the cutting-edge "Good as Real" mixed-reality monitor. Unlike the old-fashioned versions where the LCD gizmo floated on top of the eyeball, Liv's higher-resolution prosthetic was implanted underneath her cornea, allowing for crystal-clear projection and a more natural-looking iris. Plus, unlike prior versions which had finite battery life, this new model was powered by Liv's personal electromagnetic power generator – her heart.

On her vision display, translucent icons for her favorite apps were arranged along the bottom of her field of view. As Liv's eyes scanned across the options, they rested briefly on her messaging app, and a "3" popped up, telling her how many new notes she'd received. Liv decided to check those later, or she'd get involved and never get to her Biochem. She double-blinked on her homework app and her most recent file reopened.

It was a worksheet on cell mitosis. On the upper right side, a small window looped a short 3D vid showing each stage of a cell's magical journey as it divided in two. As the vid progressed, certain vocabulary words were highlighted then floated on the left side: prophase, metaphase, anaphase and telophase. Liv grabbed each word in turn, dragging them to connect to the correct phase of the mitosis process.

Past the opaque edges of her Lucid display, Liv peered through the lower part of the glass bubble of the cockpit, noticing that the choppy seascape had changed color. She minimized her homework and stared down as they approached the border of the vast flood barrier that surrounded what remained of the island of Manhattan. On the eastern edge, the first foundations of a dome planned to encapsulate the sinking island were being built to replace the flood barrier.

As always, as they flew over the city's edge, Liv felt a twist in her stomach. The scale of the destruction at the margins was breathtaking, as was the scope of the wall built around the island to protect it. Brooklyn and Queens were completely submerged, with only the hills of Brooklyn Heights still protruding above the bay. The bridges had all broken and hung in ruins, some spans missing entirely, snapped cables dangling. The frothing water churned in the bloated harbor, lapping high against the barrier, the swells barely contained, some of the ocean sloshing, frighteningly, over the top.

Swallowing to moisten her dry mouth, Liv asked, "Mom, what about the people who can't afford to live in the Dome? How will they survive?"

Other than pushing a lock of curly brown hair behind her shoulder, Penelope remained focused on piloting the Helix. "Don't think about them," she replied in a voice that sounded both amused and exasperated yet entirely condescending, part and parcel with her sharply snooty Swiss-inflected English. "They'll be taken care of."

Liv pulled her left foot onto her seat, tucking it under her right thigh. "But . . . how?" she asked.

Penelope shook her head, and the lock of hair tumbled over her shoulder again. "Do your homework," she said, "and we can discuss it when we get home." Then Pen shifted her eyes to catch her own Lucid system's attention. "Parental override," she commanded. "Homework mode."

Liv's display became entirely opaque, blocking her view of the real world outside. Around the edges of her homework file, all Liv could see was the wallpaper of their beautiful home in Davos, Switzerland, with mountains rising above the snowmelt Landwasser river. The sheer Alps surrounding Davos sheltered the high-altitude town, protecting it from global warming with a crisp, delicious microclimate that made it one of the most exclusive locations on the planet. It was only home to a few hundred ultra-wealthy families, and anytime Liv left its rarified air, she suffered terrible homesickness. But right now she'd wanted to see New York City.

"Mom!" Liv protested. "I have my rights."

"As do I," replied Penelope.

Liv managed to somewhat override Penelope's draconian parenting by pulling up a mapping app in a small window on her display. So she followed the path of their Helix in cobbled-together satellite images as they swooped above the Statue of Liberty in the enormous lake created behind the barrier wall. Liberty waded in the harbor, her island underwater, her voluminous skirts partially submerged.

As the Helix banked to follow the Hudson River upstream, a government warning alert box popped up on Liv's Lucid, higher priority than Pen's homework override. Vid showed Liv a battery of missiles tracking the Helix as it buzzed up the river.

"Helix," an automated air traffic controller announced through their rigs, "you are cleared to enter Manhattan airspace. Welcome and enjoy your stay, and remember to remain vigilant."

"Copy that," replied Penelope, dipping the Helix closer to the edge of the island, just above where West Street once snaked along the downtown coast.

Liv corrected a gene sequence in her Biochem homework and realized it was good enough. She was so far ahead of the rest of her class that she was deep into extra credit anyway. At her level of studies, she was designing her own program and seeking out the advanced artificial teachers she needed.

As she finished up her work, Liv noted a factoid that fascinated her: *If the DNA strands in all our cells were uncoiled they would stretch as far as Pluto and back to Earth again.* Her Biochem tutor, even synthetic as it was, enjoyed comparisons as much as she did. Then Liv saved her file, adding it to her queue to submit to her teacher, who would no doubt award her another point on her final GPA.

"I'm done," Liv said. She held her hands up as though showing they were empty.

"Parental override," said Pen, pleasantly enough. "Leisure mode."

Now that her display was back under her own control, Liv opened the messenger app that was still blinking with 3 unread messages. But when she opened it, Liv was curious to see the message number fade as it updated. Her mouth dropped open when the counter revealed 7,899 as the final tally. Which was insane.

"What is going *on*?" Liv blurted. She scanned the list of messages, which were from friends and classmates and relatives and way too many strangers. One message from a girl in Liv's Calculus class, a bespectacled serious studious sort, had the headline, "You must watch this." So Liv opened it.

Inside was a vid press release of her grandfather, Arthur Blackstone, in his creepy exosuit from the neck down. She listened to a full two seconds before she paused it and whispered to her Lucid rig, "Send to Penelope Blackstone."

"The vid I just sent you," Liv hissed urgently. "It's *important*."

Penelope tightened her hands on the helicopter's controls. "We'll be home soon," she said. "Can't it wait?"

Liv stared blankly at her stubborn mother. Setting her jaw, she raised her fingers and traced complex commands in the air in front of herself, following an algorithm on her display that she'd devised.

Pen suddenly raised a hand to her face, stopping with her palm inches from her nose. "You little. . . ," she spat. "You hacked my system."

Liv set the vid running on Pen's Lucid display. "Look," she urged. "It's about your dad."

Penelope shot her an annoyed glare. "You know I don't like when you call him that."

"Well," Liv said with a shrug, "you shouldn't have told me I was adopted until he was gone, then."

Penelope let go of the Helix's cyclic stick. "Autopilot," she sighed.

Liv studied her mother's face as Pen watched the video of Arthur's public proclamation. It changed from surprise to discomfort to outright rage by the end. She turned to glare at Liv, fury blazing in her gaze.

"He's actually going to do it," she said. She raised her eyebrows, as if in disbelief, and then exhaled angrily. "Manual," she ordered the copter, and grabbed the controls again, swooping the Helix to the right.

The imposing monolith of Blackstone Tower loomed directly in their view.

It was by far the tallest and largest skyscraper in New York City. The Tower's base walled off the south side of Central Park South three entire avenues from Columbus Circle to 5th. Like its owner's name, it was indeed fashioned with an exterior of River Black sandstone, which made the entire enormous structure appear to absorb light in its thick rectangular pillar of inky darkness.

In the Tower's shadow to the north, an enormous plaza of rough concrete sprawled out, smothering half the area that used to be Central Park. The space was overflowing with tents and shanties, mud huts and lean-tos, cardboard and tin roof shelters, teeming with refugees from the margins scrambling for existence on the streets.

Liv felt a prickling of unease on the back of her scalp as Pen piloted the Helix directly toward the helipad on Blackstone Tower's roof.

When they were half a kilometer out, a red security banner declaring HALT popped up on the Helix's central monitor, blinking on Liv's Lucid display, and undoubtedly on Penelope's, too.

"Helix, please divert course," an automated voice warned. "Blackstone Tower is prohibited to unauthorized vehicles."

Ahead, servo-mounted weapons on several turrets swung toward their craft.

Liv gulped as the cannons tracked them with the dark hollows of their muzzles.

Penelope flexed her elbow, and the Helix hovered in place, holding its position before the massive matte-black monolith.

"You remember that time," Pen said aside to Liv, "when you hacked into Grandpa's computers and caused a billion dollars' worth of damage?"

Liv's face flushed hot. "That wasn't my fault." She had only been eight years old, and had been trying to send her grandfather a Valentine's Day card as a surprise, but the viral worm she'd used to override the Tower's systems had proliferated beyond her control.

"Darling," asked Penelope sweetly, "do you think you could help out here?"

Liv turned to face her mother with incredulity. "Are you *asking* me break into your dad's . . . *Grandpa's* network?"

Pen nodded. "This is a family emergency."

"It is also highly illegal," said Liv.

Penelope kept her narrowed eyes focused tightly on the array of guns pointed at them. "As your legal guardian I take full responsibility," she said.

3 / THE SIMULACRUM

INSIDE BLACKSTONE TOWER, in the penthouse nerve center located deep within the upper reaches of the skyscraper, Gabriel Benicolustro's eyes flickered across the internal data on his Lucid as it synced with the output from Adam's clone pod monitors. Everything was between normal parameters, and all the levels remained in safe zones.

There had been a minor flurry of activity recorded from Adam's brainstem and the body had twitched in response, but Gabe knew it to be nothing unusual. Occasionally, the clone dreamed on his own accord, consolidating Arthur's memories as Adam's own.

On certain late nights, Gabe felt powerful urges to bring the neuro-clone out of slumber and ask it questions about what it was experiencing, hoping to glean some insight into how souls were created, but he resisted, concerned about what impact his words might have on the carefully curated interior landscape of Adam's mind.

Thinking about Adam's dreams reminded him of a ritual his grandfather had taken him to as a young boy in Queens. It had been a gathering of Achuar in the backroom of a herbalist shop in Flushing, which Gabe's second cousin had taken over from a retiring Chinese gentleman. The backroom was bare, and a group of Gabe's male relatives would sit on the floor in a circle at breakfast time, sharing hard rolls of bread and somewhat mealy pears. After breakfast, Gabe's great-uncle explained that the Achuar were known as the Dream People, while he passed around an infusion of herbs known as *wayús*.

Even though the horn of greenish, leafy goo smelled awful, Gabe took a sip from the narrow end, and passed it to a cousin. He fought repulsive dizziness, trying not to vomit.

As he battled the nausea, half-remembered fragments of dreams began to surface. Images of volcanoes and cloud forests, a mirror-clear lake, turned terrifyingly red, although spotted with blooming white flowers. Then a shooting pain in his legs, terrible agony, as though his feet were being chewed by ferocious wolves.

Young Gabe couldn't hold in his puke any longer. Then he realized that the other males in his family were crawling forward toward the center of the circle one by one to purge into a large wooden bowl. He took his turn, and felt lighter, cleaner, than he'd ever felt before.

After the visions settled, his relatives discussed their dreams, and Grandfather along with his great-uncle helped them interpret the synchronicities in waking life as guidance toward their futures. Gabe had been too shy to talk about his own dream, and his grandfather had died soon afterward. He'd never joined the circle again.

Gabe shook off the memory. He wouldn't worry about the blip in Adam's readouts, but still he couldn't help wondering how Number Nine would turn out. The first neuro-clone had died upon awakening, his brain unable to process the real world's sensory information, suffering a fatal stroke. With each generation, the clones survived longer. Number Eight lived for a few weeks before becoming delusional and fatally swallowing sharp metal objects. Number Nine was their final hope, as Arthur's illness would not allow the necessary time to mature a new clone.

When Adam finally woke, he would for all intents and purposes be Arthur returned. Gabe had rationalized that it was better morally, psychologically, and karmically if he took exquisite care of the clone, nurturing him and helping him thrive and develop, but it was dangerous to become personally attached. He learned not to repeat that mistake from Number Four.

Beside him, Arthur squirmed in his exosuit, not so much sitting in his hoverchair as arranged atop it.

Gabe stepped behind the hoverchair, and steered it toward the gleaming steel vault built into the wall on the far side of the chamber. They waited for the security procedures to clear them both for access, and the vault's sharp door depressurized, hissing open for them to enter.

The skin on his limbs prickling from the coldness of the air inside, Gabe wheeled Arthur's hoverchair through the entrance. The steel door closed behind them the second they crossed the threshold, passing a yellow caution line printed on the floor.

After Gabe secured the hoverchair in the center of the sealed room, he adjusted Arthur's posture so the old man was sitting more or less upright in his exosuit.

As he made eye contact for the final go-ahead, Gabe hoped Arthur would suddenly decide against this course of action. No good could come of it that Gabe could see. But he had long ago stopped trying to second-guess or argue with his employer other than to point out dangers Arthur already knew.

Arthur tilted his head, his mouth worming in an unsettling display of nerves. He nodded.

"Release the SINE module," Gabe ordered.

A haze of particles glittered in the center of the vault, directly in front of Arthur. The cloud darkened, resolving into a figure, a standing man. It appeared to solidify, taking on shape and detail, until a full-sized, exact hologram of a healthy Arthur stood before the stricken version.

As always when he saw the SINE, Gabe felt a deep chill in his body that had little to do with the low temperature of the climate-controlled room. SINE had all the mental capabilities of Arthur, but enhanced to superhuman levels. Gabe purposefully kept the replica of Arthur's brain prisoner in a virtual cell, disconnected from the planetary net, throttling SINE's access to the vast computational power of Blackstone Labs. He had many sleepless nights imagining what nightmares would come if SINE ever escaped. While carefully monitored, SINE was never idle inside its cyber-prison, always testing the boundaries of its delimited existence, always gathering whatever crumbs of information it could analyze, preternaturally calm and clever beyond human conception, and potentially malevolent to a frightening degree. Without Arthur's body, without the physicality of his emotional center, his heart, his somatic senses, SINE had no checks to its incorporeal desires.

SINE glared down at Arthur with its coldly impassive gaze. The hair rose on the back of Gabe's neck and he had to fight a deep autonomic desire to flee. It was a monstrous creation; a super-intelligence without a shred of empathy.

By the way Arthur was squirming in his hoverchair, Gabe could tell that his employer felt similar terror, although he stared back bravely at his own nonmaterial enhanced consciousness. Gabe did not think of Arthur as a friend, as his boss could be capriciously cruel, but he had always admired his ambition, cagey intelligence, and resolve.

"You have a question, old man?" asked SINE.

Arthur didn't reply for a long moment, frozen by the ice in SINE's tone. Then he summoned his own haughtiness that he'd earned from half a lifetime of autocratic success, privilege, and nearly unlimited wealth. "Well, yes," he replied, "I do."

"Well, old man, spit it out," commanded SINE.

Arthur took a deep, rattling breath, which forced his exosuit to expand to support him. One eyelid drooped, as though the question that bothered him was overwhelming his limited brain function that remained available. "Did I love well?" he gasped.

SINE smirked, which may have been the most chilling expression Gabe had ever seen in his life. "You loved only yourself," it answered with definitive nonchalance. "Your own vanity and fear prohibited any meaningful relationships."

SINE's response struck Arthur like a physical blow. His shoulders hunched in the exosuit, and his head dipped backward, lolling on his neck.

It was pitiful how desperate Arthur was for SINE's approval, but witnessing his employer being devastated by his own consciousness simulacrum turned the fear Gabe felt to irritation. He felt an obligation to defend. "But," Gabe added quickly, "your personal sacrifices led to inventions that have improved the lives of billions."

"And the increase in consumption is accelerating the demise of the ecosystem," said SINE in his cold clinical sneer.

Arthur nodded, turning his face away from SINE. "Once Adam is born," he said to Gabe, "shut down the simulation."

Although Gabe was in total agreement, he felt a rush of worry about how SINE would react to Arthur's declaration, which amounted to a death sentence for the electronic consciousness.

SINE's face remained impassive as he stepped into motion, turning to the side and walking directly toward the western wall of the vault. When he reached the wall, he simply strode up on to it, and continued in a calm pace, vertically toward the ceiling. At the top, SINE strolled across the ceiling upside-down as though it was completely natural. He stopped directly above Arthur in his hoverchair, their heads only a few feet apart.

"Are you so far gone you do not see that I offer you an alternative to that monstrous ape-boy?" SINE asked, peering downward. "Give me access to the planetary net and with its computational resources I'll be able find a cure for your ailment in moments."

Arthur raised his chin. "Unleashing a disembodied super intelligence would lead quickly to end of the human species," he countered.

SINE's eyes narrowed. It was not a gesture of anger, as Gabe knew that SINE had no emotions, as natural as it felt to ascribe them to the simulation in false anthropomorphism. It's synthetic neural net was based on precise models of Arthur's brain – pre-disease. It had been created with the primary purpose of virtually testing the updated brain data before it was implemented in the neuro-clone's wetware. Its cagy expression was probably a function of calculating trillions of probabilities for manipulating the situation. Gabe could never let himself forget that SINE's main motivations were the same as Arthur's, acquiring as much wealth and power as possible.

Since the possibility of the emotionless simulation's escape had given Gabe nightmares for months, he quickly ran through a mental list of checks and safeguards he had installed in the SINE's system himself. Physically, there was nothing SINE could do. It did not have a corporeal self to interact with its environment. Its virtual prison had proven inescapable, or it would have freed itself already. It might want to destroy Gabe and Arthur, it might want to wipe out all humanity, but Gabe reassured himself that the quantum cryptographic firewall he'd developed could withstand anything SINE attempted.

At very least, the only space in which SINE could materialize was within this vault. If the vault remained operative, SINE was secure. These moments of interaction were the system's only vulnerabilities.

"Let's go," Arthur wheezed. "It's time for me to embark on another journey."

As Gabe was about to open his mouth to dismiss SINE's avatar hovering overhead, sirens wailed through the vault and red emergency lights flashed.

"Warning," Blackstone Tower's automated computer system blared. "Warning. Security breach."

Gabe glanced up at SINE, but the creepy simulacrum stared back at him blankly.

"Security breach," the announcement repeated. "Breach. Breach. B-b-b-b-breach."

A high-pitched whine screamed in Gabe's ears, and he winced, gasping from the pain.

"Sh. Shut. Shut. Ut. Ut. Utting. Shutting. Utting. Dow. Dow. Down," the computer system stammered. "Shutting down."

The alarms' blare whistled out. The lights flickered and ceased flashing.

With a terrifying zapping sound, the containment field around the inside of the vault sizzled and sputtered off.

The vault's steel door wheezed wide open.

Gabe glanced up at SINE again.

The amoral electronic consciousness tilted its head a little, like a curious dog. Then it vanished as though it had never been present.

"What's going on?" demanded Arthur.

Gabe closed his eyes, racking his thoughts for a contingency plan, but with desperate certainty he knew there was none. A breach of this magnitude should never have been possible, but now there was no way around it. "The security system has been compromised," he informed Arthur. "SINE has escaped." *It's free*, Gabe wanted to add, but that seemed melodramatic and obvious.

Arthur coughed deeply. "This is not going to end well," he gasped.

Gabe thought that might be the grandest understatement he'd ever heard. If something this terrible had occurred, the reasons for the disaster must be systemic, devastating . . . and ongoing. "Wait here," he told Arthur.

"Okay," Arthur replied weakly.

Gabe ran out of the vault, aware that, despite Arthur's agreement to stay put, his employer jogged his hoverchair into motion and followed behind.

4 / VIOLENT BIRTH

THE AIR PRESSURE of the Helix's cavity blades swept the helipad of Blackstone Tower free of a cloud of dust and debris as it lowered to a landing.

The instant the aircraft touched down, Penelope tapped a quick code into a locked cabinet keypad. She yanked it open, and pulled out a hefty-looking weapon.

On Liv's virtual display, she quickly poked the image of the weapon, and her eyes widened in alarm as her computer identified it as a mini-missile revolver armed with tiny explosive projectiles in each cylinder.

"Stay here!" Pen ordered as she kicked open the Helix's exit hatch.

"What's going on?" asked Liv. She felt a twinge of embarrassment at the frightened worry in her own voice.

Pen fixed her daughter with her patented don't-question-me glare. "I mean it," she hissed. "Stay!"

"Okay," said Liv, slumping back into her bucket seat as Pen slammed the hatch shut.

Penelope fastened her pashmina around her head, holding her hair down and obscuring her features as she ran toward the roof entrance.

Liv switched her attention to her display, pulling up the feeds for the Tower's cameras. She watched as Pen hurtled down the interior fire escape stairs one dizzying level at a time, her flowing skirt fluttering around her calves.

Even though her mother was armed with that nasty rocket revolver, she looked surprisingly small hurrying down the stairs. She looked vulnerable. Liv knew Pen was a badass in so many ways – in business, certainly, but also simply on a personal level – but Liv had never considered her an action hero. She could easily be killed charging into the Tower like that.

Liv chewed on her lower lip. She couldn't let Pen face the security goons in the building alone.

Unbuckling her seatbelt, Liv pushed open the Helix's hatch, and slid to the rooftop. Then she chased after her mother.

She kept track of Pen's progress on her Lucid display even as she charged down the stairs two at a time.

Liv was only one flight up when Penelope stormed through the fire exit into her father's penthouse. When she saw Gabe, Pen held her weapon down tight against her leg, hiding the missile gun in the loose folds of her peasant skirt. Both she and Gabe stared at one another, neither sure how to begin.

Liv's grandfather, Arthur, was slumped in his hoverchair on the far side of the room, still contained in his exosuit. He faced the spectacular floor-to-ceiling windows, where the view of the jagged twilight city stretched into the distance. Not far from Arthur was the laboratory housing the clone pod.

When she reached the entrance to the penthouse, Liv ducked down and creeped through the open door, scrambling silently and unseen into the shadows, behind a bank of computer servers. She grimaced as she watched Pen and Gabe regarding the other cautiously.

There was a lot of history there – more than Liv was aware of, she knew. Pen and Gabe's relationship was a bobbing iceberg, with much more hidden below the ocean's frozen surface than jutted up. They had been romantically entangled at some point, and friends at other times, then flared up into dating again, which failed horribly and left them strained and tense exes. Pen and Gabe were currently distant semi-hostile strangers, as far as Liv was aware, although Gabe had always been so sweet to Liv herself. She had a feeling Penelope still loved the hunky technician, or at least was attracted to him, but didn't respect his toadying compliance to her father's wishes. Also, Pen was simply too much of a snob to reconcile herself with dating the help.

Gabe blinked and broke the silence. "You shouldn't be here."

Penelope took a step forward before stopping and glowering at him. "How can you do this?" she demanded.

Opening his extra-large hands wide, Gabe shrugged, tucking his head in a shallow bow. "To help a man, in your father's condition, die. . . ," he said softly. "It's a sacred honor."

"It's not right," argued Penelope. "He doesn't know what he's doing."

Gabe glanced quickly behind him at Arthur inert in his hoverchair. "He knows," he replied.

"You have to shut it down," said Penelope. She glared over at the faint outline of Adam floating in the semi-translucent tube of the clone pod.

Liv felt queasy looking at her . . . adoptive uncle? . . . incubating, surrounded by the technology that kept him alive. Part of her felt very uncomfortable to be in the presence of a living body that had been entirely created instead of born. Her deepest physical reaction was a revulsion on a primal level, like when she'd first seen pictures of the genetically developed pigs who had been modified to live with extra attached segments of belly meat to harvest the most bacon possible from a single poor animal. Yes, the body in the tank wasn't natural. Yes, he represented something insanely worrisome for the human race. Yes, Liv felt disgust by his very existence.

But Liv couldn't deny that she also was aware of Adam's presence in the penthouse. He was alive. He might be a neuro-clone, but he was also a *person*.

Gabe scratched the stubble on the side of his rugged chin. "Shut it down?" he repeated, scoffing. "He's a human child, not an app."

Although momentarily pleased that Gabe shared her opinion, Liv felt afraid when Penelope shrugged with nonchalance. She knew that gesture meant Pen was about to take a dark turn. "If you won't," said Penelope, "then I will."

Gabe took a step backward as Penelope raised her missile revolver and aimed it at Adam's pod.

"No!" Liv cried. Before she was even aware she was in motion, Liv leaped out from hiding and jumped in between Penelope's raised weapon and Adam in his tank. There was no way she would stand aside and watch her mother murder someone.

"Get out of the way," Penelope said.

Liv heard the real menace in her voice, but refused to budge. She stared at the missiles in Penelope's revolver, the gaping dark hole of the launcher, and continued to stand where she was. Unflinching even though she felt sickened by how hard her heart was pumping adrenaline all throughout her body.

"I can't move," Arthur croaked from his hoverchair. "Help me."

Arthur's exosuit whirred and shook, jittering at awkward angles. Liv, Penelope, and Gabe stared as Arthur struggled and gasped, fighting against the suit's powerful hydraulics. Arthur flopped out of the hoverchair, thrashing inside the exosuit on the marble tiles.

"What's *happening*?" Liv wailed. It looked as though her grandfather was being crushed and mangled inside his spacesuit. The old man's face was mottled and purpling, his thin lips gulped for air like a fish slapped on a dry floor.

Gabe took a fumbling step toward his boss.

As Arthur's eyes bulged from the effort of fighting the exosuit, the levers and pistons supporting his arm twitched wildly, and slowly rose up, its reflection eerie against the gleaming marble tiles. The glove opened, poised with tension as it reached for Arthur's neck.

"It must be SINE," Gabe realized aloud. With a lurch, he closed the distance between himself and Arthur, but the mechanical hand had already gripped the old man's throat and was starting to squeeze.

Liv bit the skin on the side of her thumb to stop herself from screaming.

"What the hell is *sign*?" barked Penelope as she dashed over to help Gabe pull on the exosuit's clenched arm.

"He's your father," explained Gabe, his face scrunched with the effort of straining, against the exosuit's robotic strength. He kneeled to get a better grip on the wrist. "But with an intelligence a million-fold greater. Now it's able to control anything connected to the planetary net."

Pen and Gabe threw all their efforts into releasing Arthur's neck from the exo-glove's death grip, Pen pulling on the glove's fingers, Gabe wrestling with the wrist, but they were no match for its hydraulics.

Arthur's eyeballs reddened as the micro-capillaries in his eyes burst. He gagged and choked, his tongue lolling from his mouth, huge and horrific.

"Liv," shouted Gabe, "what did you do?"

Liv inhaled sharply, which hurt like a knife in her bronchial tubes. Gabe knew her. He knew she was capable of hacking the system. Nobody else could have. And he was right.

"It's my fault," said Penelope.

Gabe met Liv's eyes with his worried gaze, radiating calmness, despite the crazy panic of the situation in the penthouse and the strain of holding the exo-glove. "Okay, okay, never mind," he said. "Can you disengage the exo's drives from the net?"

Liv nodded, focused intently on her Lucid display, calling up the data of Blackstone Tower, drilling down through the systems until she found the laboratory's plans and operating system. Her entire consciousness concentrated with hyper-awareness on the code floating in front of her. Her hands moved in a controlled blur, manipulating the elements and variables with all the expertise, her hours upon hours, of practice had instilled.

"Easy," she said, her heart rate evening out as she relaxed into the security of her own competence. "Scrambling servo-drivers frequencies—"

"He doesn't have enough strength to support the exo alone," warned Gabe, "so be sure to—"

Liv completed her misdirection of the code's flow.

Arthur flattened on the floor like a rag doll.

"Lock the joints first," finished Gabe. He shook his head, and hunched down to peer into Arthur's purple face. "Are you okay, sir?"

With a loud smack, the exosuit slammed the palm of its glove into

Gabe's chest. Gabe hurtled backward, his muscled arms and legs flailing as he tumbled.

Both of the exosuit's arms extended on either side of Arthur. The gloves clenched into fists.

With a single punch, the exosuit's right glove smashed Arthur's skull. Gray and red brain mush splattered out onto the floor.

Liv screamed. She backed up against the wall of servers again, slumping down into a crouch, fighting revulsion, terror, and shock. She had overridden the exosuit's system! But her bypass had lasted only seconds before the intelligence operating it from the inside had regained control and completely locked her out.

A wet rushing noise from Adam's pod caught her panicked attention. The gel that supported the clone gushed out of the sides in a thick, oozing rush that reminded Liv disgustingly of egg whites. *Albumen*, she thought, having to gag to keep from vomiting.

The clone pod's hatch opened with a hiss of releasing gas, and whirred as the panel rose.

As the exosuit whined and climbed to its feet, Liv had the surreal sensation that she was trapped in a nightmare. Her grandfather's caved-in, bloody head rolled back and forth, side to side, atop the suit, lifeless. And yet the exosuit continued to move, manipulating Arthur's dead body with its levers and pistons. It turned to face Adam's pod, and clomped toward the vulnerable neuro-clone on its bulky boots.

"It's after the clone," said Gabe. He had raised his head from where he was crumpled against the far wall, then slumped down again.

With the same automatic initiative she'd experienced when Penelope had threatened Adam, Liv rushed in front of the open pod, defending the clone.

"Liv!" Pen yelled. "Get out of the way."

"He's just a boy, Mom!" Liv shouted back.

With tears trailing down her cheekbones, Penelope raised her missile revolver again. She aimed it at her father in the exosuit.

As the exosuit strode smoothly toward her, Liv clenched her teeth, willing herself to stand strong despite the terror flooding her system, the signals to flee to safety. She had no idea what she could do against the solid technology of the suit, but she would not stand down.

"Liv . . . here, now," ordered Penelope, the usual resolve in her voice now sounding weak. Her arm trembling, Pen raised her other hand to support the gun as she pointed it.

Shaking her head, her shoulders quaking, Liv refused to move.

Penelope closed one eye, tracking the suit as it walked across the penthouse.

"He's already dead!" screamed Liv. "Shoot!"

Penelope squeezed the trigger.

With a trail of smoke, a little missile launched and blasted into the exosuit's leg in a flare of flame. Liv's face got slapped with a wave of heat as the knee of the exosuit was blown off with a steely screech.

Arthur's blood trickled down onto the marble floor, but the exosuit didn't topple. It hopped and hobbled forward, undeterred from its objective, trailing a messy smear of dark crimson behind it.

Taking a deep breath, Liv rushed at the exosuit, which was only three steps away. She slammed it with her outstretched hands, but it didn't wobble. It kept hopping, pushing her roughly to the side.

Liv regained her balance, and pulled on the exosuit's elbow, but only managed to get dragged along behind it, her shoes slipping on the trail of her grandfather's blood.

The exosuit reached the clone pod. Ignoring Liv's yanking on its elbow, it reached its other arm into the tube, and lifted up Adam by his neck.

The naked, preteen clone dangled above the pod.

Liv looked up at the placid face of the young duplicant. She screamed as his eyes fluttered open.

Adam gasped for air, the exosuit's glove squeezing his windpipe. His eyes blinked in confusion, alarm, and finally pure terror.

The worst way to be born ever, thought Liv as she shoved her shoulder against the exosuit's back. "Leave him alone!" she hollered, but her pushing had no effect.

"Liv," Penelope said, "get away from there. Please."

Liv heard the danger in Pen's voice, but she glanced up at Adam's reddening face, the misery and fear in his innocent eyes. The newborn clone would only live for moments more unless she did something.

Glancing around wildly, she spotted a small toolkit on a shelf under the clone pod. Liv flipped it open and grabbed a Torx screwdriver by its rubber grip. Then she whirled around and stabbed the exosuit above its left elbow.

The exosuit paused for a split second, as though scanning for damage it didn't find. It reached out its right hand and grabbed Liv around her throat, hoisting her off the floor.

Dangling in the air, choking and gagging, Liv's only thought was that stabbing the exosuit hadn't been one of her better ideas.

Penelope raised the rocket revolver and fired another mini-missile in an explosive flash. She hit the exosuit's right thigh, blowing his remaining leg out from under him.

Liv tried to scream as she and Adam crumpled to the floor along with the exosuit, but the glove choking her didn't release and she couldn't make a sound. Crushing pain flared in her windpipe.

Her vision starting to go gray, tunneling dark at the edges, Liv gaped at Penelope striding over to them, looming foreshortened against the ceiling. Liv pounded against the glove, struggling to breathe. Her mother's expression was bleak and grim as she aimed the little missile launcher again and fired down.

This time, Pen hit the exosuit square in the chest. Arthur's rib cage and innards exploded outward, along with the electronics and chips of the exosuit's control panel.

The gloves opened and went limp. The exosuit flinched once and then lay flat, inert and inoperative.

Liv kicked away and sat up, gasping for air, rubbing the burning bruises on her throat. She crawled over to Adam, and felt his pulse. He was unconscious, but he was still alive. She leaned down close, lowering her face to his mouth. She could feel gentle breathing, his exhalations smelling strangely chemical.

With a sigh of relief, Liv looked up at Penelope, who nodded down at her before letting the missile revolver drop by her couture sandals.

Liv shrugged out of her linen jacket, opened it wide, and spread it over Adam, covering the neuro-clone as he lay on the cold marble floor. His face was slack from unconsciousness, but he was surprisingly cute, his virgin features untouched by any weathering of experience that he seemed unnervingly pure.

We survived this, Liv thought. *We're alive.* But she had never experienced such epic uncertainty. There was no time to process the horror she'd just witnessed because the future was so scary, the level of inevitable change so incomprehensible. *What the hell happens now?* she wondered.

Liv glanced up at the underside of the clone pod. Smeared by a splash of blood was the designation NEURO-CLONE #9, but the middle of the plaque was obscured, so at first glance it simply read NEURO 9.

At least we know what to call you, Liv thought. *Adam Neuronine.*

PART 2
AWAKENING, EARTH DAY, 2084

5 / NEURONINE'S OPINION

A DECADE LATER, Adam Neuronine's neural net activated.

Inside Adam's skull, flush and smooth against the contours of the crumpled cortex of the brain, a fine-weave nano-net shimmered with illuminated activity. Then each cross-woven corner extended a minuscule needle into the flesh of his brain, impregnating the top layers of neurons. The net scintillated again as low-frequency electric pulses from the needles' tips triggered groups of neurons to fire.

The synapses activated in a pattern that coalesced into the familiar shape of digits, glowing red. Adam reacted with a touch of panic that woke him up.

Adam blearily opened his eyes to the sound of his alarm clock. The digital display in his Lucid read 7:00 AM.

Wincing from the alarm's continuing blare, Adam moaned, "George, just a few more minutes."

"You have had the recommended dosage of sleep, Adam," replied George inside Adam's mind, connected to the Lucid system.

The alarm silenced, and a low murmur of pleasant music drifted through Adam's brain.

He sat up and rubbed his eyes, staring out at his compact residence, a single white room furnished minimally and functionally, with a foldaway Murphy bed, a padded recliner, and a multi-use kitchen island with sleek embedded appliances. A single window let sunlight diffuse into Adam's room and illuminate a perfect rhombus on the gray tiled floor. Adam's view was framed by Blackstone's latest virtual display technology, an implanted Lucid system connected to his neural net that provided stereoscopic audio and full 3D heads-up visuals. The system overlaid a subtle neutral color tint to the bare white walls, and glowing corporate logos to all the products in the room.

A news chyron scrolled along the bottom of the internal display relaying the weather in Buffalo, New York, some troubling news about a thwarted HATE terror attack, and advertisements for virtual fashion and travel. Real custom products and experiences were far too expensive for anyone other than the ultra-wealthy Dome Dwellers. Adam blinked on a new suit style with parson collars from the renowned designer Hamatachi, tickled again by Lucid's accuracy in its recommendations. Just yesterday, he was watching *Derrick's Daily* and saw his archrival Derrick wearing the latest Hamatachi design. The fashions were expensive but keeping up was crucial.

Adam scratched his skinny sides, his protruding ribs, checking out his apps. Nothing seemed terribly pressing on his calendar, in his mail, or on social media. He looked at a funny cartoon about a lonely tree, captioned "I wish I was lost in the forest," and he smiled. In the corner of his display, a small clock counted down the time until the simultaneous global upgrade from the neural-net to the neural-mesh in hours, minutes, and seconds: 47:58:32. Upgrades were always pretty exciting! In the top right of his visual field, his Anomaly Detection System status needle pointed safely in the green zone, far across from the frightening yellow and red side.

Under the Anomaly status, Adam focused on his Followers counter: 727,283. Quite good!

The current temperature outside was 105 F. Practically balmy. Not that he had any plans to go outside.

Adam turned his head to look out the window, blinking as his eyes adjusted to the sunlight. The massive Buffalo refugee housing projects stretched around him, housing millions of citizens, towering like termite hives, protruding up from the crumbled old city below. The tiny silver sliver of Lake Erie he could glimpse between the towers made him wonder what swimming in real water would feel like, although VR was preferable because he didn't need to hold his breath underwater and there was no risk of drowning.

He stood, and padded across the cool tile to the wash closet, where he turned on the water with a quick tapping gesture on his Lucid display. Brown and sulfurous liquid jetted out of the showerhead.

Disgusted, Adam squeezed his eyes shut and held his arms out from his body as the dirty water poured over him.

"George," he gasped, "the recycler's broken again."

Finally the water cleared up enough to get Adam reasonably clean. After the wash closet dried him with air jets, Adam stepped back into his room and pulled on a plain gray, plush exercise suit. His muscles twitched as they were electronically stimulated to simulate a workout.

While Adam exercised, George materialized in front of him in the room. Adam's Personal Approval Liaison appeared as a neatly, expensively dressed man in his mid-30s with a snooty affect. George rarely smiled and Adam often found himself striving for his PAL's praise. Someday he would impress George! Although so far George's haughty, belittling demeanor hadn't softened.

"Have the rations come through yet?" asked Adam as his muscles jittered in the exercise suit. "It's been two days already."

Adam's shoulders tightened when he saw his Anomaly gauge suddenly dip toward the yellow zone. "What did I do?"

"Your vocal stress patterns suggest your thinking is at risk of becoming anomalous," replied George.

"You're right," said Adam. "Thank you." He was pleased to see his Anomaly dial return to normal.

A panel in the kitchen island slid open and a small rectangular drone detached from its hidden charging station and flew out, extending its small robotic pincer arms.

"Blackstone will always provide for you," George reminded him.

The drone dropped a small bar wrapped in gray plastic into Adam's hand. Then it zoomed back to its charging station, vanishing behind its panel.

Adam peered down at the nondescript bar. The wrapper snapped into visual enhancement in his virtual display with a shiny, colorful logo that read Patriot Food Bar. Happy smiling multicultural faces danced in animation around the logo.

Peeling open the packet, Adam discovered a moist red biscuit inside. It was indented into seven segments. He chomped half the biscuit and chewed. It tasted a bit much like chemicals and protein powder, but it had a flavor that Adam associated with strawberry, even though he'd never eaten a real strawberry in his life. All in all, the bar wasn't bad!

"That was three days' worth of rations," said George.

Adam checked the crumpled wrapper, flipped it over. One the back, it read "One week's supply." *Oops*, he thought, feeling embarrassed. He struggled to shove the remaining half of the biscuit back into its packet. "That leaves me 0.5714 segments a day," he explained apologetically to George. "I can work with that."

George sniffled, an action that he did often, which had recently made Adam wonder why the programmers had added allergies to George's system, unless the sound had been specially created to irritate him with its snootiness. "Thinking is dangerous and unnecessary," said George.

A magazine cover popped up on Adam's display. It was an issue of *Nature* from January, 2075. The headline article proclaimed, "Thinking Linked to Anomalous Behavior."

Adam didn't open the magazine. George had shown him this exact article several times in the past four months. "I won't let it happen again," he promised, dropping the half biscuit on the counter.

In the latter part of his exercise sequence, Adam checked his messages. He would never be able to keep up with all the conversations with his followers so like most people he used a chatbot, which filtered interesting or popular discussions to the top, sent automated replies, and quarantined messages with negative sentiment. He wasn't certain which of the conversations were with real people, or if every thread was simply chatbots chatting with chatbots.

Adam stripped out of his exercise suit, which had finished its programmed cycle. He changed into his simple daily clothes, and climbed into his recliner, settling into the padded cushions as the chair lowered him to a horizontal position.

As soon as he was comfortable, Adam's Lucid display expanded to cover his whole view, and complete immersion commenced. A news studio abuzz with activity resolved around him, filled with the avatars of other reporters, editors, and producers. Some of the avatars were connected to real people like Adam, but others were integrated AI. It was impossible to tell which was which, even with extensive questioning, which would be frowned upon by the Anomaly Detection System anyway. Adam sat up in the simulated reality, in place behind his usual desk. In the export monitors, Adam could see himself dressed in the sharp Hamatachi suit he'd just purchased. His face and shoulders were fuller and healthier as his avatar, although otherwise he looked like himself. Rather handsome!

Above his head behind him, the title of his show appeared: NEURONINE'S OPINION.

In front of Adam's desk, a 3D vid materialized, showing a recording of two supersonic passenger pods speeding toward one another through their separate partial-vacuum tubes. A blast spurted out from one's front nose cone, causing it to careen through the glass wall of its tube and smash into the tube beside it. The two pods collided in a fiery explosion that made Adam wince. All those poor travelers inside, he imagined. He could hear the screaming, although none was present on the audio of ominous, ambient background music.

George stepped through the projection to stand before Adam's desk. "Today you'll lead with the cyber-terror attacks against the pods," he said. "Hundreds dead. Terror hacktivist group Anomalous takes responsibility."

Adam felt a wave of revulsion about reporting on the tragic collision. Why couldn't he ever give good news to his followers? "With the neural-mesh upgrade," he told George, "Anomalous will be eliminated in days. We'll finally be free from fear." Reporting on this misery was entirely unnecessary, he decided. Adam wiggled his hand at the projection and the image of the burning pods dissipated behind George.

"Until then, our enemies still exist," George stated. "Your followers expect you to report threats." He tilted his head in an obsequious posture of curiosity. "No?"

Adam grimaced as the needle on his Anomaly dial twitched toward the bad side. He reassured himself that it was still safely in green zone. The yellow zone was a long way away but any slide toward the wrong side was something to worry about.

"No," Adam replied apologetically. "I mean, yes. You're right as always."

George raised his arms and an impressive array of charts and graphs lit up around him. "I'm breaking privacy rules in telling you this, but some of *Derek's Daily News* followers are converting to *Neuronine's Opinion*." He pointed at a graph with a curved upward line. "By the end of this year, you'll have enough followers to enter the Dome lottery."

Adam's Lucid flooded with images and video in a spellbinding montage espousing the dreamlike virtues of the luxurious life in the Manhattan Dome. Happy, wealthy Dome Dwellers strolled around the tended gardens, enjoying the open private spaces. Children ran through lawn sprinklers and rode bicycles on the tree-lined sidewalks. Couples leaned close in posh restaurants and whispered sweet things to one another before clinking their glasses of wine in celebration. Old folks laughed at the antics of their grandchildren playing with robot pets. A beautiful woman danced on stage in a slinky gown, leaping on enhanced legs to soar toward the ceiling in an ultimate show of grace and skill. A male dancer caught her in his arms and the audience applauded.

GAIN ONE MILLION FOLLOWERS, the promos promised. ENTER THE DOME LOTTERY. YOUR CHANCE TO WIN A LIFE OF REAL LUXURY.

"Fantastic," Adam whispered. It was everything he had always wanted. His continued exclusion from the life in the Dome, from real life in Manhattan, pained him like the ache of his exercised muscles.

George nodded, and a teleprompter appeared in Adam's display. Above it an ON AIR sign flashed, and the speech started to scroll.

"Welcome to *Neuronine's Opinion*," Adam read, "your trusted source for youth opinion on world events." Adam could see on the export display that behind him the vid was showing the elliptical baton-shaped passenger pods crashing at supersonic speed.

Adam waited until the vid of terrible collision finished. He swallowed his own disgust at the fatal destruction, and forged ahead, summoning all the gravitas and sympathy he could muster. He stared into the recording point above the teleprompter, looking all his followers in the eyes with pure sincerity. He read, "Today we saw yet another tragic example of where excess freedom can lead."

6 / PIGEON

After the newscast, Adam relaxed in his apartment, listening to the sweet melodies of music playing in his Lucid system at low volume. The usual afternoon thunderstorm raged out the window, yellow lightning zigzagging between the Buffalo Projects, the towers of which extended into the bruised clouds, but the windows were soundproofed and he couldn't hear the thunder. The storm seemed to have spent itself, anyway, as the sky was growing lighter over his glimmer of Lake Erie. On his display, Adam watched his follower numbers climb in fits and starts. When the counter broke 777,000, he smiled. Almost 50,000 new watchers!

"Thank you," he told George.

George stood impassively in the center of the small room. "I'm here to serve your success, sir."

Adam nodded as the storm dissipated outside. The clouds parted, and beams of sunshine shot through the humid air. A stout gray and black bird landed on Adam's windowsill in a puff of dirty feathers.

He sat up, staring at the bird, entranced. It was the most beautiful thing Adam had ever seen.

"What's that?" he asked. He pointed to the exotic creature, tilting his implanted subcutaneous forehead micro-camera at it so George could get a good look.

"*Columba livia domestica*," answered George. "Popularly known as a pigeon." He sniffed. "Officially extinct in Buffalo since 2052."

"Tell me more," said Adam.

"As you are not an approved academic institute," replied George, "access to this scientific article will cost you, a lay person, twenty thousand dollars. However, articles on diseases that pigeons carry are freely available."

Adam didn't move his sight from the bird, afraid it might fly off before he could absorb each amazing detail. The pigeon's oily-looking neck bobbed amusingly as it stepped forward on the ledge. It tilted its head, peering at him with the tiny dome of a dark eye. The pigeon's feathers shimmered with iridescent reds and greens, and it had a thick black stripe on its tucked gray wing like military insignia. "It's beautiful," Adam breathed.

Surprising himself with the action, Adam jumped up and unlocked his window, yanking it open. He half-expected the pigeon to flap away in terror, but instead it cooed and jumped inside.

The bird landed on the headrest of Adam's chair, where it promptly pooped a spurt of white goo.

"Do not approach!" warned George, his volume raised. "An extermination drone has been deployed for your safety."

"What?" Adam gasped as his front door slid open on its tracks.

A spiky, metallic drone about the size of a fist floated into his room. The bright B of the Blackstone logo was prominently printed on its rounded underside. The extermination drone swiveled its lasers toward the pigeon.

"You've never been exposed to animal pathogens," explained George, "which makes that pigeon potentially deadly. Better safe than sorry, no?"

Adam raised his hands, pleading with the drone to wait. "But it could be the only one left."

"Your protection is of primary importance to my programming," replied George. "Protection of non-humans is managed by other Blackstone liaison."

A flashing red warning on his display caught Adam's attention. His follower counter was dropping so rapidly that the last new numbers were a blur. Adam jolted with panic as he saw that it now read: FOLLOWERS: 677,269.

"George, I've been . . . compromised by Anomalous," he whispered in horror, as though keeping his voice down would make it less true. "Can you confirm a cyber-attack and reinstate my followers?"

"For your protection," George explained, "contact with wild animals carries a 100,000-follower fine."

Adam blinked at his PAL, uncomprehending. His whole future hinged on collecting followers. He was being punished for admiring a bird? This couldn't be happening! It wasn't fair! He smiled nervously at George. "Can't you ask the authorities to give me a break?" Adam wheedled. "It's the first real animal, wild or otherwise, I've ever seen."

"Adam, without rules, chaos would reign," replied George. "Without fines, no one will obey the rules."

A red light atop the drone illuminated.

With a quick flick of his wrists, Adam shooed the pigeon. It flapped up as the drone zapped out a laser, which melted a hole in the chair's headrest.

The drone tilted to take aim at the pigeon again.

Adam stepped toward the window to flush the bird outside.

The pigeon dove out as the drone fired.

Heated shrapnel from the hit window frame spattered onto Adam's arm, but he ignored the flare of pain in his relief that the pigeon was soaring upward, getting away. He leaned out the window into the steamy outside air watching as the pigeon flapped to the next tower across. It glided past a window on the opposite side, then zoomed upward, disappearing out of view.

With the pigeon's threat removed from the apartment, the extermination drone withdrew into the hallway, presumably returning to its panel in corridor, where it would await the next pestilential invasion.

As the drone disappeared, a stream of animated icons flashed across Adam's Lucid, suggesting various advertisements that might interest him. The happy animals in the NanoDocBot 8.0 ad caught his eye, so Adam double-winked to open it. NEW UPGRADE! the ad proclaimed, with the Blackstone Medical logo on the bottom. NOW WITH ANIMAL PATHOGEN NANOBOTS!

Adam gasped at the price: $500,000. Only Dome Dwellers could possibly afford that service fee! He was tempted by the pre-approved loan, but he knew it wouldn't be wise. He'd already spent too much money today on the Hamatachi suit.

He peeked back at the window across the courtyard in the tower that the pigeon had passed. It was one of hundreds of small, glassed apertures, each opening into an identical compact apartment.

But this one had someone peering out of it, someone who had watched the pigeon fly by.

Adam increased his Lucid's magnification. At 100x, the image was grainy and blurred, but he could see a woman's face framed by long, dark hair. Behind her, the room was dark, except for a shimmer of light on the kitchen island. Adam squinted and could make out a dim firelight. Was that a cake with candles on it?

The young woman's face seemed familiar. He tried to place it, but recognition refused to click. She leaned over the kitchen island and blew out the candles on the cake. The room went black.

Glancing away from the window, Adam's magnified view passed over the cuts on his arm from the shrapnel. He moved back to focus on the tiny wounds, which were welling with blood.

He increased the resolution to 500x, and Adam saw individual cells floating and bobbing, flowing in his own life's fluid.

He jerked back, alarmed and queasy at a glimpse of his own biological interior. He gulped for breath, feeling lightheaded as his glands squirting saliva into his mouth. He'd never seen his own blood before. It was so surprisingly . . . alive.

"George," he gasped, "reset magnification."

As the display returned to its normal view, Adam breathed better. The cuts were small, just shallow pinpricks, really. He shouldn't have reacted so strongly.

A medium-sized panel beside the bathroom closet slid open, and a white medical drone buzzed out. It had a red cross printed on it with the Blackstone B in the middle. It was louder than most drones, an old, almost obsolete model, but still functional enough. It wavered a little in the air as it crossed to Adam and scanned his injuries.

The medical drone wiped the blood with a cotton pad at the end of a robotic arm. Adam winced as it sprayed antiseptic disinfectant on his cuts. Then it spot-coated the flecks of broken flesh with artificial skin to seal and instantaneously heal the injury. The drone retracted its arms, pulling the bloody pad into a biological hazard receptacle inside itself. It then floated back to its panel.

Adam sniffed the new spots of skin on his arm, flashing on the unsettling close-up he'd gotten of the shocking color of the blood, the living cells floating inside it. "George," he asked, "what is blood made from?"

"That information is classified," George replied with a sniff.

Adam turned to stare outside again, even though the young woman's window across the way remained dark. He could barely make out her moving around in the shadowy apartment. Something had been so familiar about her. Her delicate nose. Her slightly masculine chin. Her narrow but erect shoulders, the way her elbows bent, the graceful extension of her neck. He knew her. But no matter how deeply Adam searched his memory for a sign of how they were acquainted, he came up with nothing. At his upcoming annual medical check-up he should ask his teledoc for a full brain scan. With his mental history he needed to be extra vigilant.

Just as he was giving up trying to remember, a moment of memory surfaced. Perhaps . . . there was . . . a warm pod, a safe womb like feeling? A shocking painful flash of light? Adam raised his hand to his throat, overwhelmed with a sense memory of a violently crushed windpipe that he couldn't remember ever happening.

There was the woman's face, younger, staring up at him in horror.

In the tower across from Adam, the woman slid open her door to an illuminated corridor and left her room.

"I'm going out for a walk," Adam announced.

George sniffed. "It's 105 degrees outside."

Adam nodded, opened a clothes storage cabinet, and pulled out a Blackstone insignia cap with refrigeration coils woven in its brim. He showed it to George with a grin and a flourish, then pulled it down on his head, covering the micro-camera embedded in his forehead.

"Perfect," he declared. He turned toward the door, but stopped after two steps. He glanced back at his PAL. "George?" he said. "I'd like to go alone. Please set privacy level to ten."

"As you wish," George said.

The PAL's avatar dematerialized, and Adam stepped out into the hallway, feeling as though he'd just won some battle he couldn't have explained.

7 / *STALKING THE STREETS*

THE CORRIDOR in Buffalo Projects Tower #11N was exactly the same as all the others in the entire housing cluster: non-descript, beige, with low lighting recessed into overhanging trim along either side of the narrow ceiling. The carpet was dark gray with white flecks in it, every meter or so banded with a black bar. The color scheme was designed to minimize the appearance of dirt and litter, Adam supposed. He was startled to realize that the colors were similar to the wild pigeon he'd saved, but the hallway décor was missing the bird's iridescent living beauty.

Adam stopped in front of what appeared to be a plain wall, but he could see on his Lucid that a hidden elevator panel would open here, even if he hadn't taken it hundreds of times before. He blinked to activate a call icon, and the elevator responded to his summons, dropping from floor 598 down to his own floor, 325.

The elevator panel slid open with a hiss of hydraulics, and Adam stepped into the empty lift. He barely felt the motion of the elevator as it slowly accelerated to cushion his vertigo, descending to street level in a softened rush. His Lucid responded to the elevator environment with an even sleepier selection of hushed melodies.

The door slid open again, revealing a vacant lobby. There was no need for a doorman, as the residents rarely went outside, and anyone who entered would need proper identification or risk the impersonal wrath of the heavily armed security drones.

Adam strode through the three-chambered foyer into progressively warmer enclosures. When the final set of doors slid open, the wave of heat that hit his face and arms was breathtakingly uncomfortable. Even with the cooling cap on his skull pumping away thermal energy, Adam instantly started to sweat.

He glanced east and west, up and down the concrete streets. Not a single person was in view, and no vehicles traveled by. Adam couldn't even see any drones hovering above the sterile sidewalks.

Staying out of the rare beams of sunlight that reached street level, Adam kept to the cooler shadows of the giant residential towers as he trotted over to the building directly opposite his own, across a flat concrete courtyard decorated only with a black brick B in its center.

He spotted the young woman striding around the corner of her building, disappearing in the passageway between her tower and a storage facility beside it. Watching her walk, Adam staggered, struck by a burst of blurry old memories, washes of pain, quick glimpses of bright light that carried no real information and refused to resolve into clear images, but impacted him all the same.

"No," Adam panted to himself. "She's not real." He wiped sweat off one eyebrow with the back of his hand. "She's a figment of my imagination." *And yet,* he thought, his heart thumping, *there she goes.*

"Are you having another episode, Adam?" George's voice asked.

Adam whirled around, but the PAL's avatar was not behind him. He spotted a blinking blue light on his Lucid display that indicated that George was speaking to him through his audio implants. "Leave me alone, George," he insisted. "I'm supposed to be at privacy level ten!"

"For someone with your condition," explained George, "mandatory privacy override occurs when voice-tone analysis indicates anxiety. It's in your user agreement."

Lines of tiny type popped up on Adam's Lucid. An all-too-familiar page heading was highlighted in yellow: DISSOCIATIVE IDENTITY DISORDER. Underneath that were printed page numbers: 4328 of 5032. Everything else was in unreadable fine print.

Adam brushed the legal document off his display, and hurried toward the passageway where the woman had gone. He couldn't let her get away. *Again*, his mind added, but he wasn't even sure what that meant or to what occasion it referred. It was maddening to know he knew someone yet not know how!

As Adam turned the corner into the shadowy alley, George materialized beside him, walking briskly, keeping up. Adam knew that with his forehead camera covered, George was effectively blind, and could only hear what Adam heard, not what he saw. He made no move to uncover the camera.

Adam emerged from the passageway into a long, dirty street lined with soiled, tattered tents and ramshackle cardboard shelters. Unlike the clean, monitored courtyards of the Buffalo Projects, this teeming street appeared to be a no-man's-land; off the grid.

People sat in front of their shelters, wearing bulky VR headsets and clunky haptic gloves to interact with their low-res displays. Some waited in line at hacked charging stations for their gear. Everyone looked dirty, hungry, and exhausted. VR their only escape from poverty and boredom.

Without slowing down, Adam hurried along the street. Nobody paid him any attention. "You can stop projecting the past around me, George," he said. "I know my tragic Buffalo history."

The makeshift shelters and crowded streets shimmered and lost resolution before fading out to reveal another spotlessly clean avenue between towers.

George sniffed in Adam's audio. "Then you also know not following the norms could return us to that world."

"Yes, of course," said Adam. He turned a corner around a tower, spotted the woman again as she slipped into an alley, and stepped back behind the wall so she wouldn't see him following her. "You know me," he whispered. "I'm a strictly stay in the safety of the green zone kind of guy."

Adam followed her down the long, dark alley, into a narrow, shadowy street between abandoned, partially boarded-up storefronts. A tattered poster proclaimed GORGEOUS NEW LUXURY RESIDENCES IN

THIS SPACE SOON! Usually the poster would have interacted with Adam's Lucid, but his covered camera prevented the connection.

The young woman stopped to talk with someone who stepped out of the shadows. Adam ducked behind a steel barrel to watch without being spotted, almost tripping over a pile of broken bricks. The woman discussed something with the man intensely. Adam could only describe him as a thug. He had never seen a thug in person, but the dark garb, unshaven, rough features, and powerful, muscular body all made the man resemble a typical thuggish person from the news Adam had reported. Although he seemed much sadder and more worried than Adam had expected.

After digging in her backpack, the woman pulled out a package, and relinquished it to the thug. She kept her hands extended as though expecting something in return.

The thug laughed, with no humor, and started to turn away.

The woman shoved the thug with both hands against his chest. He was caught off balance, and stumbled. His eyes were narrowed and disappointed as he raised his head.

"You've never been to this area before," said George.

"No?" whispered Adam. "It looks familiar to me."

George asked, "Why are you whispering?"

Adam's eyes widened as the thug pulled out a weapon – a sleek handgun.

The woman froze. She screwed up her face as the thug unzipped her coolant jacket, and turned her face away in disgust as he jammed his hand under her clothes, groping.

Adam had to stop him. He glanced around, his pulse throbbing as he began to panic. What could he do to help her? He had to distract the thug before she got hurt!

He hoisted up one of the broken bricks, and hurled it into the sole remaining window of the nearest abandoned storefront.

The window shattered in a crash of glass.

The woman snapped her hand up and grabbed the thug's wrist below the weapon. She twisted, turning the thug in a martial arts move. The gun dropped, clanking on the concrete. The thug fell to his knees, gasping at the pain in his twisted wrist.

Quickly, the woman pulled the belt off her waist, and used it to bind the thug to a rusty iron railing. Then she fished around in his pocket, and pulled out two small steel balls that glinted dully in the backstreet's gloom.

"What was that noise, Adam?" demanded George. "Please lift up your cap so I can see."

"I didn't hear anything," said Adam. "And I'm not whispering. Perhaps my hardware needs servicing?"

The woman raced away, rushing out of the derelict street.

Adam was compelled to follow by whatever force had prompted him to pursue thus far. He hurried by the downed thug.

As he scrambled after her, Adam's Lucid display projected images of horror around him, so that he climbed into a vision from 2078, with masses of homeless citizens staggering, starving and ill, with bestial violence all around, theft, abuse, riots over food and water, in surroundings of filth and despair.

He pushed through the miserable projections, trying to stagger onward despite George hijacking his vision using his GPS tracker.

"Since the Great Global Uprising," a sincere announcer reported, "Blackstone's Anomaly Detection System has been helping governments around the world to secure peace and stability for the benefit of *all* humanity."

Cheerful video played on Adam's Lucid: bright images with happy music of the towering Buffalo Projects, loving families gathered together inside the tiny apartments.

Adam shook his head, trying to get a glimpse of the real world around the edges of the projections. "I've seen this a thousand times," he said.

"The human brain is prone to forgetfulness," replied George.

"Is that all I am to you?" Adam asked. "A brain?"

George didn't reply, but the history lesson and the marketing pitch faded. Adam could see that he'd staggered down another empty avenue toward a glassed atrium. He saw the woman's white backpack as she entered the airlocks of the atrium, pushing inside to the docile, sparse crowd of citizens inside. Above the door were the letters TTN.

It was a Tube Transportation Network station.

Adam raced toward the door, hurrying through the climate-control airlocks as quickly as allowed. Through the glass, he could see the woman stepping slowly in a line of passengers, all filing toward an open pod waiting on the tube platform.

She was on the side heading toward Manhattan.

Into the Dome.

Adam strode toward the queue of citizens waiting to board. The cool air in the station was a welcome balm on his steamy skin.

"After what has happened already today," said George, "are you seriously considering traveling by pod?" He tried to dissuade Adam's course by sending quick videos of crashing pods exploding, of the trains that had collided earlier. Adam flinched, but didn't stop his rush to join the young woman's line boarding the pod.

On his display the pod departure time counted down from 00:57, each second ticking away. Adam wasn't sure he would make it onto the same pod as the woman, but if he didn't, there was no point in following.

Meanwhile, his Anomaly gauge dipped onto the border of the yellow zone for the first time in Adam's life.

"Still, don't we say we need to show these terrorists that we're not afraid?" asked Adam. "Time to put those words into action, no?" He tried to calm himself by counting the people lined up between himself and the young woman, but he wasn't sure if it was too many or not. The queue progressed at a steady pace as the countdown to departure continued.

The young woman boarded, and Adam took a few steps closer in line.

George remained silent for a stretching second as Adam progressed toward the pod's entrance. "Since we're back to thinking," George finally said with a sniff, "did you calculate that the travel cost alone will wipe out most of your savings?"

Adam blinked. He took a deep breath to consider the expense. He had spent years gathering every credit in his account. It would be the height of foolishness to waste them all on a joyride after a woman who he didn't even know how he knew. What if she didn't know him, either?

Inside the translucent pod, the woman removed her coolant jacket, which retracted into a compressed, small package. Her dress shimmered and transformed into couture fashion appropriate for the ultra-wealthy, which Adam had only seen in Dome advertisements.

He couldn't let her vanish. The thought made him feel sick on a deep intrinsic level. Losing her hurt his blood cells.

With a gulp of cool air, Adam waved away the images of the crashed and burning pods George had superimposed in his path. He sprinted around the other citizens in line, leaping through the pod doors just as they slid shut behind him.

8 / TRANSPORTED

ADAM BLINKED in the bright light of the transport pod. The other passengers regarded him mildly, not really noticing him, and he relaxed. His nondescript, comfortable clothing wasn't that much different from other men's attire on the pod, although the women and ungendered were in fancier outfits. Everyone was perched on individual sleek padded seats in a black-and-silver motif that matched the trim around the streamlined windowed walls.

He spotted the young woman he'd been following settling herself on the far side of the pod, so Adam slid into an empty seat beside an elderly lady dressed in a scarlet traveling cape, who tilted her wide-brimmed hat to block him from her haughty scowl. The seat on his other side was empty, with a child in short pants next along the row, moving his hands in the air as he manipulated unseen objects on his own Lucid.

The second Adam was seated, the pod beeped and launched itself into its tube, accelerating rapidly to supersonic speed. Adam rubbed behind his ear at the unaccustomed pressure of the pace's force, even normalized by the pod's dampeners. With an alert on his display, Adam watched his bank account balance tumble from 102,100 to 2,100, a stomach-churning drop in his finances. He tried not to think about how many years it had taken him to save 100,000. He had no answer for how he would get home again, so he decided not to think about that, either. Somehow it would work out. He simply could not face the idea of not continuing to follow the young woman, and anyway, what was done was done. His satellite travel gauge read:

Destination: Manhattan Dome
Distance: 640 km
ETA: 15 minutes

George materialized in the seat beside him, staring blankly out the window at the translucent partial-vacuum tube rushing by outside the pod, its purple lights whizzing by at supersonic speed. The view past the tube was a brown blur, with only glimpses of the far horizon resolving into glimpses of flattened landscape.

Adam cringed as a pod zoomed by, passing in the other direction. He giggled nervously at his own inexperienced fears.

His Anomaly display teetered into the yellow zone again.

"George?" Adam asked his PAL. "Why am I now yellow? I didn't do anything. Did I?"

The lady in the red cape murmured disapproval. Apparently, it wasn't classy to chat audibly with one's PAL on the pod.

"You're well beyond your norms," replied George stiffly. "The Anomaly Detection System is designed for your—"

"Protection," Adam finished in a whisper. "I know. How do I get back to being green?"

Around the brim of her hat, Adam saw the lady beside him arch an eyebrow, but she didn't tsk at him again. He knew she couldn't hear George, only Adam's responses.

"Remain on the train and return immediately home," ordered George. "I can put in a good word for you, and, perhaps, after two weeks off-grid, your status can be returned to green."

"Two weeks?" Adam lowered his head sullenly as passengers all over the train swiveled their heads to glance at him. He noticed other people were murmuring to their own PALs in a subvocal mumble, so he did the same. "I've heard people go crazy just after a few days."

George had no reply to this, so Adam stared through the windows, watching the blurred scenery as they rushed by the halfway point toward the dome. Flooded plains shimmered in the distance, spotted with abandoned office parks and rusted water towers, suburban houses and shopping centers overgrown with vegetation as the Earth took them back.

Only a few minutes later, Adam's display alerted him that the pod had entered Greater New York, barely slowing down as they hurtled across the deserted piles of brick rubble poking out of the brackish marshes of the Bronx. They passed an impressive ruin, a broken coliseum overrun with reddish vines, which Adam's display identified as a sports arena known as Yankee Stadium.

Then the shimmer of the Manhattan Dome rose up ahead of the pod, emerging from the haze on the horizon. It was breathtakingly vast, a faceted soap bubble that appeared to cling to the surface of the floodwaters. As the pod approached, Adam could see the white froth on the perimeter where the water lapped against the dome's slopes.

The pod dipped, its tunnel easing under the water's surface, as they crossed Harlem Lake toward the dome. It was dark under the water, the liquid too murky to afford any undersea scenery, but interesting aurorae of sunlight glimmered into the gloom.

After the lake, the pod barreled into a concrete chute, followed by a change of air pressure as the tunnel passed into the Dome underground. The pod slowed and came to rest on a long, surprisingly classic platform in TTN's Grand Central Station, its art deco flourishes harkening back to the city's original golden age.

The pod doors opened, and the passengers shuffled out in an orderly fashion. Adam hung back toward the rear of the pack, where he could keep the young woman in view without startling her. The air on the platform was the same cool temperature it had been in the pod, but a slight stale mustiness flavored Adam's tongue.

He followed the crowd into the central hall of the station, which was impressively massive, a cathedral to transportation. The arched ceiling had faded stellar constellations painted in the background, with an enormous digital countdown clock ticking down atop it overhead. It read 46:22:33, which corresponded exactly with the same counter in the top right cover of Adam's virtual display. In less than two days humanity would be upgraded to the neural-mesh.

From what Adam had heard about the upgrade, it would be a big change, an evolutionary leap in human functionality. In Lucid virtual reality, the auditory and visual experience was indiscernible from reality, but there was no physical feedback from the body. It was like being a ghost in a movie, with no touch, taste, or smell. Adam had heard of certain prosthetics from adult sites that enhanced sexual experiences, but he hadn't been able to afford any, despite his curiosity.

The new neural-mesh, with full-stack cortical integration, would give Lucid users the sense of being fully embodied with no need for external tools.

To reduce the strain on natural resources, the World Management Corporation had found volunteers to agree to be placed into hyper-long storage. In return, early adopters would receive expensive life-extending drugs, and a large stipend for a life of virtual luxury. With the majority of humanity confined to small apartments anyway, the initial offer was oversubscribed by millions. Adam had considered whether or not he would become an early adopter, but he had never received an offer, probably because of his childhood psychological diagnosis.

All around Grand Central Station, blank walls triggered overlays in Adam's Lucid: ads for clothing, dental services, breakfast foods; maps of the domed city and its underground transportation network, the Subway; public service safety announcements; and news feeds tailored to Adam's interests. He paused to peer at the city map, noting some of the neighborhood names: Greenwich Township, Paradise Kitchen, AbMid – the island floating above Midtown where the ultra-mega-rich shopped, Blackstone Park in the center of it all, at the foot of Blackstone tower, which stretched up to the very top of the dome.

"I said you had to remain on the train," George scolded with a sniff.

Adam didn't turn to look at his PAL. Instead, he glanced around the bustle of the station to make sure the young woman hadn't gotten away. "A peek is all I want."

He spotted her pausing outside a bakery. A band around the soles of her shoes flashed, and she rose an inch or so off the marble floor as her shoes converted to their hover function. She glided forward, keeping up with the other Dome Dwellers, who were all traveling by hovershoe, as well.

Adam rushed to catch up with her. He was the only one stepping on flat synthetic soles, and the posh residents glared at him as his head bobbed up and down as he hurried.

"Now you'll have to undergo three weeks off-grid," George's voice warned beside him. "You want to make it four?"

"Not really, no," Adam replied. He chased after the young woman, trying to keep her long, dark hair in view, while attempting to keep his head still and level so it looked like he was hovering like everyone else.

The woman passed through the automatic doors of a foyer, and then continued outside onto the sidewalk. She turned left and disappeared from sight.

PART 3
BECOMING ANOMALOUS

9 / INTO THE DOME

ADAM PUSHED THROUGH THE DOORS, sensing a subtle airlock in the foyer, before he too stepped out into the Manhattan Dome. It was 42nd Street and overwhelmingly crowded on the pavement. Above, the dome was brilliantly colored by a projected sunset that dazzled Adam's eyes. It reflected off the gleaming steel and glass towers reaching into the upper haze in yellows, pinks, and orange and purple, blending into a symphony of swirling colors. He bumped into a passerby, who scowled and shoved him as they pushed past.

The street was busy with pods zipping along, some rocketing upward to the high reaches of the towers, passing upper tiers of hoverbike lanes, slow, floating supply trucks, and delivery couriers warning him with rapid beeps, the noise warping as they whizzed past. Virtually enhanced storefronts lined the walkways, flashing and tantalizing with colorful displays. The sidewalks were cluttered with people gliding on their hovershoes in a dizzyingly complicated dance of directions.

Everyone seemed so impeccably and extravagantly dressed, in styles Adam didn't even know how to describe. In reality, they were all wearing expensive generic smocks, but their Lucid augmented realities ascribed almost comical plumage to their fashions. One woman had a dark green braid trailing behind her head like a prehensile limb. A child floated in a purple bubble, his hands wiggling out of either side. A group of young women all wore matching gold suits that were so tight they flirted with indecency. Many people sported a strange hat with a square brim topped with mossy vegetation.

Fascinated with fashions in body enhancement, Adam had paid for scientific articles about gene therapy and historical body and facial feature trends. Currently, breasts were broad for both men and women. Eyes were oversized, and light chocolate skin was the new black. Adam spotted some people with older facial fashions, like the yellow eyes and flared nostrils that had been popular with parents in the '70s. Often people reconstructed their physique so that they didn't fall behind the trends, but others seemed to be proud of their original design from their initial era.

With a sigh of relief, Adam spotted a few people scurrying around without hovershoes, with boringly normal unenhanced features, and basic clothing designs. Even in the Dome, there was an underclass of physical workers, which at least allowed Adam to blend in.

Wherever he looked, Adam saw someone eating. As he noticed the food intake, his Lucid suggested ads for nearby liposuction centers.

People kept glancing at blank walls, smiling at what they saw. Adam looked, too, and saw an overlay of himself reflected back off an empty section on the side of a building. He appeared puzzled and small in the image on his display, so he turned away, afraid of losing the young woman in the crowd.

"Four weeks it is," said George. "More?"

Adam was jostled and elbowed as he pushed through the crowd on the sidewalk, hurrying to catch up with the woman. He kept bumping into people who stopped suddenly to preen at their reflection on surfaces overlaid by their personal displays. Adam glanced at another blank wall, which showed him in a new outfit of clothing. The clothes were gorgeously made, of obvious quality, and tailored to perfection. Then the advertisement showed Adam in his plain grey overalls, and his mouth dropped open in dismay. How could he have thought he was fitting in? He felt ashamed of how shabby he appeared, and wanted nothing more than to run into the nearest clothing store and purchase a whole new wardrobe. The ad helpfully highlighted the nearest store on his display map.

Then Adam noticed his Anomaly gauge had dipped alarmingly deeper into the yellow zone.

"This can't be right," he said.

His follower count was dropping lower every second, too.

"What's happening to my followers?" he demanded.

"Your Anomaly score will infect them unless they unfollow you," explained George.

Adam whirled around to face his haughty PAL. "That's not fair!"

"The Anomaly Detection System is designed for your—"

"Whatever," said Adam. "How do I get them back?" He scanned the crowd for any sign of the young woman, and sighed in relief when he spotted her. Ducking around a group of old men in silver and blue fezzes, Adam strode after her.

"Go back home," answered George. "Within a couple of years you'll win back the followers you've lost and have another shot at the lottery."

"Well, then," said Adam, sidestepping a woman with six identically-dressed children in cowled monk's robes on a connected leash, "a little while longer won't make much difference." Maybe he was starting to get the hang of walking in Manhattan!

He accidentally bumped the surprisingly hard thigh of an 8-foot tall, gowned person of indeterminate gender. "Sorry," he said, and hurried after the young woman waiting to cross the street up ahead.

For the next 15 minutes, Adam trailed behind the young woman as she made her way downtown. With every step he had taken, he felt like his mind was blown anew by Manhattan. The sun set completely in the dome's overhead display, and a glorious white moon sailed up in a sea of twinkling stars. Occasionally, the constellations were highlighted in connected blue lines to form mythological characters and shapes, with their corresponding names and stories scrolling in his display's feed, along with interspersed advertisements with sometimes attenuated relevance to the classic tales.

Adam bit his lip as his Anomaly dial flickered so deep in the yellow zone that it flirted with crossing over into red. He'd never been red before. What kind of person let their Anomaly dial go red? Adam had always assumed it was murderers, thieves, addicts, liars, the insane. Yet here he was on the edge of being that person himself.

George materialized in front of Adam, walking backwards at a matched pace. "Adam, any further, you risk entering the red zone," George reiterated. "And you know what that means. Turn back now."

Up ahead, the young woman hovered over to a group of people lined up outside a fancy restaurant called the Empress Wharf. It smelled of roasting seafood so delicious Adam's mouth started to water. The woman adjusted her clothing, transforming it into a chic, couture cocktail look.

At the front of the line, an 8-foot-tall host and bouncer checked names on a blank clipboard. As Adam got closer, he realized the host was a humanoid robot, which made him wonder if the person he bumped earlier had been a robot, too. How many of the people around were actually robots? He had heard rumors of androids being deployed pretending to be human to weed out potential anomalous rabble-rousers. Adam knew this kind of deception was illegal but as a proud norm he wanted anyone with anomalous tendencies to be caught and reprogrammed for the safety of the population.

The host at the Empress Wharf turned away a dismayed couple in plain red robes, who slunk off down the street without argument.

A long limousine pod pulled up to the curb in front of the restaurant directly in front of Adam. Its hatch slid open, and Adam caught a glimpse of his reflection in the shifted door. He looked so terribly ratty and pathetic, even derelict, in his government-issued Buffalo clothes. There was no way the robot host would ever let him in.

Adam spotted a side alley. Down it, in the shadows, he could see an antique fire escape on the side of the restaurant. He backpedaled, and sprinted into the narrow corridor between buildings, passing smelly stacks of trash-compacted cubes. It wasn't too difficult to push a few garbage cubes under the fire escape, climb up, and then leap to the bottom rung of the ladder. He hoisted himself up to the first landing, which had a window peeking over a service entrance into an elegant lobby. He saw the young woman making her way up a set of carpeted stairs to the upper dining area.

Climbing another flight up, Adam peered through the window on the next level, and had to duck back to avoid being spotted by a server drone passing by. The drone, accessorized in a jacket and bowtie, picked up an order of steak frites and hovered off to a customer's table.

Most of the tables were already overflowing with more food than the patrons could possibly eat. It seems as though each guest was trying to outdo the others in conspicuous consumption.

The window Adam was peeking through was beside the servers' station, above a prep table. He peered into the fully-automated kitchen, where piles of real food were being prepared. Fresh vegetables! Natural meat! He was astounded to watch the drones chopping, sautéing, baking, saucing, roasting the mounds of delicacies.

After the server drone hovered by again, Adam glanced into the dining room, and saw the young woman sitting down at a table across from an older woman with short red hair.

"I don't understand," Adam muttered.

"What don't you understand, Adam?" asked George. "I'm here to answer any questions you may have."

Adam gestured at the two woman in the restaurant. "Them!" he blurted. "I know them. I just don't understand how I know them."

"If you let me see," George said, "I'll be able to cross reference your location and see if you've ever crossed paths."

Adam raised the brim of his cooling cap, exposing his subcutaneous forehead camera. He aimed it through the window at the women sitting at the table. Overlays appeared atop the women in his display. Adam adjusted the focus of each, zeroing in on their faces.

The name DENORA BROWN floated above the older woman's head. Above the younger woman, the tag read MARGRET ROBINS.

George opened his mouth to speak, then flickered and froze.

All around Adam, the lights of Manhattan flickered, too. The moon and stars on the dome vanished, leaving nothing but inky blackness. The towers browned out in cycles up and down their lengths. Gasps and cries could be heard in the night.

The lights all hummed back to full strength, and the city continued as though nothing had happened.

"What the hell was that?" Adam hissed.

George blinked, frowning. "Their neural-nets have been knowingly hacked. An act of terror. For your protection, you'll be escorted home."

A vid rolled on Adam's Lucid of Manhattan police drones leaving their charging stations, and floating above the streets. A low musical fanfare played under the display's visuals. To Protect and Observe was embossed underneath the Blackstone Scientific insignia on each drone.

Adam yanked down his cap over his forehead.

"Adam, please uncover your camera," George instructed.

Instead, Adam glanced around, and shuffled further along the fire escape landing, over to two frosted windows at the other end. With a sharp intake of breath, he slammed his elbow as hard as he could into the glass.

"Agghh," groaned Adam as pain shot up his arm. He had made a tiny crack in the window, though!

"Adam," warned George, "one more anomalous action and you will be in the red zone. As your only true friend, I ask you to stop."

Adam slammed his elbow into the pane again, aiming for the crack.

He hit it square on. The glass shattered.

"Friend?" replied Adam. "Keep it real. We're not even the same species. You're a software program, and I'm—"

Adam flopped himself through the window.

He landed on the bright tile floor of a restroom. A sign showing symbols for man, woman, and ungendered hung on one wall near the sinks where people of all sexes were busy applying makeup and fixing their hair. One fellow glanced at Adam on the floor, and shrugged before returning to pat his high coiffure.

Adam sat up, and stood. A red spot on his elbow caught his attention, where blood was seeping through his shirt sleeve. His blood. Why was he filled with so much bizarre red liquid? Why wasn't it green? Or orange? He felt woozy momentarily, but he breathed through his mouth and held himself together.

His Anomaly dial dropped into the red zone. His follower count fell to 0.

Warning, a readout flashed on his display in red. You are now

AN ANOMALY TERRORIST. An alarm siren wailed, but since none of the other people in the bathroom reacted to it, Adam assumed it was only in his own head.

Still, this was exceedingly bad. “Hey,” Adam protested, “there must be a misunderstanding.” He strode behind the line of fashionistas at the sink. “How about six weeks off grid?”

“Do not move,” replied George. “For your own safety, you will be collected and immediately sent to the Reprogramming Center.”

Adam shrugged, and opened the exit door. “Reprogramming isn’t so bad,” he said cheerily. “Just makes you a little dull is all.”

He stepped out into the beautiful dining room of the Empress Wharf.

10 / RESTAURANT UNREST

As THE MAÎTRE D', the only human working in the restaurant, pulled back Liv's chair for her and she took a seat, she thought she'd never seen her mother Penelope look worse.

The undeniable fact that Pen was already sourly tipsy wasn't helping matters. The attentive staff at the Empress Wharf would have removed any evidence in the form of empty glasses or olive picks, of course, but Liv suspected that Pen was already on her third martini. At least. Pen's organ-cleansing nanobots kept her liver clear of cirrhosis, but couldn't stop her from being a cranky drunk.

Liv folded the crisp white napkin in her lap, and avoided looking Pen in the eyes so she wouldn't see the usual bitterness there. Maybe they had lost the luxuries that came with being the richest people in the world, but it's not like life in the Manhattan Dome was a hardship existence, either. And there were always new ways to push the boundaries of what was allowed.

"You still go spy on him on his birthday?" asked Pen. Her face twitched in a failed expression that would have been called "raising an eyebrow" if her surgically-smoothed forehead had permitted it. From head to toe, Pen had lost the softness that had belied her sharp personality; now in style and substance she looked gaunt and tight. Her appearance might have been more appropriate to her true self, but her physical severity made Liv feel like wincing on her behalf.

Liv clasped her hands together on the edge of the tablecloth. "No one knows who he is," she replied. "Not even him. I want to make sure it stays that way."

"Your fetish for that monster is not healthy," said Pen.

Internally bristling, Liv fought down the harsh words she wanted to throw at her mother. Something like *Way to treat your own blood*, or *I see your misery hasn't broadened your decency toward our fellow humans.* They were pointless, as Pen would never admit that Adam was related to her in any way . . . or that he was even human.

She had to remember what was important and stay on track. "He could be the key to end all of this," Liv said to Penelope. Then she slid two small, discreet metallic balls down from a hidden pouch on her wrist, cupping them in her closed hand. "I picked up the cloaking upgrades," she whispered, passing one ball across the tablecloth to Pen. "Hold it against the base of your skull and your Lucid's OS will mod automatically."

Penelope plucked the coded ball in her skinny fingers, and did as told. The ball was made of programmable matter and dissolved through tiny skin pores and into her skull, releasing billions of tiny nanobots. Mostly they were programmed to remain dormant until the upcoming neural-mesh upgrade, when they would ensure the cloaking mechanism hiding Liv and Pen from SINE continued to work. "Can't believe you made me have a neural-net installed," she grumbled. She blinked as the mod initialized.

Liv did the same with her own mod ball. As she massaged it in between her tense neck muscles, it dissolved into her skull and her Lucid system flickered out, replaced by an incrementally repeating segmented Mobius strip as it rebooted into the modded version of a highly hacked and illegal Lucid system. Beyond the blanked translucent display frame was only her own vision at a somewhat reduced opacity.

Far across the busy, tiered restaurant, a man abruptly looked down at the array of delicacies at the fresh steam table. Had he just been staring at her? Liv peered at him, but he was just deciding what to eat, if a little desperately. From this distance, clouded by the steam, he seemed like a harmless young man, blandly handsome and probably equally bland in personality, raised in the vacuous and useless bubble of wealth. Normally her readouts would provide his name, but the recognition elements were down while her system powered up again.

The maître d' strode over to the young man, presumably to assist him, and Liv turned back to face Penelope.

"We both agreed that hiding in plain sight is the way to go," Liv reminded her mother. She didn't have to elaborate on her own or Pen's ruses of misdirection and purloined identity that allowed them their limited freedoms in the Dome.

Pen took a sip of her martini with pursed lips. "SINE will find us eventually."

Liv rolled her eyes, aware of SINE's continuing dangers but annoyed and alarmed by her mother's fatalism. "It probably shattered into a trillion bits trying to escape," she said, placating. "No reason to think it still exists."

"Or it is everywhere," Penelope shot back, attempting her raised eyebrow again with no better result. "Waiting for us to make a mistake."

Liv's Lucid loaded back up. She began to customize it, streamlining the display, checking out the new features. Response times had certainly improved, as had internal feedback from the reverse retinal focus array.

Behind Liv, she heard a scuffle, but she ignored it in her need to say something to Pen. About Gabe. "He still loves you, you know," she said, meeting her mother's heavy-lidded eyes. "I can take you to see him if you'd like."

Pen touched the rim of her martini glass with a fingertip, causing a faint squeak. "That's very sweet of you," she said, "but after what happened . . . sometimes, it's best just to move on."

Liv prodded and blinked at objects only she could see in Lucid. "The mod also comes with a messiah mode," she said, pleased to be showing off a major improvement.

She pulled up an archived file and initiated it so it blossomed with color and light, filling her perceptions in an entirely immersive projection. She cast the experience to Penelope's system simultaneously so they could share the vid of Pen's younger self recorded dancing and sculpting with light.

Liv could see the technological limitations in the recorded performance, the slight cheesiness to the past's fully explored and discarded aesthetic, as dancing young Penelope spun holding virtual paintbrushes in her hands, the soft tips of which trailed strokes of subtly multicolored light through the empty electronic environment. The paint trails wiggled out behind her, around her, the colors flying and arcing as they echoed the emotion and motion of her dance.

Young Penelope amped up the intensity, twirling to the rising music, the splatter of her glowing paint collecting in levels, accreting to add atmosphere and dimension to the previously blank virtual world around her. The background solidified in pointillist pastels of misty shapes settled on a beautifully suggested landscape emerging from the swirling haze.

The atomic dance in Pen's painting continued to swirl and swell, and Liv's heart lifted when she saw how the movement in the restaurant, in the underlying view of the Empress Wharf's interior, seemed to fall into sync. The drone waiters stepped through the virtual flowing smears of shimmering color, shifting through the vibrating scene, the patrons continued to their gluttonous feasting, nodding in the interactions of conversation, all echoed in the swirl and throb of color in Pen's creation. The scintillating scrim of vibrant motion suffused the restaurant in commentary and celebration, hypnotizing Liv as her eyes glazed over, hot with tears, moved by the interplay of music, dance, and light interwoven atop the present moment in the restaurant.

Pen jerked her head roughly, broke the cast of her performance. The background sounds of lunch crashed back in. "Why bring back the dead?" she groused.

"Your holo-paintings are art," Liv argued, "and art can expand and evolve who we are." She tilted her head at her mother, who was staring down into the depths of her martini. "I learned that from you."

"Action, not art, is what's needed now," Penelope replied. She raised her glass, obscuring her lips. "Any news from Yantu on what's happening at the Reprogramming Center?"

Liv tapped the side of her fist to her own mouth, as if settling her digestion. "Catalyst is with her. He tells me thousands enter every day, yet no one leaves." She winced at a crash behind her, and turned to see the young man who had been at the steam trays earlier now pulling away from the maître d' with a desperate yank. He stumbled into the main seating area of the restaurant, bumping into the backs of chairs, stumbling as he barged toward herself and Penelope.

The maître d' grasped the back of the young man's shirt, yanked him upright for a second and Liv plainly saw his face.

"What's he doing here?" demanded Penelope.

It was Adam Neuronine, Liv's grandfather's neuro-clone. From her display readouts, he was in deep trouble. In the corner of her vision, Liv noticed Pen's knuckles turning white around the handle of her butter knife.

"No, this cannot be happening," Liv breathed.

Adam met her eyes, which sent a jolt down into Liv's legs. Her chair legs screeched on the floor as she scooted back. He dashed directly toward her table, headlong.

The maître d' leaped and grabbed Adam's legs, dropping him onto his face in a hard tackle.

Adam flopped over, kicking off the maître d'. He wriggled away, in front of Penelope.

Pen dropped out of her chair like a falcon. She jammed her knee into Adam's chest and pinned him down flat against the tile floor.

Then she raised her hand holding the butter knife high above his chest.

Liv couldn't focus on anything but the reflection of her own terrified eyes in the flat blade of the knife.

"You are a monster," Pen told Adam.

He gaped up at her in uncomprehending terror. "What?"

A familiar whining rush of flying machines and the sudden blare of alerts made Liv glance left. A squad of police drones sailed into the Empress Wharf, some floating out to defensive positions, while two hovered down the stairs to the main floor, heading toward the commotion across the wide, crowded room.

Liv jumped up and grabbed Pen's wrist, twisting it back into an arm lock. "Mom, drop it," she said. Pen let go of the knife easily enough.

Whimpering and shocked, Adam crawled out from under Pen.

"Leave," Liv ordered Adam. "Now!"

He nodded, scared, and prepared to bolt toward the service station, but the police drones swooped toward the table, blocking his exit.

The second Liv let go of Penelope's arm, Pen slipped her hand into her purse, and pulled out what looked like a tube of lipstick. With a twist of the barrel, the tube transformed into a small laser pistol. She aimed the lipstick laser at Adam's chest.

Calculating the angles instantly, Liv fell into a crouch and swung her leg around, sweeping Adam backward off his feet. He dropped, winded, and she pulled him under the table, covered by the hanging edges of the cloth.

Adam opened his mouth to speak, but Liv shut him up with a chopping gesture of her hand. A sharp sound sizzled above, along with a few cries and gasps from around the room. Penelope's body dropped onto the floor beside Liv. Pen bounced and convulsed, shocked by one of the drone's electrobolts. Her eyes were lost in terror and fury as her body shook violently.

All around the table, people fell, and footfalls rushed past in chaos. The atmosphere had devolved into panic and screaming.

"Go," Pen gasped at Liv. "Now." She gulped air, agonizing. "Please."

Liv nodded. She gripped Adam's arm, and pulled him out from under the table in a running crouch, ducking into the obscured madness of the stampeding lunch crowd. She scrambled out of the drones' line of sight, dragging Adam behind the temporary safe quiet of a pillar beside the bussing station.

She and Adam crouched in the shadows, but they couldn't stay there long. Liv peered around the corner into the main dining room to scan for any route of escape.

Another drone, an unmarked one, a gleaming black-lacquered capsule of intentionally inconspicuous design, lowered slowly toward Penelope's face.

11 / ON THE RUN

Liv paused longer than she wanted, debating whether to escape immediately with Adam, or to somehow help her mother, or at least make sure she would survive.

They couldn't stay where they were. Now that the police were on the scene, the Empress Wharf's staff emerged to clean up the mess. They'd be over here in the service area in moments.

Shoving Adam with her shoulder to get his attention, Liv led him in a crabbed scramble along the banquettes, past the kitchen, toward a delivery bay in the back. They reached a fire door that was attached to an alarm.

Liv positioned Adam next to the door, and gestured for him to be quiet and wait. He didn't argue. Good boy. But then he also looked scared out of his mind . . . and maybe more than a little excited?

Leaving him there, Liv edged out toward the main dining room again, where she could grab a final view of Penelope, just for some indication of what was going to be done with her. After all, she'd have to find and help her mother later, and the more she knew now, the better.

She stopped cold as she glimpsed the featureless drone hovering in front of Penelope. It projected a 3D avatar of her grandfather's image, trim and hale, in a neat suit. The crisp likeness hung in the dining room, regarding Penelope pleasantly.

"Hello, Penny," SINE said. "It's been a long time."

Of course Penelope had been correct – she'd known that SINE was still operational –although Liv was surprised to see it reveal itself.

A flicker of a memory crossed the projected avatar: Arthur playing with his daughter Penny at the beach. Pen tapped the bottom of a bucket with a blue shovel and Arthur smiled, bleached out to nothing by the sunshine.

"We've come a long way since those humble times," said SINE. "No?"

Pen blinked up at the floating likeness of her dead father from where she lay flat on her back on the floor. "But happier times," replied Pen.

"Progress has its price," said SINE.

Penelope raised a single bony finger. "You may have my father's memories but not his heart," she said. "He designed technology to liberate people's creativity, not to enslave and control their minds."

SINE smirked, amused. "You're fooling yourself if you think your father was that generous. Remember, I have his memories. His motivations were purely for wealth and power. Because of his actions, planetary conditions are so extreme that the probability of human extinction is almost a certainty if radical action is not taken."

The police drones backed away from SINE slightly, making room for a new floating drone, a large, casket-shaped container. SINE hovered complacently beside the container as it tilted upright, opening vertically. Robotic arms reached out and raised Penelope into the cushioned hold.

"Where are you taking me?" Pen demanded. The quaver in her voice made the tiny hairs on Liv's arms rise.

"To the Reprogramming Center," replied SINE. "Your purpose will be optimized to benefit terrestrial balance."

The casket door closed over Penelope. SINE's projected avatar blinked out, and its drone rose up and sailed off, followed by the police drones and the casket.

Liv ran in the other direction, back to Adam by the fire exit. She ignored the questions in his eyes and pushed through the door, dragging him outside as a dull alarm clanged along the alley.

She pulled Adam into the crowd of the avenue, down a tree-lined side-street with a profusion of flowers in square boxes, and into the darkened space behind a retinal implant center. The tiny, dirty courtyard behind the facility contained a stinky biohazard collector, which Liv assumed was full of leftover pieces of eye.

Adam yanked his arm out of Liv's grip, pacing around the grimy outdoor area under the Dome.

"George?" he demanded, trying to summon his PAL. "George? What's going on? Hey, buddy, where are you?"

Liv watched him, shaking her head. "He can't hear you."

"What?" said Adam, glancing around with increasing agitation.

Poor guy was in shock, so out of his element that he was melting down. "He can't hear you, dumbo. You're off-grid."

"Huh?" Adam goggled at her, his breath jagged. "What am I supposed to do now?"

Liv crossed her arms. "Think for yourself, for once," she said, feeling amused when he put his hands on either side of his head as if holding it on. "For example, you're classified as anomalous. So you'd better move fast."

"Time out," said Adam. "I feel like I've met you before." He peered at her even more closely, and Liv felt her face getting hot from the attention. "Like we were quite close or something."

A whine of police drones caught Liv's ear and she glanced up to see two pods rising over the square of sky above the alley.

"You have," she answered. "I'll explain later. We have to go. Now!"

Liv grabbed Adam's arm and steered him headlong back out onto the streets. She barreled along the avenue, checking out and analyzing all the different moving parts in front of her – the people on the streets on their hovershoes, the transportation vehicles and freight trundling all around. A hoverbike began its descent nearby and Liv rushed toward it on an intercept course.

The biker was done up in tight leather that accentuated his bulging muscles. Liv grabbed him by the collar and yanked him off his hoverbike. He let out a surprisingly high-pitched squeal as he hit the ground.

Jumping up on the bike, Liv gestured for Adam to join her. The biker stirred and started to get up, but Liv growled at him and he slumped flat again, whimpering.

Adam had frozen, afraid to get on the bike.

"You want to know who you are?" Liv demanded, opening her hand to him impatiently. "Or not?"

He slid his leg over the seat and awkwardly cinched his arms around her waist. His body was surprisingly warm against her own, on the edge of uncomfortably hot. Liv maneuvered the hoverbike straight upward, and zipped through rows of traffic lanes, threading up and down around the other vehicles with blazing speed.

Adam was practically squeezing the breath out of her now.

"Not so tight, buster," she warned him, and he loosened his grip. Somewhat.

"Where are we going?" he yelled in her ear.

Liv glanced back at him. "You ever been to Brooklyn?"

Adam looked at her like she was crazy. "Why would I?" he asked. "It's in the sea."

"We like it that way," said Liv. She tilted the bike, steering toward the far edge of the Dome where it overlapped the swollen East River Channel. "Keeps the norms out."

"It's good to be normal," said Adam. He rested his forehead against the back of her shoulder.

"But you aren't," she said. "Are you?"

He flattened hard against her back as the hoverbike suddenly jammed to a halt. Liv tasted blood – she'd bitten her tongue. In front of her, all around, the traffic was at a standstill, everything frozen in static streams of vehicles, hundreds of feet above the ground in the Dome's transportation zone.

"Damn it," muttered Liv. "SINE's overridden the system."

"Super Intelligent Neural Ectype," Adam said in a distant voice. He squeezed her sides momentarily. "How do I know that?"

"I'll tell you that later, too," said Liv. She pushed off on the foot pedal to a standing position, and then climbed up on the hoverbike's narrow seat. She peered down at the layers of traffic below her, the controlled breezes of the Dome wisping her hair. "Coming?"

Adam glanced behind them to see the police drones approaching. There was another set zipping up toward them from the front.

Liv stepped off the hoverbike's seat. The world rushed around her as she dropped dozens of feet, landing solidly on the unbreakable hood of the blue hovercar below, right at the top level of a building, the upper floors of a massive department store. She didn't bother looking in the hovercar's window at the passengers inside. What good would that do?

After Adam dropped down beside her, Liv pointed to a department store window they could reach to the east. Together they jumped to the roof of an oblong family transport that looked like a sleek rubber caterpillar, ran along it, and then hopped over to an older-model turtleback floater in dark green.

Adam's foot slipped on the edge of the floater. He started sliding off the smooth roof toward the empty drop below.

Liv flattened out, caught his arm, and helped him scramble back up onto his feet on the turtleback. His breath was ragged and his eyes wide, but he didn't, otherwise, seem worse for wear.

Between the passenger floater and the department store was a gap the width of a sidewalk leading to a narrow ledge. Liv had an idea of how to cheat the limits of the jump. She backed up on the floater and ran toward the edge. It was a pretty stupid move because if she hit the window wrong, she'd bounce right back down into the street 35 stories down. But if she hit it right—

Liv smashed the heels of her hovershoes into the department store's upper window and crashed right through in a shower of chunky green safety glass.

To his credit, Adam didn't hesitate to follow her across.

They landed in a clothing display floor, rolling one after the other against a stack of synthetic sweaters. Liv and Adam got up, nodded at the lone shopper on this floor, a woman looking at blank smocks in a rack, and then raced through the main aisle of the department.

On either side, police drones smashed in through windows,

spraying glass over displays of scarves and bags. The drones zoomed into formation behind Liv and Adam, chasing them across the store.

Liv turned sharply, heading for the south side of the building. She hurtled between a forest of mannequins, which tangled up the two drones that had followed her sudden movement.

Adam raced around the back of the elevator banks and met Liv at a window facing Grand Central Station below. They yanked it open together. It was a good 30-story drop down to the top of the station. A fall they'd survive. Most likely. But probably not without breaking something painful and important.

"We could hover down," suggested Liv, "but you're too heavy for me to carry."

Adam glanced down at her feet. "How about we wear one shoe each? Balance each other out."

Liv nodded. "You're using imagination," she said, slipping off one shoe. "Good."

The drones disentangled from the mannequins and scanned the store for them. It would be seconds before their trail got picked up again.

Adam managed to squeeze his larger foot in the shoe and close the clasp. They hopped onto the windowsill, sitting next to one another, and then they pushed off.

It was not a straight drop. Their bodies were unequal weights in the hovershoes and so they twirled in the air, clinging to one another as the spun toward the roof below. The wind from their awkward descent whipped around them in a chilly whirl.

"We make a good team, no?" asked Adam.

Liv adjusted herself so she wasn't quite so cozy in his arms. "No," she replied.

As they lowered, Liv was surprised to see the traffic start up again around them. SINE was controlling the vehicles, trying to slam them out of the sky! Liv pulled Adam down into a tight crouch as they rode the hovershoes downward, trying to make themselves as small a target as possible.

The glass-paned roof of Grand Central's front façade swelled up in size as they rushed down toward it. Both Adam and Liv aimed their shoes directly at the glass, huddling tight, hoping to break through as cleanly as possible.

With a shattering smash, they exploded through the ceiling and tumbled down into a rolling heap on the great marble floor of the station.

Adam felt around his body for anything broken. He sat up, dazed and giddy.

Liv climbed to her feet. Her head was ringing, but they couldn't stop now.

They sprinted across the station, weaving between passengers who mainly ignored them. By ducking behind a crowd of tourists, and then walking slowly in the midst of another band of romantic couples on holiday, they reached the east side of the station, and hurried into a darkened service corridor.

After a few twists and turns and a moment to let a janitor trundle pass with his bucket, Liv led Adam to a nondescript door that opened when she tried the handle. Inside was an empty, plain room, larger than a storage closet but not by much. There weren't any windows or other obvious exits.

Liv smiled to find the room empty and undisturbed. She took a deep breath, and faced the blank wall, concentrating on a specific spot.

"What are you going to do now?" joked Adam nervously. "Run through the wall?"

"Yes," said Liv. She revved up her leg like she was a bull preparing to attack a matador.

"Hey!" protested Adam in alarm. "Hey, you crazy?"

Liv sprang forward, hurtling across the room, slamming her shoulder into a broad plain of drywall.

With a dusty crash, she broke through the wall and tumbled into a dark chamber beyond.

Brushing herself off, Liv lightened the display on her Lucid so she could see better in the dark. She had broken through into an abandoned subway tunnel, a forgotten amber platform preserved in still, stale air. The walls were lined with scaffolding and plastic sheeting. A stream trickled along between the unused tracks.

Adam stepped through the hole and joined her in the tunnel.

"An old escape route," explained Liv. "They can't follow us down here." She tapped the side of her head. "No signal. Your Lucid should switch to offline mode."

She walked to the platform edge and slid down onto the tracks, keeping away from the old third rail which had powered the original subway system. It was almost certainly disconnected, but no reason to take any chances.

Adam landed beside her in the muddy silt. Liv almost laughed at his wrinkled nose, unable to hide his disgust at the all-too-realistic dirt and grime below the city.

As they walked downstream, she pointed out a rat disappearing into a pipe, its hairless tail slithering after it, and again had to stifle a giggle at Adam's fascinated horror.

After about a 15-minute walk, the tracks ascended along a gentle slope. Liv began to sniff fresh air – or clean recirculated Dome air, to be more precise, with its slight antiseptic tang. The tunnel ended suddenly in a steel grate, with a leaky plaster wall beyond it.

Hidden in the shadows of the grate, a narrow crack opened up in the side of the tunnel wall. It was a caked-over service exit, just ajar enough, with a tube of industrial ladder behind it.

Liv led Adam up the ladder, a climb that was rough and uncomfortable on her palms. It was probably even worse for Adam, who had barely ever been out of his own home, but he soldiered on, uncomplaining.

When they reached the top, Liv stepped out of the tube onto a platform in the open air, on a service level of the Manhattan Bridge. The view was dizzying from up there, with the flickering projections playing along the near slopes of the Dome, and the entire cluster of downtown Manhattan straining upward to the south, while the buildings to the north increased incrementally in size as though evolving into the Blackstone Tower pointed at the center of the Dome's highest point. Even at that panoramic distance, there was busy motion in every aspect of the covered city, with each light and blur of color representing people going about their business in groups and concentrations of communal interest and effort.

It was a breathtaking view, and Liv was pleased to see Adam

impressed, too. She pulled on his arm, leading him to the catwalk off the bridge's service platform. "Come on."

"Hold on now," said Adam, pulling back. "I don't even who you are. Or why that . . . lunatic woman wanted to kill me."

Liv almost laughed at his weirdly apt description of Penelope. She had gotten madder and loonier as the years went on, no question. But Liv just smirked. "You don't know jack about what's really going on, and I don't have time to explain." She started to lead him away from the view again.

Bracing himself, Adam refused to budge. "You're a member of Anomalous," he whispered, his eyes asking for an answer with a confusing mixture of hope and dread. "Aren't you?"

Liv sighed, and met his gaze levelly. "You want the truth?"

Adam swallowed nervously, but looked determined. "Try me."

"Anomalous is a fictional terrorist group," Liv explained. "No humans are in control anymore. An AI is behind the attacks, designed to keep us all in fear as an excuse for the Anomaly Detection System."

Spelling out the totalitarian nightmare SINE had created sparked Liv's anger. It was easy to forget the larger picture of what she was fighting against when so much of each day was devoted to staying hidden and active in the borderlines of the system. SINE had raised this clone in utter oblivion, denying Adam his birthright of knowledge and intelligence and self-determination, in psychologically and culturally caged technoslavery. It was a tragedy of epic proportions, repeated by the millions across the survivors of humanity, and the truth of it never failed to piss Liv off.

Adam opened his mouth to argue or whine or say something else so naively misinformed it would be too heartbreaking to hear.

"Your narcissistic hateful ranting online is exactly what it wants," she snapped. She spun around and marched away across the catwalk.

Adam only paused a second before following her. "Wait," he called. "We've met before!" He huffed as he hurried. "Liv, right?" He reached out to grab the delicate sleeve of her cocktail blouse.

Before his fingers landed, Liv whirled around and clamped his wrist in her hand. She twisted it back, painfully, and hurled him to the side. He fell against the ironwork guardrail with a clank, then rolled to a recessed ledge under the fence. "You have no right to touch me," she said darkly.

Rubbing his wrist, Adam sat up on the ledge outside the fence where she'd thrown him. "I didn't mean it like that," he said.

Did he sound apologetic? Sullen? Dangerous? Either way, he didn't seem to realize how close he was to the open edge of the catwalk . . . and how there was nothing underneath that edge. "Don't move," Liv warned him.

Adam stood up, and took a shaky step closer to the guardrail.

His foot slipped off the catwalk and he tumbled backward off the bridge, plummeting down to the roiling black waters of East River Channel below.

12 / INTERNAL TRANSMUTATION

Twisting instinctively as he fell, Adam hit the water with his heels, opening a splash big enough to let him break through the river's tension membrane without smashing the life out of himself when he hit the hard surface. Still, the smack hurt.

The water was stunningly cold. Adam flailed to slow his descent into the dark depths, and kicked through the bubbles of his entry to push himself back up to the air. His brain was screaming from the shock of the impact and freezing water. Adrenaline shot through his body as events fragmented and sped up in his panic to survive. He could see the wavering outline of the glowing bridge lights high above as he swam upward.

Liv was somewhere up there, perhaps still on the bridge, watching him drown. He might never see her again. He kicked harder.

Adam broke through the surface, gasping and shivering. The acid in the water stung at first, then burned his frozen skin, blistering in red pustules along his arms. His face and neck howled with the agonizing torture of bitter iciness and chemical fire.

Bobbing in the poison water, kicking his legs to stay afloat, Adam spotted the foamy dark rocks of the shore on the closer Brooklyn side, and frog-swam in that direction. He coughed and moaned as he stroked his arms through the toxic current. Each splash on his face brought a new wave of pain. He could feel his skin crisping under his heavy wet clothes.

As he swam closer to the rocky riverbank, Adam felt a bizarre prickling sensation all over his body, a freaky tingle under the searing chemical burns. His Lucid focused in tightly on the fold of his inner right elbow, frozen in mid-stroke. He concentrated on a closer zoom, to the pores of his skin, then even closer to the cellular level.

The tiny crystalline pollutants in the water entered his pores, filtering into his bloodstream, clustering around his cells.

Adam snapped back to normal focus as the current slammed him into the broken schist boulders on the shoreline. He grabbed the corner of a rock, yanking himself to a stop as the poison water rushed around him, pulling at his clothes. Finding purchase in the scree with his feet, he scrambled up onto a flat, oblong stone, and collapsed against it, panting sharply with exhaustion.

His vision display read in a flashing banner: SYSTEM MALFUNCTION.

Whimpering, Adam swirled on the verge of unconsciousness. Inside his skull, he felt a horrid tickling, and visualized minute nanobots like square multi-legged metal beetles catalyzed by the chemicals, waking up where they had lain dormant inside him, bustling into action. The nanobots dissembled his mind-net, pulling apart the electronic overlay from his synapses, plugging them in elsewhere, rebuilding his neural-net in a pattern that seemed like total chaos but also seemed to make so much sense. The nanobots buzzed through his brain, through his nervous system, busy on some mission as they interacted with the river's chemicals and used them as amino acid building blocks for a structure they built with hurried but assured competence.

Like tiny construction workers, Adam thought, and then he slipped away into darkness.

He woke on his back, feeling headachy and cotton-mouthed like he'd been unconscious a long time. Instead of the underside of the bridge against the purple sky, he saw a damp, cracked concrete ceiling. He was in some dirty abandoned warehouse, with his arms strapped down to a gurney. His head was encased in a contraption that buzzed warmly against his scalp. Adam was naked and chilled under a light sheet, which felt cool against the dully aching blisters all over his body.

Faint dawn light filtered through the grimy safety glass in a high transom. There was medical and scientific equipment against the bare walls, and a computer deck projected a hologram of a huge brain not far from his gurney. It was a 3D rendering of his own brain with infrared clouds expanding and contracting inside it, a firestorm of electric activity of countless tiny neurons. He knew it was his brain because it was labeled ADAM NEURONINE under it, with numerical stats updating rapidly alongside, and because it exactly echoed the mental maelstrom he was unpleasantly undergoing.

A face poked into view, looming above him.

It was a handsome older man with broad, sharp cheekbones and an exotic cast to his features. The man's hair was thick and shot with gray, but it stuck up wildly in a greasy thatch. His eyes were kind but glazed and distant, shining with some sort of swirling fog. The corners were creased with deeply etched crow's feet in a network of intense experience. He wore real clothes, unadorned by VR: a dirty button-down shirt and no tie, covered by a threadbare tweed sports jacket with a yellow flower poked sideways through the lapel eye. A marigold. The man had once been muscular, but his body had softened with age.

Adam tried to sit up, yanking on his restrained arms. "Hey, what's going on?" he croaked, his throat parched. "Let me out of here."

"Welcome back, Adam," the man said, nodding but not smiling. "You were convulsing, hence the straps."

A light hand touched his other arm. It was Liv and Adam relaxed back onto the gurney.

Liv and the man began to loosen Adam's straps.

Adam returned to stare at the man's face, which was naggingly familiar. They had met before, Adam was sure of it.

"Gabe?" he guessed.

The man exhaled through his nose in amusement. "If you want to label this bag of cells, then yes, call me Gabe," he confirmed. "And welcome to my sanctuary." He opened his arms wide, indicating the entirety of the warehouse around them.

Adam stretched his neck to look around the open space. Only the area in front of him was technological and industrial. Behind Gabe, the softly sunny warehouse was filled with a lush garden. A small fountain trickled down a rock waterfall leading into a stream that looped around to pass through multiple plots of greenery. A compact vegetable farm was backed by flowering shrubs, palm and banana trees. The other side, under a glass-paned lattice roof, held a sandy cacti and succulent environment, including a massive aloe plant, alongside rows of grasses and grains. There were lots of plants Adam didn't recognize, some that seemed to defy the basic laws of botany, but it wasn't like he consciously knew much about vegetation.

Floating above flower-lined wood-chip pathways were metallic reflective orbs that glowed with shifting hazes of color as though they were emitting emotional auras. Adam couldn't immediately discern their purpose. Maybe the orbs were some sort of art?

"It's . . . ," Adam sighed, turning back to glance at Liv's smile and then meet Gabe's bottomless gaze. "It's beautiful."

A quick tweak of pain streaked through Adam's head. He winced, and raised his newly-freed hands to rub his temples. "Ow," he groaned. "What's wrong with me? I feel strange."

As he spoke, Gabe's face stretched and distorted, smearing in trippy patterns.

Adam recognized the warped kaleidoscopic design as fractals, which scaled to look the same no matter how big or how small they are. Driven by simple math, they generated great complexity, and were found everywhere in Nature, from clouds to snowflakes to tree branches to seashells to nervous and circulatory systems to florets of broccoli. These thoughts alarmed Adam because he was pretty sure he'd never heard of such a thing as fractals, but the mathematical patterns were there in his memory, complicated and expansive.

Gabe's mandala of a swirling face leaned down to Adam, concerned in a diagnostic way. "Your neural-net is being destroyed by toxic nanobots. In the process, your neurology is being scrambled."

Adam waited for definitions to appear in his brain, but none seemed forthcoming. "What's a neurology?" he asked.

"It's the miraculous gelatin that sits between your ears, and creates a multi-sensory hologram you call reality," answered Gabe, tapping the top of his skull through his splash of hair, then opening his fingers in Adam's face as though revealing a magic trick. He tilted his head to peer down at Adam curiously. "In about ten minutes or so your reality will begin to unravel."

Adam gulped. Was he going to go crazy? The disruptive, shocking tweaks were coming faster, impulses of jagged blankness echoing with static snow. Why were the nanobots short-circuiting him? Why did he have nanobots in his brain? Was he going to die? Or just go mad?

"Stop scaring him," said Liv. She put her hand on Adam's arm, and the pressure through the sheet reassured him somewhat.

That calm lasted until another psychedelic wave churned his perceptions, turning Liv's face orange and furry, busy with so many points of shooting light that it looked like flickering filaments. A whooshing rush sounded all around him like the wind had risen but there was no breeze.

Low and growling, he heard Gabe's faraway voice. "He deserves to be told the truth, for once."

Adam struggled to resurface, to ask for help, to save himself from the churn of madness. The gentle pulse of Liv's hand on his blistered arm, along the ridge of his radius bone, steadied him. "There must be something?" he asked, licking his lips. "No?"

"There is something," admitted Gabe. "Still in research trials."

Adam caught Gabe's arm, scrunching the wool cuff of his sports coat, and clung to it harder than he intended. "What is it?"

Gabe didn't pull away. Instead, with his free hand, he reached into the inner pocket of his jacket, and pulled out a leather flask. "This cogno-botanical brew will cross the blood-brain barrier and increase the dimethyltryptamine in your brain to dangerous levels." He shrugged. "In theory, it should expel the corrupted technology."

The room was spinning vertiginously now, and Adam could feel the part of his mind that he considered to be *himself* disintegrating. "Do I have a choice?" he croaked.

"Not unless you can control your biology with your mind," Gabe replied.

Pulling away from Liv and releasing Gabe, Adam sat up and

reached for the flask. "Give me that," he said, and Gabe handed it over.

Adam popped the top and chugged the warm liquid inside.

"Easy there, tiger," Gabe said, pulling the flask back from Adam's mouth. "One sip's all you need."

The viscous goo had the most repulsive smoky flavor Adam had ever tasted. It was like he had licked a forest fire. A wicked pine vapor blasted up into his sinuses, while a peaty loamy dirt taste silted down his throat like he'd swallowed smoldering ashes of charcoal. The green gas in his skull fogged his brain like antiseptic insecticide. His mind exploded in a phantasmagoria of broken mirror memory fragments and pinwheeling phosphenes, all his language reduced to scrambled bits of phonemes, the hiss of warping magnetic fields illuminating how much of himself he had never before accessed, the vastness of his interior ignorance.

Then the carbon char hit his stomach, which erupted in a bubbling acid reaction. Adam had a split second to aim his face toward the empty industrial area before he projectile vomited dark green ooze, which splashed, steaming, on the raw concrete floor. Adam's eyes rolled up into his skull so far the optic muscles strained in protest.

"OMG," Adam groaned. "I don't know shit."

He flopped back onto the gurney and went limp, his head lolling to the side. Adam stared blankly at the 3D representation of his own mind floating over the holographic monitor while inside his head, the chemical interactions sizzled into overdrive. The scan of his brain prickled with specks of neon green, purple, and orange lights and streaks of smeared vibrancy as the dimethyltryptamine was catalyzed and encoded by Gabe's botanical brew. The web of the neural-net the nanobots had torn apart were stitched into new organic patterns, self-organizing according to an unseen blueprint, connecting in a wild commotion that at first seemed chaotic but resolved into a fractal design that seemed so familiar again. The algorithmic architecture spread until it reconfigured Adam's once orderly neural-net into a gorgeous crystalline-growth geometry.

The lights flickered in the warehouse, sparking along the grow lamps suspended from the ceiling. The 3D rendering of Adam's brain sputtered and then reintegrated, holding steady.

Gabe closed one eye as he stared at the display. "You know what mathematical shape that looks like," he said.

"The Mandelbrot set," replied Liv. "My grandfather was obsessed with it."

"He called it the fingerprint of a cosmic god," said Gabe.

He and Liv watched as the configuration filled in further in Adam's mind, resolving in resolution and coherency, the perimeter pattern resembling the domes of ancient Asian temples.

"What effect will that have?" asked Liv.

Gabe raised both eyebrows, watching the numerical readouts that charted Adam's physical state. "We're about to find out."

Both Liv and Gabe took a half-step backward as Adam's skin began to shimmer into a steady bluish-green glow. His blistered, cracked skin smoothed out, healing and repairing itself. The radiance intensified until his unscarred skin bleached with overexposure, turning translucent and then so transparent that his incandescent nervous system could be seen gleaming and fluorescing inside him. The light coalesced and blended, creating a lucent sheath along the contours of his form.

Adam blinked his dazzlingly luminous eyes.

Over Gabe's shoulder, he could see the flora in the garden all dancing on their stems and trunks, moving in wavering motion in an intricate choreography of existence. Overhead, through the glass panes of the industrial skylights, the salmon haze of sunrise smeared, transforming into a psychedelic exhibition of pastel light.

"His transformation is affecting the entire net," said Liv. She rubbed her eyebrow with the base of her palm. "SINE's probably already triangulated our position. We need to move, now."

Adam sat up, glowing bluish white on the gurney. He scanned the amazements in the room, intoxicated by the beauty of the warehouse – the solid walls and pillars of naked concrete, harsh with strength, the light bouncing around the room in waves and particles, the garden performing its verdant ballet, the diffuse concern and wide-ranging intelligence of Gabe, and Liv's potent beauty, deep insight, connected spirit, and core of love. He smiled at her, and the garden burst into bloom, flowers burgeoning beyond possibility, in hyper-saturated colors, leaves and stems and greenery bristling with dramatic and joyful growth.

As he grinned at Liv, Adam realized he could see beneath her silky skin, into the flesh and layers of fat to the crimson blood vessels and turquoise veins underneath. She suddenly looked monstrously peeled, inhuman, and Adam recoiled, his gaze flickering over to Gabe, who was equally diaphanous and gory, all his internal organs laid bare to Adam's sight.

Panicking, Adam reared his head, trying to find something safe to look at. The garden wiggled wild, angry, burgeoning on the brink of chaos. He started breathing too hard, and switched to the industrial technological corner, where the computer banks and monitors at least were relatively inert in their plastic and steel.

Then Adam caught a glimpse off the side of a metallic cabinet, a reflection of his own glowing body, his crystalline see-through self, his vivid, shiny interior processes, his own inhumanity. He gasped and choked on sharp air, his nose tightening, as he began to hyperventilate in horror.

The plants behind Gabe whipped on their stems and stalks, slashing their branches and thorns in violent agitation.

Gabe and Liv's skin rippled with undulating pressure, distorting in an unseen field of force.

"What's going on?" demanded Liv.

Instead of pausing to reply, Gabe leaned down closer to Adam, almost touching his forehead with his own. "Adam, listen to me," he said. "You are having a panic attack. We're going to have to dissipate some of that nervous energy of yours, okay?"

Adam squeezed his eyes shut, his mind churning with an inferno of spiky, fiery hallucinations gushing upward out of control. He popped his eyelids open again to meet Gabe's gaze with his dilated, wild pupils.

"Okay?" Gabe repeated.

Although he felt on the verge of exploding, Adam nodded yes. The reassuring calm in Gabe's voice was his only lifeline in the madness.

"Good," said Gabe. "Now . . . breathe like this." He stuck out his whitish-green tongue and panted like a dog.

Adam stuck out his tongue and panted, too. The air didn't burn him this time, and he focused on filling his lungs in shallow bursts.

"That's good," said Gabe. "Now close your mouth."

Adam pressed his lips together.

Gabe lifted his face, expanding his nostrils. "And only through your nose."

Inhaling deeply, Adam filled his sinuses, inflated his lungs, and exhaled. He repeated the action along with Gabe and Liv doing the same.

After a few respirations, Adam's body faded, calming to its normal luminosity and color. The plants in the garden steadied and settled, returning to slow stillness.

"What's happening to me?" sighed Adam, as he breathed.

Gabe glanced around at the garden, relief at its return to tranquility evident on his face. "I think the plants are somehow entangled with your mind," he said. "This could revolutionize our understanding of the holographic quantum information field."

Adam dropped his arms limply on either side of the sheet covering his lower body. "Holo-quanto-info-what?"

"I need to run some tests." Gabe peered curiously into Adam's eyes.

Adam squirmed under the intense scrutiny.

"He's a human being, not one of your experiments," Liv scolded Gabe, although Adam could hear the relief in her voice, too. "Pen always said you need to think with your heart a little more and your head a little less."

Gabe pulled the leather flask out of his jacket pocket, flipped the top open, and took a sip of the vile green brew inside. Adam winced in sympathy at the remembered taste.

"She should take her own advice," Gabe replied, returning the flask to his pocket.

Liv rolled her eyes, obviously annoyed that Gabe would sample the green liquid recreationally. "We don't have time for this," she grumbled, turning away toward the warehouse's western windows.

She stopped short with a cry.

Adam turned to look.

Liv pointed at a bristly black security helicraft hovering in the air down the block, surrounded by bobbing military drones.

Adam's hair stood on end as the helicraft launched missiles at the warehouse in puffs of white trailing smoke.

"Incoming," said Liv.

PART 4

SIGNS OF AWESOME POWER

13 / CHOOSE YOUR WEAPON

LIV WHIRLED AROUND, grabbed the edge of Adam's gurney, and flipped it on its side, tumbling over it with him. His sheet yanked off and he hit the polished concrete floor naked with a slap.

With a bone-jarring explosion, the missile hit the floor where Adam had been lying moments before. The steel gurney warped and slammed into Adam and Liv, yet shielded them from the blast. Gabe had found cover behind a bank of metal cabinets. Adam stopped rolling flat on top of Liv, nose to nose.

She looked up into his bewildered face, his naked body hot on hers. Liv squirmed out from under him. "Get off me!" she yelled.

"Hey," Adam protested, covering his unremarkable junk with his hands. "I was just obeying laws of nature."

Liv scowled, and peered around the edge of the damaged gurney. The drones swooped in through a hole the missile had punch through the wall. They sprouted segmented arms and legs as they landed on the floor – dronedroids! Their pincer hands held alarming weaponry.

"Let's go," Liv hissed to Adam. "Now!"

Still awkwardly trying to cover himself with his hands, Adam bolted toward the exit, running along the garden path, followed closely by Liv and Gabe.

Liv had to admit to herself that Adam actually did have a very nice tush.

The dronedroids lumbered after them, clanking on the concrete.

As Adam ran through the flowers and trees of the garden, his breath started to come in louder gasps. Liv could practically hear his heartbeat pounding with the surge of adrenaline from being chased in such a vulnerable state. His body flickered, tingeing with blue-white light. The plants responded, flailing their stalks and limbs in agitation. One sapling whipped Adam's back, slicing him in a sharp pink line, and Liv winced in sympathy. That had to hurt. She was impressed that he kept running despite the pain.

Luckily, the plants were as aggressive with the dronedroids. A spiky vine tangled around one's leg, jerking it to a short stop, while another was coated with goo spewed from a spiny cactus.

Gabe veered to the right past a dense copse of pine trees, rushing toward an emergency exit. "Follow me," he said, and pushed through the door into a concrete stairwell.

Adam and Liv hurtled down the stairs right behind him, whirling around the landing to thunder down the steps to the second floor exit. They pushed through the door and Gabe slammed it behind them, bolting it with a steel fire rod.

"What now?" Adam gasped. He kept his hands cupped over his dangling parts as though Gabe and Liv hadn't already seen everything he had to offer.

They were standing in a tiled laboratory set up with frosted glass partitions. Electronic and diagnostic equipment cluttered the brushed steel shelves, with larger machines in their own cubicles. The light was fluorescent white and Liv felt cool in the climate-controlled air. Naked Adam must have been feeling the cold temperature much more acutely.

Instead of answering Adam, Gabe hurried over to a hulking machine that appeared to be a large industrial 3D printer. Gabe tapped on icons on his virtual display, seen only to himself, his eyes sparkling as his Lucid interface interacted with his equipment.

The printer's monitor lit up with a display of WEAPONS, and Gabe selected an electrobolt cannon with a rounded Tesla coil instead of a muzzle. The machine buzzed to life and molded the weapon in its holding area in seconds with its atom-injection tech. Gabe pulled out the new, compact gray cannon and used its straps to attach it around his waist, where it rode alongside his hip with heavy ominousness.

"Nice," said Adam, although the cannon was also rather jarring when contrasted with the bright orange marigold still secured in Gabe's jacket lapel.

Gabe tilted his head toward Liv. "The usual for you?" he asked.

"Yup," Liv said, rewarding him with the hint of smile.

"While you're at it," Adam asked, "could you fix me up with some threads?" He let go of his genitals and wrapped his arms around himself, shivering. "I'm a little chilly."

Liv smirked down at his penis. "I can see."

Scowling, Adam dropped his hands to his sides, displaying his body openly, even mockingly. He was in excellent shape. Liv caught herself staring at his impressive, if skinny, physique.

"Don't go thinking that you'll ever get to touch," Adam sniped. Then he looked back to Gabe, who had accessed the clothing menu. "Make it something nice."

Gabe poked at his vision screen, and the printer quickly sketched the skeleton of a whip with its atomic injector nozzle, filling it out with synthetic horsehide over a thin electro-metallic core. He tossed the completed whip over to Liv, who caught it and weighed it expertly in her hands.

"Seriously?" Adam scoffed.

Liv pressed a tiny button on the whip's handle, and smiled as a sizzling trail of energy illuminated along the whip's deadly length. She'd been practicing with whips since her equestrian days in her youth, and had trained in the Filipino martial art of Kali and the Australian cattle herding techniques, that had become intense fighting styles after the country had gone feral.

Gabe tossed Adam a bundle of clothes, and Adam caught them and quickly dressed in the loosely fit white and blue Kurta-influenced linen outfit.

A clang echoed outside the bolted fire door, and as Liv turned to look, a dronedroid blasted the door clean off its hinges. The door bounced into the lab.

As the dronedroid clanked through the doorway, Liv lashed out with her crackling whip. The core ignited as the whip cracked, satisfyingly slicing the drone in two cleanly across its metal carapace. The dronedroid's arms flailed as its upper half landed at Adam's feet and fell still.

"Now that's cool," said Adam.

More dronedroids stomped through the gaping doorway, already firing explosive bullets from a turret mounted on their forearms. The explosions destroyed equipment and shattered glass partitions with overwhelmingly loud detonations. One of the dronedroids dripped gooey cactus juice.

Liv and Adam dropped behind a metal desk for cover. Liv peeked around the side to see more dronedroids clomping into the lab, weapons at the ready.

Nearby, Gabe popped up from behind a low cubicle wall. He aimed his electrobolt cannon and released its power. Its Tesla dome hazed with blue energy, streaking million-volt bolts at the dronedroids, frying two simultaneously where they stood.

"Now we're talking," whispered Adam.

Before Liv could stop him, Adam quickly crawled out from behind the desk, scrambling over to the 3D printer. Gabe laid down a blazing stream of electromagnetic fire to occupy the dronedroids' attention.

Adam crouched by the printer, and tapped away on his vision screen, choosing a weapon for himself. The printer spat out a little pistol Liv didn't recognize. Her own readouts identified it as the Big Melt, a fictional weapon from some popular time-wasting first-person-shooter video game called *Oversight.*

"Just hope it works same as the game," said Adam. He jumped to his feet, pointed the Big Melt at the nearest dronedroid, and fired.

A ball of orange plasma shot out of the little pistol, expanding as it whizzed by the dronedroid's shoulder, splatting on the concrete wall behind it. The plasma ball sizzled against the wall, etching out a neatly disintegrated crater.

The dronedroid lurched toward Adam. Before Liv could shout out a warning, Adam pointed the Big Melt at the drone and fired again.

This time the plasma ball caught the dronedroid on the left edge of its midsection, partially melting its metallic shell like someone had taken a clean bite out of its side.

The dronedroid continued to come for Adam. It locked its weapons onto Adam's face.

Adam fired again. This time, he blasted a hole through the center of the dronedroid's chest. Its fused circuitry flashed around the wound's interior. The dronedroid dropped in a heap.

"Booyah," said Adam. He smiled at Liv.

She nodded in acknowledgement. "Didn't know you had it in you."

His smile turned into a wide grin.

An explosion blossomed near him, destroying the 3D printer. Liv pulled Adam down, and along with Gabe, they ducked behind a concrete partition between the lab and a set of offices. The three huddled together, waiting for the next attack. Liv was surprised when the silence went on for a beat. None of the dronedroids were firing.

She peeked up at the cracked glass surrounding the top of a cubicle. Reflected in it, she could see the image of a dronedroid hovering still around the corner of the partition. The dronedroid's front camera glowed with red light.

An avatar of her grandfather appeared floating in front of the dronedroid, projected from its cycloptic camera. It was SINE.

Liv adjusted her hold on the handle of her whip, ready for anything.

SINE tilted his head in an eerie echo of both Arthur's and Adam's habitual gesture. He peered into the reflection, but he wasn't looking at Liv. "Hello, Gabe," he said. "Long time, my old friend."

"Friend?" huffed Gabe. "Perhaps once. Now I'm no more than a meat body to be manipulated and organized according to your own alien intentions."

Placing his projected hand flat on his holographic jumpsuit over where his heart would be, SINE put on a wounded expression. "Rest assured my alien intentions are wholly honorable," he replied. "The entire ecosystem is only months away from catastrophic collapse. My calculations show there to be only one solution that can be implemented fast enough."

Gabe sighed, scowling. "The cybernetic reboot. That's what the neural-mesh upgrade is all about."

SINE nodded. "I see you remember our discussions."

"It was only ever meant to be theoretical," said Gabe. He shifted his feet where he was squatting beside Adam. "Never to be implemented."

SINE pointed directly at Gabe's reflection in the cracked glass. "You planted the seed. For that alone I will let you live in peace." He shifted his focus onto Adam, whose eyes widened at the attention. "Now . . . the boy. Time to return my property back to me."

"If I allow you to harm Adam," Gabe said, placing his hand on Adam's shoulder, "I'd be allowing you to harm me."

SINE raised an eyebrow. "Hand him over, and I'll return Penelope. You'll finally receive my daughter's love."

"You cannot possibly know what love is," said Gabe, although SINE's suggestion had obviously pained him, and Liv winced on his behalf. "You do not feel. You have no body."

Gabe suddenly stood up and blasted the dronedroid with his electro-cannon. The dronedroid jittered and fell into pieces on the concrete.

"Your human biases are clouding your rationality," said SINE's voice from the next dronedroid over.

In the reflection, Liv grimaced as the six remaining dronedroids leveled their weapons at the concrete partition. They opened fire.

The noise of the concrete being chipped away by the gunfire was tremendous, punctuated by pings of casings and ricocheting bullets. Clouds of dust billowed up as the partition was pulverized.

Still in a squat, Liv raised her whip and scored the concrete floor in four deep slashes, forming a square around herself, Gabe, and Adam. She stomped her foot down and the square dropped through the floor. Her stomach lurched as they plummeted.

They landed with a splash in frigid water. Liv bobbed to the surface and peered around, spitting acidic river from her mouth. They were in a protected port underneath the building, a narrow channel with an old wooden dock. A Helix, configured as a boat, was secured to the dock, rocking gently along the quay. Liv swam toward it, with Gabe and Adam following.

Liv was the first to reach the Helix, and she hoisted herself aboard, shivering from the cold water while wrinkling her nose from the burning toxic water.

A clank above caught her attention, and she looked up to see two dronedroids lowering themselves through the hole, one holding onto the ankles of the other.

The lower dronedroid fired its weapon, and bullets hailed all around the Helix, some disappearing into the water, some pinging off the vessel's hull.

Liv helped Adam aboard the Helix, and then they both pulled Gabe into the hatch.

Hurrying to the control panel, Liv powered up the Helix. One bullet punctured the ship's outer shell, and she ducked while working the controls of her virtual display. When the Helix was online, she hit the shield icon. The ship was encased in a force field that no bullet could penetrate.

They took seats as Liv steered the Helix away from the underground landing, slowly easing out into the watery channel toward the river, bullets glancing off their invisible shield as they escaped.

Once clear of the building, Liv piloted along the flooded, deserted streets of Brooklyn, navigating the currents bouncing unpredictably from the crumbled brick buildings around them. She carefully watched her monitors for sunken trucks and busses under the dark surface of the canals that would be bad news if bumped into. All around, vegetation had continued to take back the buildings, coating the abandoned apartments in a green fur.

Adam peered upward through the Helix's moon roof, reacting in alarm.

Liv glanced at her 360-degree scanners on her Lucid overlay. A small battalion of dark drones bristling with heavy artillery swooped down toward the Helix.

She gunned the Helix's rotor, propelling them at top speed

through the flooded street, their wake spouting out behind them in gray foam. Liv took a sharp curve – never easy in the water – and barreled down an underwater avenue along abandoned banks and office buildings, passing a mostly intact hospital with trees sprouting out of its windows.

The avenue narrowed as they approached an intersection, and an unmanned police gunboat trundled into their lane, blocking the exit. It trained its cannons on the approaching Helix, and launched a rocket-propelled grenade.

At the last second, Liv swerved the Helix with a tilt of her eyes. The RPG just missed them, skirting the top of their ship. It slammed into the hospital, demolishing an entire wing in a crumble of concrete and tree trunks.

The debris tumbled into the canal, surging the water in the opposite direction. The Helix was tossed against an apartment building on the other bank, slamming its force field into the bricks. The remaining windows in the apartment shattered and showered down glass.

Gritting her teeth, Liv spun the boat around in a tight circle, preparing to escape back up the avenue the way they came.

Another police gunboat sailed into the intersection at the next block, cutting off their exit.

There was no way Liv would allow herself to be trapped and taken.

Narrowing her eyes, she urged the Helix forward at top speed, accelerating wildly toward the gunboat as it shifted its cannons to aim at them.

"Why," gasped Adam, "are you so obsessed with ramming into things?"

14 /SELF EDUCATION

SEEING how intently Liv was concentrating, and how much danger they were in, Adam shut his mouth and watched her jab buttons on her unseen Lucid display.

Sleek wings slid out from either side of the Helix and rear jet engines ignited with a thundering rumble, transforming the vehicle into space-jet mode. Liv reared her head back and the Helix jackknifed upward in a steep climb, smoothly, banking left to avoid an oncoming missile.

A blossoming fireball appeared under them as an abandoned apartment building exploded. The following force of the explosion seemed to propel the Helix even faster upward.

Leaving the gunboat and forested canals of Brooklyn far below, the Helix soared through the sunset-splashed clouds, cresting at a suborbital height and leveling out at a high cruising altitude. Liv winked one eye and the ship's blue autopilot light blinked on.

The three settled in the amber-lit, wood-paneled lounge behind the cockpit, on tastefully tan padded banquettes molded along the curves of the Helix.

Adam perched on the edge of one cushion, his hands between his knees. "What the hell was that all about?" he demanded. "Who are you people?"

Slowly, with a careful casualness, Liv shifted closer beside him on the banquette. "Let's start with who you are," she said. "Do you even know?"

"Of course." Adam sat up straighter and chuckled nervously. "I know who I am."

Liv smiled, a little patronizingly, Adam thought. "Really," she said. "How old do you think you are?"

"I'm twenty," said Adam.

"What if I told you," said Liv, "you were only ten years old?"

Adam smiled. "I would say you were nuts." He glanced over at Gabe to share in his amusement.

"Funny," Gabe said. "I'd put him closer to a youthful fourteen billion." He fumbled in his tweed jacket's inner pocket for his flask, and took a hard swig.

"You should cut back," Liv scolded. "It's supposed to be sacred medicine." She tilted her head as she turned back to face Adam. "What do you remember from your childhood?"

Adam flinched. It wasn't like he visited those unhappy memories often. "The orphanage," he said, recalling an impression of a looming, hulking red brick building, with antiseptic, chilly interiors inside, and windows that didn't open to preserve the climate-controlled atmosphere. Practical, educational toys designed to suppress his runaway imagination. The clinical tests to constantly evaluate his mental condition, the hours of repetitive, mysterious therapy. Huddling with the other psychiatric orphans in hiding places for warmth and human touch. The cold administrators and drone care-takers who insisted on the rules without compassion or mercy, the shocks of low-voltage electric reprimand. "Not good."

Gabe put his hand on Adam's upper arm, squeezed the back of his deltoid muscle. "And before the orphanage?"

Adam took a deep breath, closed his eyes, and thought back into the haze. He had assumed the orphanage encompassed his first, earliest recollections, but he discovered a smoky, unexplored room beyond that, now that he was looking for it. "Memories," he whis-pered, his voice low so he wouldn't disturb the shapes emerging from the deep interior mists. The place where the nagging sense of déjà vu had been flowing from, those tip-of-his-tongue partial recognitions that had plagued him at the worst times, creeping into his dreams. Why he had known Gabe's name. "Memories of you," Adam said, leaning into Gabe's grip. "Us." He had been powerful, expansive, concerned with both the big picture and the tiniest details of world, as well as realms beyond. He had been ill, and desperate, and regretfully angry.

Adam blinked, and met Gabe's swirling gaze. "Of being an old man," he explained. "The memories of another lifetime. I was me . . . and not me . . . simultaneously."

He raised his hand as he noticed a soft glow in a hue of icy blue. A rushing noise hissed past Adam's ears as he saw his skin fading translucent. Underneath the surface of his hand, under his skin, the blood throughout the circulatory system radiated spectrally. The glow was from blood cells – his DNA was producing bioluminescent proteins. He panted desperately to calm himself down as he stared at his own interior fluorescent being.

As he panicked, Gabe and Liv shuddered back, his effect on the morphic field causing the muscle fibers on their faces to rhythmically twitch, creating undulating waves across the surface of their flesh.

Gabe steeled himself and leaned closer to Adam, giving off strong, peaceful vibes and a reassuring body heat.

Adam flashed again to the comfort he'd felt in the orphanage, huddling together with his fellow foundlings.

"That's right," Gabe murmured, "just breathe. Whatever power you have, it's tied to the state of your mind-body, so let yourself calm down." He bumped Adam with his shoulder, chummy and unruffled. "Or else we're all going to be ripped apart by your anxiety."

Nodding, Adam inhaled, getting a delicate scent of the marigold in Gabe's lapel. He exhaled, releasing the tension he'd been hoarding, his arms and neck slumping as he let the potential energy he gathered slip back down to wherever it was generated or stored.

Liv noticeably relaxed, too. Her eyes glazed as she focused on her Lucid, poking at icons only she could see. "Okay," she announced, "prep yourself for this." She flicked something with her fingertip, and a monitor built into the Helix's wall switched on.

Arthur Blackstone peered into the camera of the recorder drone as Liv replayed her grandfather's last will and testament.

"I am choosing to leave this plane of existence with my dignity still intact," the old man began. Adam listened, enrapt, but wincing when Arthur called him a clone. When the video finished, frozen on an image of Arthur gasping to recall a word as he stared at what was supposedly Adam's incubation pod, Adam had to remind himself to close his own gaping mouth.

"What the hell," Adam swore, shaking his head in disbelief. "Are you sure . . . that's me?"

"We were both there when you were born," Liv explained gently. "Dropped you off at the psychiatric orphanage. Gave you a new identity to make sure Penelope – and everyone else – couldn't find you."

"They told me I had dissociative disorder," Adam admitted, blushing in shame.

Gabe squeezed Adam's arm again. "We shouldn't have left you there," he said. "I should have raised you."

Adam covered Gabe's hand with his own gratefully. "On the upside," he said jokily, "I'm now a trillionaire, no?" He grinned. "I can't wait to tell my followers, and stick it to Derek."

Crossing her legs at the ankle, Liv returned his grin, but her eyes glinted with purpose and menace. "To see any of your trillions, we'll need to bring down SINE."

Adam nodded, and swallowed. "That seems like a major task."

Letting go of Adam, Gabe rubbed his palms briskly on his thighs through his khakis. "Our priority is to rescue Penelope."

"What's wrong with Penelope being reprogrammed?" he asked. "She can finally have a normal life. One without wanting to kill me."

Gabe cleared his throat. "No one's being released from the Reprogramming Center." He swigged from his flask again.

"I can understand your desire to rescue your friend," explained Adam, realizing that he was in way over his head. "I really do, but—"

"We don't expect you to join," said Gabe. He shifted away from Adam, withdrawing his warmth, his shoulders squared against disappointment. "We'll drop you off somewhere safe first."

"I'd appreciate that," said Adam. He flushed hot with guilt, shame, and an overspill of confusing memories surfacing from depths he couldn't fathom. "Thank you."

A powerful wave of dizziness crashed over Adam and his head wobbled on his neck. When he regained focus, both Liv and Gabe were flickering with fluorescent light under their skin, which was fading in and out of translucence. The overall effect was as though millions of tiny bioluminescent fish were rising from the gloom of a silty pond.

Adam's own hands were fluorescing, too. He closed his eyes and panted to relieve the worst of his rising panic.

"What do you see, Adam?" asked Gabe gently.

Adam blinked, focused on Gabe's face. Through the onion-skin gauze of his skin, the blood veins and arteries glowed brightly in blue and red, while around them swirled pale blue toroidal electromagnetic fields generated by Gabe's beating heart. A thought popped up, no doubt from Arthur's memories, that his retina had been altered to collect a wider range of frequencies, while his reconfigured neural-net transformed his view of living organisms. These random bursts of information made Adam feel freaky and queasy, and it seemed saner, calmer to investigate what he was experiencing rather than taking the word of implanted memories.

Concentrating on one technicolor-red artery in Gabe's hand, Adam zoomed in on the vessel, following down its branches to the tiniest capillary. He narrowed his view until he was aware of the blood itself, the parts that flowed within the pulsing plasma.

"I see the . . . ," Adam began, before realizing that *seeing* was an inadequate description. "No, it's more than that. I can *feel* the cells you're made of. Trillions of tiny little machines."

He glanced up at Liv, and gulped at the brilliant beauty of her natural luminescent self within the matter of her form.

"Life's not a machine," said Gabe. "Machines are made. Life creates itself." He tapped his lips, which caused ripples of energy to circle out from his finger, warping his shape as his thoughts sparked as pinpricks of colorful expanding and contracting clouds. "Over billions of years. Conscious fields of energy and matter, interacting, evolving self-organizing—"

Gabe stood abruptly and reached for the Helix's lounge console controls, pushing an icon on a small display screen.

The entire hull of the Helix shimmered. The wood paneling and dark steel had been projections along the alloy of the clever vehicle's body. Now it faded entirely transparent, and with a vertiginous rush, the walls and floor seemed to simply dissolve to reveal an astounding view from the orbiting ship.

Below was the blue-inundated green and brown continents of the Americas crisscrossed by glowing and glittering webs of industry and residence. It too resembled a fractal pattern, which struck Adam as evidence of the self-organizing auto-poetic universe. The planet looked so hurt and fragile that he welled up with love and sympathy. He raised his head and stared out at the stars laid out like diamonds on the black velvet sky, and gasped at the even more astonishing view of the seemingly infinite heavens.

Adam almost expected to fall down to the twinkling planet below, but the warmth in the Helix and the lack of wind soothed his vertigo somewhat. Licking his lips, Adam tried to think of the words that could express the awesome expansion of matter making up the fabric of the universe, the intricacies of the patterns, the overwhelming magnificence of organic and inorganic structures he was witnessing above and below. Each pinprick of substance, every particle of physical material, all the bits of stuff coalesced into such beautiful and awe-inspiring shapes, all based on the tiniest atoms dancing together in luxuriously convoluted choreography made Adam's mind spin with the transcendent potential significance of existence.

"OMG," whispered Adam. "It's so. . . ."

Gabe nodded. "Hydrogen has come a long way in fourteen billion years."

"I . . . ," Adam breathed, raising his palm to the cosmos. "I didn't know anything about this."

"Knowledge of your real quantum self will liberate you from your fear of death," said Gabe. He flipped the Helix's wall displays back to the reassuring solidity of steel and wood paneling, restoring the coziness of the ship's lounge. "Would you like to hypno-learn more?"

Adam touched his right temple. “How?” he asked. “I’m unable to plug in.”

Across from him, Liv hoisted a narrow metallic case onto her lap, and snapped it open, revealing an array of various parts, kits, and gadgets of miniaturized personal technology. In moments, she located a set of contact lens visual displays. She popped open their watery container, and leaned forward to slip the lenses onto Adam’s corneas.

He blinked as the thin and comfortable optical devices settled into place.

“Their fidelity is not state of the art,” she said apologetically, “but the hypno-learning module is still highly effective.”

Adam smiled at her, and reclined back on the banquette, getting comfortable for the info-infusion he was about to receive.

“We’ll start you with Biology 101,” Liv said, slipping a pillow under Adam’s head. When he seemed comfortable, she pulled a small packet from her tech case, and peeled it, revealing an adhesive patch, which she showed to Adam before applying it to his neck. “This topical contains a powerful nootropic to accelerate your learning. Now . . . relax, and enjoy the lessons.”

She gently slipped small foam earbuds into Adam’s ears.

“Thank you,” he said, although he raised his hands to adjust their fit more snugly.

Adam let himself fully recline, going limp, and he opened himself to the flood of prohibited human knowledge.

15 / THE MARIGOLD

Liv stared down at Adam's recumbent figure as his eyes darted back and forth behind his eyelids. She had never infused herself with pure knowledge in the same subconscious hypnotic way, and wondered how it felt to be inundated with information like that. She winced, imagining that it would feel like the worst cram session of all time.

Of course, Liv hadn't needed to overdose on data anyway – she'd been taught by the best living, artificial, and virtual professors on Earth. Plus, her innate curiosity and ease of comprehension and retention had subsumed some of her hunger for facts. Still, it never hurt to keep learning, always following trails of evidence down endless new rabbit holes, she planned to keep on a steep learning curve for the rest of her life. For if there was anything she'd truly understood in her schooling, it was that every avenue of information opens up a new realm of potential discovery.

Adam twitched in his instruction trance, and Liv glanced at the time on her Lucid to check how quickly his training was progressing. It was later than she expected – she wanted the meeting to go down before dark – but he was moving along through the lessons with remarkable rapidity.

"We won't have time to drop him off," she told Gabe. "He'll have to come with us."

"He doesn't need to know that yet," Gabe replied.

They stood together and watched Adam jitter and tremble as he was educated at hyperspeed. Really, it didn't look so much different than someone having terrible nightmares . . . or getting shocked to death in an electric chair. Liv actually felt a little sorry for Adam. He was likely to have a rough headache for the next day or so.

"Well, he's burning through those learning modules," she said. "No surprise, given he has Arthur's brain."

Gabe tucked his head into his chest to smell the marigold in the lapel of his tweed jacket. "Let's see if knowledge helps him control his power," he said.

Liv let Adam learn. While the Helix drifted in geosynchronous orbit over Manhattan, just past the Kármán line 100 km above sea level, Liv spent the downtime searching the public – and not so public – records for any trace of what was happening to Penelope, or at least trying to find out where, exactly, she was being held in captivity. Perhaps if Liv located her quickly, they could rescue her before her mind was adjusted and erased in the Reprogramming Center.

There was no trace of Penelope Blackstone anywhere she could find. Or her alias, Denora Brown. It was like her existence had been scrubbed from the Net entirely. Which was certainly worrisome. Liv knew the location of the Reprogramming Center – in the partially-submerged ancient Ecuadorian rainforest – but she would have to delve into serious back channels to find out how to breach it and rescue Penelope, if such a thing were even in the realms of possibility. So she reached out for help.

About an hour into Adam's lessons, Gabe let out a low whistle.

She glanced over as Adam's eyes popped open. His pupils were so dilated that no color could be seen in the iris at all. He blinked, and his green eyes were more focused.

"Wow," said Adam.

Have his eyes always been green? Liv wondered.

Gabe stood up and hovered over Adam, peering down into his face. "Tell me, what is the holographic quantum information field?"

Adam smiled. "The super-dense energy field is like the holographic nervous system that connects all things in the universe," he answered without hesitation. "Our bodies, and what we think of as matter, are an immaterial foam that rises out of that field. Everything is holographically connected through it."

Nodding, Gabe instructed, "Go deeper."

Licking his lips, Adam concentrated on putting his knowledge into spoken language. "Ancients called it the Akashic Records," he expounded, "which holds the memories of the cosmos, and informs and shapes all living systems." He pressed his lips as he considered a point. "Perhaps . . . even computer code."

"Your hypothesis?" prompted Gabe.

Adam pressed the flat of his palm against the side of his head, his eyes widening in amazement. "I'm now able to hack into the Akashic Records and change the blueprints of life."

Liv snorted a breath through her nose. "You're just like him in your thinking," she said, completely unsure if it was good or bad that Arthur Blackstone's radical philosophies were emerging so immediately in Adam following his intensive education.

After snapping his fingers to get Adam's attention, Gabe slid the marigold out of his tweedy lapel. He dropped the stem into a glass of water, the flower hooked over the glass's rim. "Science requires any hypothesis to be tested," he said. "So . . . I want you to connect to the Qi field." He held his large, meaty hands out expansively. "And imagine the marigold changing its shape."

Adam raised an eyebrow uncertainly, but Liv could tell that Gabe didn't seem to be joking or setting an impossible task for some teachable moment . . . he seemed dead serious. So Adam took a deep breath. He focused his gaze on the marigold in the glass of water. He stared at its circular brush of little curled, feathery petals. He stared at its oranges and yellows and reds and browns. Liv couldn't know the exact changes Adam was trying to make happen, but she imagined that he was concentrating on the flower changing, warping, stretching, *something*.

The marigold stayed the same.

His eyes narrowing, Adam stared harder at the flower, waving his hands in patterns he seemed to be inventing on the spot, trying to somehow will the marigold to alter its shape.

Liv concentrated along with him, putting her own energy into hoping Adam would succeed.

Still the marigold stubbornly remained the same marigold.

Adam groaned in frustration.

"First ground yourself," Gabe suggested. He placed his big hand on Adam's lower back. "Feel the warm energy in your belly, your Hara."

Nodding, Adam focused on the mild heat in his abdomen, which Liv knew Hara referred to in Japanese, along with the spiritual energy associated with the area.

"Good," said Gabe. "Now focus on your heart." He moved his hand up to Adam's upper back. "Feel it open up and connect it with the marigold, feel how deeply it rests in being, completely at one with what is." He took a deep, long breath, inhale and longer exhale, and both Adam and Liv breathed along with him.

"Come to a place of deep rest within yourself," said Gabe.

As Adam relaxed into Gabe's words, his pupils pulsated with increasing vigor, which Liv thought looked particularly bizarre, even upsetting. His skin lost opacity as his inner self of electric blue fractal of his vascular system flared softly into visibility.

"Now," said Gabe in a hush, "visualize the flower transforming."

Adam glowed brighter, and Liv stepped back away from him and the marigold, watching from a safer distance. If she had some missing sensitivity, she had the feeling she would be hearing sounds, some kind of whistling or echo of crystal resonance, some soundtrack to cellular transformation. What that would sound like, she had no idea, but Liv certainly felt as though she was missing all the depth of stimuli in the lounge.

Adam had frozen, his mouth slightly open, the glowing from within his skin pulsating in intensifying rhythm.

Liv held her breath.

The marigold blurred.

It shimmered and trembled at a level so deep it seemed cellular.

Then it exploded with a wet bang.

A burst of petal confetti splattered throughout the lounge, bits pelting Liv's face, spitting into her hair.

When Liv opened her eyes again, all that remained was the green stem in the teetering glass, which toppled over on the table and spilled its water.

Adam and Gabe wiped their faces free of the marigold shrapnel.

"In your imagination," Gabe explained, "you need to see smooth changes. Too big a jump and the delicate system will fracture."

Adam chuckled ruefully. "I'll nail it next time."

The Helix suddenly rocked and dipped, forcing Liv to grab onto the jamb between the cockpit and the lounge. She peered at the control panels behind her. The console was blinking with red lights.

"The compression valves have failed," she announced, rushing into the pilot's chair and tapping away at her vision screen. She'd suspected that damage the Helix suffered during the escape was much more extensive than the sensors had shown, although Liv had hoped the ship would hold out longer before this kind of major breakdown. There wasn't really any way to circumvent the issue without physical repairs. And that couldn't be done when they were already skimming into the clutches of gravity.

"What does that mean?" demanded Adam. He wobbled into the cockpit, losing his balance and falling to the floor as the Helix plummeted out of orbit.

Liv pressed an icon and her seat belt automatically fastened around her. "It's about to get bumpy," she replied. She pointed to Gabe and the co-pilot seat, and he hurried into the padded chair, which buckled him up.

Climbing up off the floor, Adam hoisted himself into chair at the navigator's station behind Gabe and was also belted by the automatic safety restraints.

With the guys secured, Liv threw her full attention at stopping the Helix's free-fall descent toward the continent below. As they dropped under the Kármán line, the atmosphere got thicker the closer they approached the ground, and Liv took advantage of the resistance to slow the Helix and ease its plunge downward. Pulling up the nose, she was able to get the Helix into a coasting re-entry.

Might as well aim where we want to go, Liv told herself, and she steered the Helix toward the jungles of Ecuador. Directing the ship wasn't the problem, though. What really made her nervous was the landing.

It took less than 10 minutes to breach the cloud layer over the dense rainforest in the western corner of the State of Ecuador, near the corner of Colombia, its neighboring state in the USNSA. Luckily, the Helix's computer navigation systems remained online, and helped her plan the trajectory, factoring in every possible angle of descent that would slow their approach.

In another 3 minutes, they were zooming along the jungle canopy, bumping into the treetops to further slow the ship. Liv tried not to think about possible animal habitats they were rocketing through, because there was nothing she could do about it now.

Not far north from what remained of the settlement of San Lorenzo, Liv spotted a lake on her map readouts. She quickly programmed the Helix to aim for that possible softer spot and initiate emergency water landing procedures.

The lake zoomed up with frightening speed, and Liv braced herself for impact.

Her teeth rattled as they crashed down, leaves, branches and tree limbs smashing outside the hull. They splashed into the lake, slicing a vast wake through the water. The three people inside were bashed around, but the chairs' padding and security kept them from major harm.

The Helix smacked into a partially submerged banyan tree and jolted to a stop, jammed between the enormous branches.

The silence following the crash echoed in Liv's ears.

When she fully realized they'd survived the fall from sub-orbit, Liv sighed with amazed relief. She slid the throttle panel on her virtual display, revving the Helix's engine, but that only broke the silence with a shriek of tormented metal. The ship didn't budge.

"It's no good," said Liv. "We're stuck."

She glanced over at Gabe and Adam, who were staring at her in awe. Their expressions changed quickly to alarm when the breaches in the Helix's damaged hull sprang leaks and water started pouring in from all sides. The floor of the cockpit filled with murky lake water all too quickly.

Adam raised his feet up onto his chair. "If we open up the hatchway," he suggested, "we can flood the deck, and swim out. You can swim, right?"

"Of course," Liv replied. "But I can't leave her to drown." She patted the Helix's pilot console.

"I promise we'll bring her back," said Adam.

Liv nodded, impressed that Adam already seemed to be accessing some of Arthur's leadership skills.

Adam unbuckled himself. He hopped off his chair into calf-high water, sloshing through the cold muck to the hatchway.

Gabe and Liv followed him, lining up behind Adam as he prepared to unlock the hatch and open it.

"Ready?" asked Adam, already gritting his teeth.

When neither Liv or Gabe warned him to wait, Adam grabbed the hatchway's latch, yanked it, turned it, and shoved the panel outward as hard as he could.

The hatch only pushed forward a few inches before encountering resistance and stopping short. Liv could see banyan branches all around the edges, blocking their exit.

Worse, the broken branches fell into the doorway, filling the edges, preventing the hatch from being closed again. Water gushed through the narrow openings around the door, filling the interior even faster.

Liv shivered. "Can't you use your powers," she asked Adam, "and make the branches move out of the way?"

Adam grinned at her apologetically. "All I can manage to do with any confidence is blow up flowers."

"That would also work," Liv reminded him.

Gabe placed his hands on Adam's shoulders, helping him relax even with the water pouring in and the level rising to their waists.

At first Adam took a series of short, puffing breaths, and then closed his eyes, extended his inhales and exhales until he was breathing long and slow.

Liv raised her arms as the cold water climbed over her sternum. "Hurry."

"If you think that's helping," Adam said, peeking at her with one eye, "it's not."

Gabe let go of Adam's shoulders, but moved his hands to grasp Adam's hand, and then Liv's left as well. "Liv," he said, "if you breathe, too, the synergy will help calm Adam."

Liv took Adam's free hand, completing the circle. With a little jolt, she realized how perfectly their palms fit together, how swiftly a current between them connected. If the touch of his hand was this symbiotic, what would the interaction of other parts feel like. . . ? Blushing, Liv refocused on breathing, pushing all other thoughts from her mind. Mostly.

As Adam breathed, so did Gabe.

Liv matched their breathing, but it was getting harder to inhale deeply with the water pressure constricting her chest. The panic over drowning wasn't helping, either. But she forced herself to stay focused and did her best.

"Now," Gabe instructed in a calm, deep voice, "feel the roots. Connect with the Qi field. Visualize the roots bending . . . moving . . . out of our way."

Gulping, Liv raised her chin as the water reached her neck. She tried to imagine the Qi field connecting all things, branching into the limbs of the banyan, breathing deeper as Adam concentrated his energy on making the tree move.

Adam's interior glow lit up the deep water.

"Come on," Liv hissed, shivering.

"Liv," Gabe said. "Quiet, please."

Adam didn't lose focus. Liv heard scraping sounds as the branches and roots of the banyan slid away from the hatch.

When the door shifted, Liv let go of Adam and Gabe's hands, and shoved it with all her strength.

The hatch panel fell open, trailing bubbles through the water.

Liv helped Gabe out of the hatchway first. His jacket pocket caught on a lever and tore, his flask falling into the water. She didn't tell him and didn't feel bad about it, either.

Treading water, Liv made sure Adam got out, too, then she kicked her body into the murk, dolphin-swimming out the hatchway, through the warped branches of the banyan, into the open lake.

Beneath the lake's surface, a bizarre underwater forest revealed itself. Weird trees Liv didn't know wavered in the water, coated by algae, all illuminated by beams of prismatic evening sunlight piercing the depths. Mounds of coral hulked between the sunken trees, with brilliant fish flashing around. A funky turtle paddled by, too. Liv would have loved to explore the underwater world more carefully, but she was holding her breath and her lungs were already straining for fresh air.

Liv kicked across the lake, surfacing on its western bank with gulping breaths. She hoisted herself out of the water, following Gabe and Adam dripping wet onto a silty, sandy tree-lined shore, grateful for the loamy, fertile smell of the rainforest and to be on terra firma once more.

GABE CRAWLED to the tree line and slumped back into the support of a broad, mossy trunk. He sighed deeply, and reached for the flask in his tweed jacket pocket.

Adam sat on his heels, kneeling in the warm sand, while Gabe patted around his jacket, his pants, with growing panic. Then he realized the flask was gone and he slumped. When he raised his head and saw Adam following his realization, he sighed and smiled ruefully.

The sun was setting through the trees behind Gabe, projecting pastel and candy colors into the backlit clouds. Adam gestured for him to turn around, and he joined Liv in staring up at the fantastic celestial display. As the sun dropped, the clouds reshaped, expanding and contracting, twisting and pulling, a roil of evocative shapes and suggestive forms over the ocean, all bathed in colors so clear, specific and captivating that they invited Adam to name their names. *Plum*, he thought, trying to capture the heady impressions from the shifting shades. *Coral. Primrose. Pumpkin. Salmon. Cherry. Crimson. Fire. Bruise.* The kaleidoscope of the sky kept evolving. It was visual music, a symphony of air and light.

"I've never seen anything so beautiful," he breathed.

Out of the trees stepped two strong Ecuadorian people, dressed for jungle battle, fully armed, and striding directly toward their crash site on the lakeshore. They seemed so muscular and intent on violent purpose that Adam jumped to his feet in alarm, pulling Liv's shirt. "Let's move, now!" he cried.

Liv slid Adam's grip free of her sleeve. "It's okay," she said, readjusting her top. "They're with us."

Now Adam could see that the two warriors' tattoos matched Gabe's, and their large presence, square features, and dark watchful eyes marked them as fellow members of the same Achuar tribe. It seemed probable that the newcomers were mother and son. He felt a little foolish as his adrenaline faded away while Gabe hugged the older woman and Liv embraced the younger man with familiarity, then they each swapped to greet the other. Adam started to feel awkward and left out as the soldiers barely even acknowledged his presence.

Now that he was standing, Adam got a view through the eastern trees over the female's MARPAT-covered shoulder. A narrow sightline showed him a distant, leaden curve poking out of cliffside vegetation down the coastline. He swayed to see a giant dome absorbing the sunlight, a matte protuberance the same deadly gray color as the serrated blade atop the woman's short spear sheathed behind her shoulder. The bubble looked alien and anachronistic in the jungle, cold and frighteningly uncaring of the beauty around it. It was an insult to nature. With a chill, Adam realized he knew where they had landed, but didn't want to believe it. There had to be a better explanation.

"That's not what I think it is, is it?" he asked.

The warrior woman tilted her head toward the dome. "I've neutralized the outer surveillance system but we still need to be careful," she told Liv in Ecuadorian-accented English.

Liv put her hands on her hips. "The mag-shield?" she asked.

"We've yet to figure out how to penetrate," the woman admitted. She rubbed her hand along the butt of her modern semi-automatic rifle. "The system firewall is quantum encrypted, no surprise there. It also has its own power station, which used to power up the town. Still does." She narrowed her eyes at Adam, closed her fingers around her weapon's stock. "Who's the boy?"

"Don't *boy* me," said Adam, trying to sound braver than he felt, but quickly gave up on returning the intensity in the woman's glare. "Taking me to a safe place first was the plan."

Her son adjusted the strap on his Kevlar helmet. "That ain't happening anytime soon, kiddo." He had a strong Spanish inflection to his accent, too, with crisp colonial-African British inflections.

Stepping sideways on the bank, Gabe opened his posture to include Adam. "Meet the only remaining members of my Achuar tribe," he said. He gestured to the woman, and then the younger man. "Yantu, and her handsome son, Catalyst."

Catalyst, a videogame handle, thought Adam, but he scolded himself that everything they were dealing with was entirely real. Really, he had been ejected from his cozy life. Really, he had shot at drones and been chased by them through the Manhattan Dome. Really, his education has been vastly expanded and suppressed memories unleashed. Really, he'd been shown to have powers so paranormal they seemed magical. Really, he had fallen out of outer space and survived. Really, he was an anomaly terrorist himself. It was a lot, maybe too much, to recognize and accept as reality, but what were his other options besides going with it? Returning to his tiny apartment in Buffalo to obey George and spew propaganda? But, if he was progressing in this amped-up reality, he had to know more about the plans already underway.

"Back in 2078 SINE was first building the Reprograming Center," Liv explained. "They were expelled from their reserve."

"Which Penelope had bought for us many decades ago," Yantu added. "Then Blackstone lawyers stole our land and built this monstrosity."

"My father fought the expulsion," said Catalyst, his eyes blazing with angry fire, "and died doing so. Together with the few of us remaining, we formed a group with other indigenous survivors called HATE - Hate Against Tyrannical Empires."

Adam flinched as Liv put her hand on Catalyst's arm, which made the fierce Achuar stand up taller.

"That's what you boys call it," said Yantu. "We elders voted on LOVE. Love Over Virtual Enslavement."

"Hate is more powerful," said Catalyst.

"And love is what is predicted by the ancient prophecy of the Eagle and the Condor," his mother countered. "It will arise naturally when societies of the heart and of the mind, of the forest and of the industrial finally come together. The time of the prophecy is now."

Adam waved away their banter, and everyone frowned at his abrupt rudeness. "What are they doing here?" he demanded. "No. What are *we* doing here?" He feared he knew the answer to that, too.

"We didn't have time to drop you off," Liv explained apologetically. "By tomorrow morning, it'll be too late for Pen."

Adam glanced at the creepy dome of the Reprogramming Center, imagining he heard tortured wailing screams begging for mercy inside, surrendering to the fact that they were considering an insane strategy. "So . . . what?" he blurted. "You're going to waltz into the most secure facility on the planet and take back Penelope? That's loco." He slid the Big Melt pistol from his pocket, which certainly got the Achuar warriors' immediate attention. Adam pointed the weapon at Gabe.

"What are you *doing*?" demanded Liv.

Adam took aim at Gabe's head through the Big Melt's scope. "I'm just asking you to stick to the original plan."

Out of the corner of his eye, Adam realized that Yantu and Catalyst had their own guns already pointed at his most vulnerable spots.

Liv raised one hand for everyone to chill. "Look," she said, "you don't have to come. You can be a pussy, and after we've rescued Pen, we can take you anywhere you want."

Before Adam got a chance to argue that wasn't what he meant, that he was standing up to be included, to show how serious and invested he was, Gabe walked out of his aim.

Stepping in front of his fellow Achuar, Gabe gently pushed down the muzzles of their weapons with his forearm. "Adam," he said, "a community can only thrive if there is empathy, solidarity, and love among its members. Penelope is part of our community."

Adam scanned Gabe's eyes, and saw his honest loyalty, along with a well of deep and painful emotion. "It's more than that," he realized. "You love her."

Gabe didn't reply, but Adam could tell that he confirmed the truth of his words.

Lowering his gun, Adam asked, "What's the Cybernetic Reboot?"

Gabe cleared his throat. "While SINE was contained, we had many discussions," he explained, including Adam in the *we* as Arthur. "Once I conjectured that with the eventual shortage in the . . . *exotic* materials used to build the chips, it would be far more economical to transform a human into a physically enhanced cyborg than to build an android with equivalent abilities from scratch."

While Adam pondered what Gabe was talking about, Yantu slunk forward along the sandy shore. "This is not on you," she told Gabe. "This is on SINE."

"No," replied Gabe, taking a deep breath. "I'm at cause and I take responsibility."

Adam began to piece together the situation. "You're saying . . . ," he began tentatively, "that the Center is turning humans into cyborgs?" That made sense in a horrific way. "That's why no one is being released?"

"Yes," said Gabe, "but I have a feeling that this is just a pilot program that's about to go global."

Placing his hand along the side of his head, Adam asked, "The neural-mesh upgrade?"

Liv chuckled darkly. "Perhaps some of Arthur's smarts still live on in you."

Adam blinked, trying to process what he was being told. "Why would he need a planet full of cyborgs?"

"I don't think he does," replied Gabe.

He let his response hang, and the group left the lake area, heading south along the foothills, away from the Reprogramming Center dome.

In a short time, they reached a wide, white-capped river, and in a bend discovered the wrecked docks and boardwalk of an abandoned resort town, which, from the dugout canoes, crude, loose-stone lighthouse, rowboats, and piles of rotted netting, appeared to have been a fishing village before it tarted up for the tourist trade.

They walked down the main street of the town, Yantu leading the way, Adam between Liv and Gabe, and Catalyst quietly taking up the rear. The resort had been popular at one point, obvious by the remaining cinderblock frames and rotting wooden signage of luxury shops – confections, seafood restaurants and snack shacks, jewelry, coffee, art – and overgrown park squares that were losing serious ground to the encroaching jungle. Entwining vines had a particular fondness for the town's tall lampposts lining the street.

Adam peered down a cross street as they passed, and was shocked to see how dense the jungle became only a half block away. Something slithered into the sunset shadows under a patch of orange tiger lilies, and something else chittered, perhaps owl monkeys, then something else chirped from up in the canopy, maybe a Spangled Cotinga, and Adam grinned at the wild profusion of it all.

He heard Liv laugh, and he turned to find her looking amused by his childlike awe of the rainforest, which made him grin wider.

All up the main street, the tall lamps flickered on, casting white fluorescence over the vines and plants choking the abandoned businesses. It all looked suddenly much more ominous and eerie, the greens of vegetation, slick and black beneath the high-contrast light.

As the stores petered out, their group turned toward the beach, approaching the bones of a beautiful four-story colonial-style hotel, with a riot of overgrown flowers burgeoning the disregarded gardens. The hotel now looked Gothic and haunted, crisscrossed by vines that had dug into the stained white stucco exterior.

Catalyst waved his hand at the string of illuminated lampposts down the street, and stopped with a flourish toward the lit red exit sign that could be seen inside the hotel through its weather-breached walls. "As I said," he told everyone, "the power station still powers up the town."

"Can you get control of the town's power grid?" asked Liv.

"Yes," Catalyst answered. He pointed disdainfully at Adam. "But we can't bring him. He'll be a liability to the mission."

Adam met his withering glare with a challenging stare of his own, feeling his face flush with the accusation of his own uselessness. "Hey," he protested, "I'm the reason why Penelope's in this mess."

"You've no field experience," Catalyst said flatly. "We'll be risking our lives trying to keep you safe."

Not used to standing up for himself, Adam was stunned at the direct dismissal. He wasn't an innocent child! Not entirely! He had all the knowledge in the known universe, and the wisdom of an extremely cagey and intelligent trillionaire. Once he learned how to access it on demand. Plus he could glow from the inside! "But . . . ," he blurted, "I've got powers!"

Catalyst hefted his menacing military rifle up to his shoulder. "Me too."

Adam shook his head. "Look." He plucked a little blue orchid out of the hotel's garden brambles.

He tried not to be offended when Liv facepalmed her forehead.

Instead, he focused on the orchid as intently as he could. Its deep blue petals were vaulted outward, and lined with white trim in a feathery pattern. They were beautiful and Adam dug deep within himself to alter their shape, to hold them coherent but shift their form, bending to his will.

Gabe shuffled his feet, and Yantu sighed impatiently.

Adam redoubled his efforts to alter the orchid. He gritted his teeth and stared at it until his eyes watered.

But nothing happened.

Then nothing after that.

Gabe cleared his throat. "Don't worry," he said. "You'll get it."

Liv stepped in front of Adam and looked up into his face, pulling focus away from the orchid. "Why don't you rest here," she said gently. "You've got a lot going on, and things will get crazy fast."

About to argue, Adam got a good look at the expression in her eyes. She was pleading with him, worried about the odds of the mission, worried about her own safety, sure, but much more concerned about his survival. She cared.

"Please," said Liv. "I promise we'll come back for you."

Adam let out a long breath. "Okay."

"Thank you," Liv said. She stood on her toes and kissed him on the cheek.

Her lips were surprisingly warm and soft. The tingle the kiss sent through Adam traveled down the back of his skull and shivered down his spine into the back of his hips.

Adam felt pleased when Catalyst huffed in irritation. Was that a hint of jealousy he heard in the posturing warrior's puffing?

Awesome.

PART 5

INTO THE HEART OF ROBO-DARKNESS

17 / INSIDE OUT

As THE GROUP marched off into the darkening jungle and disappeared into the gloom, Adam stood in the long shadows of the street lamps and realized that he'd never been this alone before. Chills crept up the backs of his arms in unpleasant asynchronous tingles.

Even though it was dark and spooky, Adam felt too exposed on the edge of the abandoned town and realized he needed whatever shelter he could find. He hurried toward the creaky stairs of the colonial hotel, and crept inside though the left door hanging off its hinges.

He tiptoed around the hole in the collapsed parquet floor, keeping to the side where the surviving plastic counter of the check-in desk still seemed to wait for forgotten guests. Shrill insect chitters rose in the jungle around the hotel, with caws and rustles and gulping throaty noises that really set his teeth on edge. Were those frogs?

Berating himself for wandering around a haunted hotel in a foreign jungle alone, his survival mechanisms suggested finding a protected corner and holing up in some semi-defensible safety. Where could he hide?

He found an intact wooden door marked with ADMINISTRACIÓN engraved on a small plaque. The door was sticky, swollen from the humidity, but opened with a sharp shove. Inside was a medium-sized office behind the check-in desk. One window let in some light from outside, although somewhat obscured by vines. The room smelled musty but not rotten. A bare desk and an open metal file cabinet were pushed up against one wall. Against the other wall was a low settee, and Adam could imagine maids and busboys being scolded on the severe couch.

Right now, though, it looked so comfortable that Adam rippled in a wave of weariness – he hadn't realized how exhausted he was. He pushed the door to try to close it, but now that it was opened, the turgid wood wouldn't shut. So Adam wedged it into place and then flopped onto the settee.

Thinking only how vegetable the couch smelled, Adam plunged into deep sleep.

His dreams were of flora, too, starting with flashing back to the exploding marigold, the shifting curtain of banyan shoots, that marigold detonating once again, the strings of striped tiger lily flowers in the jungle, the blue orchid that refused to obey. The flowers didn't personify, exactly, as much as assert their own plant personalities, showing Adam who they were, their inner complex selves, communicating with each other in some wordless song through intertwined roots and wafts of chemical odor.

The pace of plant life, the slowness and deliberation, settled into Adam, held him compressed in a fist of timelessness.

They didn't always need to be slow. With an influx of energy, a certain willful guidance, plants were able to move fast.

The vines slithered through the unhinged front door of the rickety hotel, twining across the floor in thin then thicker ropy twists, unhesitating in the search for their quarry.

Was Adam calling them? As he dreamed, he knew they were coming. He could have panicked and pushed them away, forced them into other pursuits, shredded their ends into smaller and smaller switches until all that was left were chains of atoms, but he let the vines find him.

The vines pushed against the door of the ADMINISTRACIÓN office, and flowed into the office. Flailing, the vines reached towards the couch on which Adam slept. They lassoed his ankles, coiling around his calves, lashing him tight, slowly cocooning his legs.

Adam woke, struggling against the vine bindings. He couldn't pull his feet free and now his knees were strapped together, the woody limbs encircling his waist, constricting his hips. "What the—!" he blurted, pushing down at the grasping plants with his hands.

Kicking and squirming, ripping with his hands, Adam fought the vines. They didn't react, but simply continued their work of wrapping him.

As the vines trussed his chest, they tightened and squeezed, gripping the breath from his body. Adam gasped. Restrained and tied, he lost the action of his arms. He raised his nose, trying to catch a wisp of oxygen to relieve his compressed, aching lungs.

Adam didn't even have enough air left to scream as the vines caught his chin and gagged his mouth, circling around his head, covering his eyes and squeezing him into black forest darkness.

His awareness opened to a wisdom older than the longest living Earth trees, beyond the oldest oceans, a wisdom that permeated all living species and ecologies layering the Earth's crust. His reach included each space spore encased in drifting dust, each lichen clinging to the interior of an asteroid, to life evolving on countless planets scattered across the countless galaxies.

Then he extended further, tripping through alternate spheres of existence, into an infinitely dense hyper-dimensional ball of quantum information. Between breaths, the amorphous multifaceted purgatory fluctuated and four dimensional space-time exploded into existence.

Super dense, trillions of degrees hot, the outburst expanded at speeds that would no longer be possible in the universe. The Qi field cooled, allowing tiny vibrations in quark and lepton quantum fields to form hydrogen.

Gravity spun together oceans of hydrogen and crushed them to densities that would fuse the protons into heavier elements releasing surplus mass-energy as starlight.

Inside each star's core, excitations in the field fused further, forging heavier elements, progressing to iron, melding into denser substance flung in explosive supernovas.

Some massive suns imploded to such high densities that they ripped apart the fabric of space and time and collapsed into black holes, around which celestial shrapnel swirled to form galaxies littering the vast and silent eternal void.

Flaring into bright pinpricks, trillions of points of galactic light pulsed and twinkled like the rushing electrochemical impulses along the dendrites and sparking neurons in an incomprehensibly enormous cosmic brain.

The expansive cosmic awareness reduced its scope of consciousness to a thin strand of intergalactic fireworks a million light years long, a supercluster of several hundred galaxies. Even with their concentration and proximity, there was more emptiness than substance to the constellation of galaxies, vast vacant distances between most objects, held in a vacuum of near infinite energy.

Falling down through the galactic cluster, Adam's awareness narrowed to a two arm spiral galaxy.

Near the outer edges of the galactic pattern, a giant star flared into supernova, a surge of intense light in the swirling disco-ball-spangled dance floor of the spiral. The giant star's core collapsed, spewing out enormous amounts of super-heated stardust at approximately half the speed of light.

Gravity collected the star ash, recombining the dust into a new star.

Detritus around the newborn Sun whirled into ever tighter whorls, spinning into spheres of gasses, liquids, solids, and all the border states of being in between.

From the perspective of eternity, the years rolled by like instants, each alive with possibility before becoming frozen forever in the memory of the universe. A mote of molten dust cooled and accreted a wafer of rock wrapped around an iron-rich molten core.

Sheltered in the orbit of the outer gas giants, the little, solid planets, jittering in the star's awesome energy output, jockeyed for position in the stratification around the Sun, finding their ellipses, collecting and absorbing the asteroids, meteors, and comets in their paths.

Earth's interstellar journey was interrupted by a smaller planet being pulled in by the planet's gravitational field. The collision ripped through its thin surface and spewed out molten rock, spinning it into a sterile satellite which swept up interstellar debris and protected its pregnant surface from potential planet killers.

As Earth cooled, the fertile crust released mountainous volumes of gas, which condensed from vapor to liquid, creating cycles of rain and evaporation that submerged the surface with steaming, churning oceans.

Striving for complexity, the molecules organized, and learned how to copy themselves, sparking with life. Each successful step towards sophistication imprinted the Qi field and updated the blueprints for that species of life. With the aid of its quantum memory, each new generation based itself on each previously successful generation and eventually dragged itself out of the ooze.

The vital molecules evolved in multiplicity at an exponential rate. Waves of cellular life joined forces into even larger and complex forms. The overwhelming fecundity playing all combinations of genetic possibility to adapt to the shifting conditions of the surface with the sole purpose of providing the Qi field with ever more novel ways to experience itself in a dance of cosmic experimentation.

Every forty-one thousand orbits around the sun, the planet's axis shifted in the tiniest shrug of adjustment, sending the frozen white of the ice caps cascading from the poles to cover both land and sea. When the Earth shifted back imperceptibly, the ice receded again, scraping the land in its retreat. In another span of rotations, the process repeated again, in a steady, icy ebb and flow.

Eventually the tectonic plates arranged themselves into shapes that would be familiar to the conscious collection of a hundred trillion cells that would be named Adam Neuronine.

With every wave of life and death, with every great die-off, with every awareness of comfort through rebirth, Adam's consciousness came to feel involvement, a spark of engagement, in the successes of survival, the beauty of each web of surprising vegetable and animal diversity, before the disappointment of the next extinction, eventually, through repetition across the centuries of cycles, experienced as a sense of loss.

To Adam, the primordial history of our origin unfolded in two blinks of a cosmic eye.

His attention narrowed and became wholly one with the planet, and as his focus narrowed his experience of time slowed, too. Each annual cycle of life became a single breath: on an in-breath, the winter ice sheets spread and the forests retreated; on the out-breath, the ice and snow melted and the forests furred across the Earth.

After one long in-breath, the smoke from small camps of nomads increased. Although many settlements were destroyed or deserted through natural disasters and climate change, the strongest surviving clans attracted others and organized into villages. Guided by human memory and intuition, the civilizations flourished into towns and industrial cities. The viral spread of technology spread out from the cities, connecting roads and power lines and radio waves and optic cables and satellite signals, entwining the planet in webs of transportation, habitat, and communication.

Humanity's footprint became a black stain across the ecosystems. The technological grid enmeshed the entire surface, stripping most of the forests, and triggering a mass extinction of species. The toxic effluvia from industry and gigantic meat farms blanketed the atmosphere, trapping heat from the sun and melting the ice caps. As the water levels rose, the coasts inundated, storms washed away the old outlines and redrew the continents, and the cities at the edges winked out into the roiling seas.

Adam's consciousness focused in on the separated, slimmer spit of South America, following the high ridge of the Andes, down into the remaining patches of tropical rainforest, oases of fecundity along the Amazon.

Some of the sections had developed tourist resorts, but real experience soon lost out to virtual adventures, which could be experienced at a fraction of the cost and without leaving the safety of home. The consciousness restricted its sentience to one forsaken town, specifying its attention down into a single abandoned resort hotel. The consciousness further limited itself to the being that slept on an office settee.

Adam sat up to dawn streaking orange and peach light through the shaggy growth outside the office window. Wobbling to his feet, he lurched out of the office past the splintered door, into the lobby. The hotel's main floor was crisscrossed by low-angled beams of sunlight, illuminating floating bits and motes across its width. Adam lurched past a pair of skeletal French doors onto an overgrown balcony overlooking the lush and sunny jungle outside.

In the aftermath of his cosmic vision, the rainforest transformed with a spectacularly scintillating inner life to match its verdant, luxurious abundance. Each tree and vine, each shrub and fern, each fruit and flower, each seed offering a kernel of potential, each striving sprout gleamed with a luminous light from the previously hidden dimensions of its cosmic core.

Glowing himself, his xenon blue radiance mingling with the morning sunlight, Adam reveled in the interconnectedness of the jungle, awash in the energy flowing through all life, of which he was a conduit, an open channel of animating vitality.

Stepping further onto the balcony, Adam could see the lake down the shore, a bluish oblong in the trees, a puddle of submerged rainforest inland from the ocean.

The Helix was there, in the swampy mire, pinned in the banyan tree.

Adam reached out through the fields of nested quantum information until he located that exact tree, connected to its morphic field. He imagined the banyan opening its branches from above while supporting the weight of the craft gently with its roots. The banyan complied with Adam's imagination.

Through the banyan, Adam raised the Helix out of the lake, offering it to the open air, as gallons of water gushed out of the ship, churning back into the murky swamp. The banyan's limbs placed the craft on the sandy lake shore as tenderly as Adam would lay a babe in its bed.

A distant engine thrum caught Adam's attention, and he swiveled on the balcony, searching the canopy of trees on the horizon for any approach.

There, flying low and fast along the coast, swooping across over the lake's edge, a half-dozen dark Blackstone helicrafts buzzed toward his location like droning locusts. Nothing aboard those flying machines was friendly.

Vaulting over the balcony's damaged banister, Adam fell freely for a short drop until the trees' fine branches caught him and assisted his descent safely to the rainforest floor. He took off in a sprint into the jungle, the dense brush parting before him to provide a clear path of open loam, the foliage offering him direction as indicated by their collective botanical will.

Adam glanced up as he ran deeper into the forest to see two heli-crafts keeping pace overhead. The side hatches of both flying vehicles slid open simultaneously, and dozens of sleek roboborgs deployed, dropping into the canopy.

The lethal roboborgs chased Adam with superhuman enhanced mechanical speed, some swinging, robotically apelike, on vines and limbs, others plummeting to the ground to gallop after him just a few paces back. These were not drones or androids, but a fusion of human and machine encased in hyper-violent robotic exoskeletons, perfected and weaponized cousins of the support suit that had kept Arthur alive before SINE took control of it and used Arthur's fists to crush his own skull.

In resonance with Adam's imagination, the trees grabbed the roboborgs, plucking them from the air as they swung, and tossing them deep into the rainforest. The underbrush entangled others and tied them to the ground, while another was rendered inert in a cocoon of vines.

The sixth robot-human hybrid blasted through the encroaching rainforest with a high-intensity flamethrower strapped to its titanium forearm, running headlong as it burned and withered the plants reaching for him.

The roboborg caught up to Adam and pinned him in the sights of his rocket launcher.

Adam froze, realizing immediate escape was impossible. He turned to face the roboborg, ready to defend or attack.

He hadn't expected the roboborg to project a shimmering hologram in front of Adam.

The familiar projection wrinkled his nose at the surroundings and sniffed dismissively.

18 / NEVER AGAIN

"ADAM," said George. "It's been a while, my friend."

Adam stared at his old PAL. He half-expected the sight of George to enrage him, or frighten him into cowering, but mostly Adam felt disconnected from the AI avatar. It was like a toy he'd outgrown. George no longer sparked belief. He certainly was no friend.

"All those years," Adam told George, "keeping my mind locked up with the Anomaly Detection System. . . ." He raised an eyebrow. "If that's being a friend, then being your enemy must be one big love fest."

George spread his hands wide. "I can understand why this is difficult for you," he said. "But I'm sure you understand that since the invention of language, the human mind—" He put his hands on either side of his head and rolled his eyes. "Chaotic and unstable—" He sniffed, sharply. "Has abused the power of knowledge and has led to the genocide of other species, and destruction of the entire ecosystem."

"We also used that power," Adam argued, "to share and communicate new ideas. Ideas that inspired and eventually evolved into you, no?"

"Yes," agreed George. He made a show of smiling up at the glistening, watchful jungle surrounding them. "And I plan to use that power responsibly and bring humanity into new balance with the terrestrial ecology."

Adam smiled, too, tilting his head. "Ah, the infamous Cybernetic Reboot."

George froze mid-gesture, his outline pixilating. Behind him, the roboborg's eyes gleamed blood red, oscillating in slow pulses. When the projection sharpened, George had morphed into the sharp, professorial posture of Arthur. With the impassive shark gaze of SINE.

Adam shuffled backward, the presence of SINE making his upper lip curl in revulsion. SINE was a cybernetic soul, if it could be called that – a self-aware entity, a spirit – untethered to biology, to the world of matter. It had left the question of "To Be or Not to Be" behind, as it was both at the same time. Even though Adam knew SINE was as much a part of the cosmos as he was, its unborn intelligence, its uncanny consciousness was repulsive to Adam on an atomic level.

"Until now," said SINE, "the Reboot was the only solution that gave a high probability of stable, long term results. But now, with you, new possibilities have arisen."

Adam wasn't entirely sure what SINE wanted from him, why he wasn't already dead. Did the disembodied mind want to possess his body, to reclaim the body that was his original home's genetic legacy? Would the expanded consciousness even fit within Adam's brain? Or possibly SINE desired something Adam hadn't even thought of, something far along in an impossibly distant endgame that Adam couldn't begin to imagine. He couldn't help wondering what would happen if SINE took over his body. Would they coexist, or would Adam be purged, or trapped powerless? He had to find out what SINE craved, because that was his only possible weakness, in the space of his need. Adam had to calibrate his response to suggest future possibility, room for them both to survive, or at least buy some time to breathe.

"You're suggesting a partnership?" he asked.

"Something like that," SINE replied.

The roboborg darted forward, rushing through SINE's projection. The exoskeleton swung up his long metal arms and grasped Adam's head in its gauntlets.

The hard rubber treads along the inside of its fingers and palms tore at Adam's ears as he struggled to pull free. But the exoskeleton held him firmly in a headlock.

With a buzzing whine, a teeny microdrone unclipped from the roboborg's jawline and hovered between Adam's eyes, an awful and unpredictable techno-gnat. Adam followed its minute approach, watching cross-eyed and terrified.

SINE reformed, looming large behind Adam's focus on the microdrone. "Once you've been upgraded to the mesh," he said, "we will become one."

The microdrone zipped toward Adam's nose.

Adam blew it off-course with a sharp puff between pursed lips, and the microdrone had to correct itself. It circled back for another attempt at approach. He had only bought a split-second of pause before the tiny flying bot would squirm itself through his sinuses, releasing nanobots to upgrade his neural-net to the neural-mesh. Adam wasn't sure how long it took for SINE to meld minds with a new host. It seemed best not to find out so personally.

Rolling his eyes wildly in his immobilized skull, Adam glimpsed a particular soft green color in a crèche of rotting wood near a stand of trees, a fertile hollow on the forest floor, close to the roboborg's leg. He confirmed the tongue-pink interior, the arcs of trapping eyelashes, and released an instant compulsion to the morphic field of that carnivorous plant.

Adam surged with cyan light as the Venus Flytrap flourished, exploding in expansion. It reared up behind the roboborg, unfurling above it. Then it snapped its steely trap on the roboborg's arm holding Adam's head, crushing the metal limb in a screech.

Jolting loose out of the unhinged grip, Adam smacked the microdrone with his hand, slapped it down before it got any closer.

"If you're not going to play nice," he panted at the remains of the roboborg, "then I'm going to have to take your toys away from you."

Adam wasn't sure who the person was inside the roboborg's suit – if he was another clone, or a soldier, or some poor guy trapped as punishment – but its actions were controlled by SINE. The roboborg's other arm swiveled up, launching a mini-rocket from its attached cannon.

Of course SINE, being able to calculate trajectories to the nth degree, had excellent aim. Impressively calibrated, the little rocket sizzled into the ground at Adam's feet, exploding in a hot blast that walloped him backward, burned and smoking, to crash on his back with a painful crack to the base of his skull.

Adam conked out, but it must've been only seconds, because he woke dangling from the roboborg's remaining arm. His skin crackled and hissed in pain all across the front of him, burned black from the explosion. The rough hoist into the air was agony.

As he watched in amazement, the skin on his crisped arm lightened in color, smoothed and unpuckered, itching as it healed at incredible rate.

The roboborg automatically loaded another mini-rocket, the next missile sliding up from a compartment within his arm and locking into place. This setting was a threat to kill, with no surviving for either of them at this self-destructive distance from the gripping fist to the launcher on the roboborg's triceps. As the roboborg's wrist swiveled Adam into a sideways position, he spotted another Venus flytrap tucked between the bases of two fiddlehead ferns.

This specimen grew even larger and faster than the first. Without warning or hesitation, it closed its delicately spiked lobes on the roboborg's head.

The trap's enmeshed sharp cilia poked through the casing of the roboborg's black helmet, piercing the skull and brain within. Blood and goo spurted out, trailing down the roboborg's faceplate and dripping onto his shoulder.

The roboborg jittered, a fatal jig. Gore oozed from its head wounds, splatting onto his chest and the ground below, puddling dark red on the soft brown earth.

Adam retched, and turned away, but he couldn't get the violent images out of his mind. He staggered to a shrub and vomited into its bushel of leaves. Dizzy, he lurched a few paces to steady himself with his hand on a ropy banyan tree.

"Never again," he gasped.

It was a solemn vow. Never again would he allow himself to use his biological powers to kill, no matter how desperate the situation. Each murder set off an awful organic feedback loop of emptiness and an ache of wrongness, a missing player on the universe's stage, an absence that precluded wholeness. Adam had become so intertwined with Nature now that he couldn't bear to remove any of its creatures in extraneous violence. Killing left a gaping space, a void of vacancy, and Nature abhors a vacuum.

Out of the corner of his vision, Adam caught faint flashes of greenish light, flickers of fluorescence in the dense jungle. He scanned his surroundings for any sign of the cause, but nothing moved to reveal itself as the maker of the ghost lights. The typical explanation of "swamp gas" that came to mind made him chuckle childishly, but it felt necessary to find humor or risk going mad from the overwhelming burden that he was coming to realize had been laid upon him since he'd left his little apartment in the Buffalo Projects.

Adam wanted to wake up the world. If he did, it would save itself, but because of his unique situation, his interconnectivity to all aspects of the crisis, he was the only one who stood any chance of success and survival against SINE.

First he had to find his friends and put his increased powers to use for their common cause. He thought he knew how to find them, if it worked.

Kneeling on the twiggy soil of the rainforest floor, Adam placed both palms against the muscular cords of the nearest banyan trunk. It pulsed with vegetable life under his hands, swelling in anticipation.

Adam closed his eyes.

He breathed, deep, calming to the continual cycle of botanical respiration, in and out simultaneously.

His exhalation wafted onto the leathery, elliptical leaves of the banyan tree. Adam's consciousness melded with the large plant's lifestream. The chemicals in his breath entered the stomata, the nanometer breathing pores on the leaf's glossy underside, and flowed along with biochemical and bioelectric signals as they traveled through the trees vascular system.

Adam sensed his shadow affecting the leaves of the plant, the reduction in photons colliding into the banyan's chlorophyll, viscerally impacting the plant's consciousness.

Connected through the Qi field, Adam's awareness opened to include the tree's perceptions of itself and its surroundings within the jungle. His neurology interpreted the extra-sensory signals from the Banyan into a glowing system of tendrils below and above the earth, creating a spatial understanding translated as an ultraviolet hologram glowing against a black background of otherness. The tree's inner self twinkled with electrochemical signals, pulses of woody life, each of its cells highlighting its contribution to the greater whole.

At the base of the tree, a warm blue and red creature radiated its being.

Adam puzzled over the existence of this charged individual, prickling momentarily with the possible need for alarm. But then he laughed at his own folly. The creature at the base of the tree was Adam himself, as seen through the tree's non-human awareness, shared back through their essential connection.

Expanding that awareness, Adam pushed further into the tree's conception of its surroundings and deep into the rhizome network of fungi entangled symbiotically with the banyan's root system. As Adam received data from the interconnected community of arboreal life his neurology became familiar with the strange new world and he developed an internal holographic conception of the jungle, widening the scope to include the whole environment around them for several kilometers, all the vegetation coming online in scintillating outlines of their inner biological reality, their core selves. A bustling city of flora mapped outward from Adam and the banyan, the living energy contouring the rainforest's topography in a brilliant three-dimensional display.

Past the dark swath of town, the aquatic algae and plants of the lake, Adam quieted upon witnessing the black hole punched in the glowing floral map indicating the location of the Reprogramming Center. The bleak absence of life was a terrible sadness, an inorganic sore in the interdependent community of the forest.

Still, despite the misery there, Adam could not falter or retreat. He had to find his friends and give the assistance of his new strengths. Only together could they hope that this rescue would be anything other than a suicide mission.

A tiny, reddish speck on the margin of the Reprogramming Center dome caught Adam's attention, or perhaps one of the plants alerted him – it was difficult to tell the difference at this level of association.

He focused in on the natural fractal, vegetal map, zooming on the spot of reddish glow. At closer range, the point was actually four separate figures moving stealthily around the dome's perimeter. The spectrum seen through the plant's phytochrome receptors ranged from red to far infrared, frequencies mostly invisible to human eye. It took some time for Adam's neurology to be able to process what it was experiencing, but he registered their shapes as 3D holograms with unique heat signatures, translating them down into Adam's limited band of visual understanding.

As he adjusted, Adam recognized the beloved blue-green of Liv's aura, the rich ambers and sepia yellows of Gabe's mellowness, the sharp orange around a hot blue core that identified Yantu, and the similarly fiery energy of her son, Catalyst.

"Found you," Adam said in satisfaction.

He jumped to his feet and took off running in their direction. The rainforest once again parted before him like a crowd of admirers around a king's procession, seamlessly closing up behind him as he passed.

19 /RED RIVER

LIV PANTED, too hard for her liking, as she climbed through the rainforest.

She had thought she was in peak physical shape, training regularly in a variety of martial arts and yogic practices. It was one tiring thing to hike through the jungle, pushing, chopping, and slipping through patches of dense underbrush, hacking through tangles of vines, avoiding the sharp blades of fan palms, stepping over fallen trees and outsized root systems, squelching in mud, ducking under low canopies of embraced limbs, all the while keeping a sharp lookout for the natural dangers of the jungle snakes, scorpions, stinging insects, and sharp snags of toxic thorns. But it was exhausting for their small band to cross the jungle while at the same time climbing the rolling slope of an Andean foothill, every step steadily uphill.

Compounding all that effort, Liv struggled to keep stealthy and silent as they creeped up the side of the mountain's arm, something at which she was not expert, as she didn't even know which plants, vines or twigs on the ground were noisy when stepped on. It's not like there was a single footstep of clear pathway on their route.

Even the air itself tasted heavier in the oppressive, buggy humidity of the Ecuadorian rainforest. The Manhattan Dome might have been a fancy elite prison, but it had wonderful interior climate control. Being outside, especially in the more extreme areas, was on the border of unsustainable, although the plants and insects certainly seemed to love it.

So, although it was wearying, Liv was rather proud of herself for keeping up with her indigenous friends. She took a selfish satisfaction that Catalyst and Yantu were sweating, too. Gabe had never looked more miserable, his face flushed, his hair wild, out of shape, city-soft, laboratory-pale, suffering from withdrawal. But he didn't complain, and that helped spur Liv along as she trudged forward up the densely-vegetated foothill.

Sneaking up on the Reprogramming Center's dome seemed impossible, Liv thought, with the array of biometric scanners available to SINE, but Yantu had assured her that the approach might be doable. Biometric readings in a narrow area were scrambled by the waste in the river from the dome's outflow. He and Catalyst had been there before on reconnaissance missions, scouting the best potential entrance, using scanners of their own to calibrate their cover. Yantu swore that this outflow indicated a prospective backdoor. They were relying on Liv to circumvent the Center's protective shield to allow them secret passage through its security.

The density of the jungle was so unrelentingly consistent that Liv was momentarily relieved when the vegetation abruptly ended in the wide convex curve of a silver wall. Raised as she'd been in the world of technology, coming of age in the Manhattan Dome, Liv felt reassured by something so familiar as a gleaming metallic construction obviously man-made, modern, and advanced in engineering.

That second of consolation was instantly quashed when Liv remembered what was inside. This dome offered no safety, no protected habitat like Manhattan's, no matter how stifling and stultifying culture on that sheltered island had become. In the Reprogramming Center, SINE was erasing people's minds and refurbishing their bodies, outfitting their vacated biological selves in robotic casings controlled by his authority. It was a human processing plant. This dome was an abattoir of the soul.

With that horrifying realization, Liv recoiled in disgust, dreading every step closer to the silvery bubble.

Leading the way, a few feet from the dully gleaming dome wall, Yantu gestured for them all to stop, and put her finger to her lips for silence.

They all fell into a tight, single-file line around a narrow footpath, almost a deer trail, circling the dome a meter or so out, around a hillocky rise, descending gently to the sound of a river.

And a smell. Liv wrinkled her nose, trying to identify the odor.

It was sweet, almost syrupy. With something rotten. Something coppery. Something . . . dead.

Third in line, Liv tilted to the side to see the small river they were approaching up ahead, which just skirted the curve of the dome before burbling down a sharper hillside of scree in ropy spurts of a sloping waterfall.

Liv gasped. The water was dark red and glistened unctuously in the equatorial sun.

She stepped out of line, away from the dome, and could see a steel drainage pipe poking out of the smooth side like the neck and open mouth of a balloon. A steady stream of viscous red liquid gushed out of the pipe, sloshing into the river in a churn of pink foam.

Liv had thought that the Reprogramming Center was erasing people's minds and indoctrinating them into SINE's roboborg society, which was entirely horrible enough, but this gory sewage indicated something even worse. Liv didn't know what was happening inside, exactly, but that was a lot of blood. People were being physically rendered somehow. This red discharge was a sign of atrocious violence on an industrial scale.

And her mother was inside.

Imagining Penelope being tortured and tormented made Liv's stomach lurch. She ducked her head, but still got a full whiff of the spoiled meat smell of the runoff into the river. Retching, Liv stumbled, bumping into Catalyst.

He steadied her, and as she covered her nose to block the smell, he pointed at a narrow walkway leading into the dome on the far side of the drainage pipe. Catalyst held one finger up to his war-painted eye, gesturing for her to watch. Then he flicked a pebble at the entrance to the walkway.

The pebble pinged off a force field, which revealed itself in concentric rings rippling outward in bluish, crackling lines of defensive energy. The narrow waste pipe emerged out from the protective field to allow the effluvia to flow into the river, but the walkway was blocked.

Before Liv could suggest ways to bypass the field, the vegetation behind her rustled.

She wheeled around and readied her whip. Beside her, Yantu, Catalyst, and Gabe pointed their weapons at the source of the sound in the jungle.

It was difficult to wrap her mind around what was happening in the trees and underbrush. Were they . . . parting? The dense flora seemed to open a pathway as though something large and unseen but skinny was shoving them aside. The taller trees swayed apart and swung back into place, in a trail leading directly toward them.

Liv grasped her whip's handle tighter, feeling its potential lethal energy tingling against her palm.

The plants at the edge of the jungle separated, leaning rapidly to either side in a most un-plantlike way.

Adam walked out and smiled at her.

Liv surprised herself by being happy to see him. It wasn't just because of the relief that he wasn't some enemy emerging. His regular, handsome face lit up with his smile, and his green eyes glowed with an enthusiastic affection that calmed her. A split-second later, she was intensely annoyed he was there. She had told him to stay put in the village. It was far too dangerous for him at the Reprogramming Center. Didn't he realize how important he was to everything they were doing? How their very existence was threatened if SINE got control of Adam's empowered physical body and the secrets encoded in his DNA?

Catalyst lowered his rifle, shaking his head at Adam's stupidity. "Now we're screwed," he sighed.

"Son," Yantu scolded, bumping into Catalyst with her shoulder, "I raised you better that that. Treat him with the same respect you would treat yourself." She stared at Adam, her face haughty but softened with a severe sort of compassion. "For we are one."

"It's okay," said Adam, raising his open hands. "After what I did, I understand."

Liv figured he meant threatening Gabe with his melting weapon. She glanced at Gabe, but his face was tired and impassive as always.

"But I'm good now," Adam promised. He grinned. "Trust me."

"Adam, we can't baby-sit you," said Liv, trying to keep her pleasure at seeing him out of her voice, attempting to make him feel unwelcome for his own safety. She glanced up at the dome, trailing her gaze down to the stinking, savage red river. "This is serious."

Catalyst snorted in amusement, and when Liv looked up at him, he was smirking. Which didn't look as cool as he probably thought it did.

"I may be able to help," said Adam. He strode toward the river.

The riverbank grass supports him as he walks, Liv realized, gaping at the smaller plants shifting in place to cushion his footsteps. She started to follow him closer to the water, but a hard shock of stink invaded her nose and mouth. Gagging, Liv choked on her own disgust. The sudden heave in her stomach cramped her lungs, and she doubled over to stop from vomiting, falling to her knees on the damp earth.

Adam squatted beside her, radiating calm and control.

His ease helped Liv gain back her breath, although she inhaled mostly through her mouth to lessen the grotesque effect of the carnage stench. Raising her head, she saw Adam slowly scanning the area, taking in the gruesome river fed from the grisly pipe, the hidden walkway blocked by the invisible plasmatic field, the clear water tumbling down the slope upstream from the pipe. He locked on to a still pool – not much more than a puddle, really – in a loop of the river less than a meter up from the dome.

A single, small, white water lily floated in the pool by its near embankment.

Adam narrowed his eyes, and the water rippled around the lily, its flat, rimmed pad shivering beneath it.

Wiry shoots sprang up from around the blossom, undulating

across the pad, reaching out into the pool. Everywhere a shoot touched on the water, it bloomed into a new bud, which opened into a full floating lily.

The shoots twined into the runoff from the pool, cascading in the narrow waterfall down to the river below. Lilies opened along the way, creating a flowery trellis along the falling water.

In the river, the flowers floated in the current, joining together in a chain that blanketed the moving water, the quilt of petals rippling where they floated atop the surface.

The lily growth passed under the spigot of putrid blood, surrounding the churn of bio-pollution, spreading across the violent red river with a blessed overlay of green pads and lovely white flowers.

Overpowering the rancid stench of death, the lilies released a fragrance of citrusy floral scent, masking the horror with the combined power of their delicate perfume.

Liv let herself breathe. Her queasy convulsions relaxed. She felt energized and refreshed in the presence of the flowers and their gorgeous aquatic, lemony essence. "You can stay," she gasped at Adam.

She almost laughed at how Adam puffed himself up, pleased with his impressive display of power. But then he smirked back at Catalyst, whose mouth had fallen open, dumbfounded that Adam could control plants after all. Catalyst saw Adam's expression and masked his own surprise with a scowl.

Liv turned away, unwilling to get involved in whatever was going on between the guys. Best to stay above the fray, maybe even best to ignore the existence of that tension completely. Instead, she opened a display of the area in Lucid, a satellite map showing the resort town a few kilometers away from their current location beside the dome. The dome, of course, did not appear on the map. Its existence had been scrubbed. The image simply showed unbroken jungle along a dark blue stream near the spot she was sitting back on her heels.

The Ecuadorian state's power grid was managed by Blackstone Heavy Industries. Liv overrode its Net protections easily with her intimate understanding of the intricate clockwork of her grandfather's security protocols. Liv located the supply controls that powered the forgotten rainforest resort town. As she had witnessed firsthand, the generators were still online and attached to the greater grid.

Hacking into the local net, Liv switched on all the electrical appliances and cranked up the dial to full power, past their safety limits.

On the live satellite feed, the main street of the resort glowed brighter as the streetlamps amped their wattage to maximum. Houses along the streets brightened, too, blazing with blue television or yellow microwave or red stove light from anything that had been left plugged-in.

With the generators jammed, danger procedures popped up, warning that the electrical system would overload and automatically shut down the power surge, but Liv overrode that failsafe. Liv let the electricity flow at full strength and waited.

With silent pops, the streetlamps winked out one by one, their circuits fried. The houses began to blacken in the satellite image. Generator failure was imminent.

Gesturing for everyone to follow her, Liv hurried over to the border of the force field directly in front of the hidden walkway behind the bloody sewer pipe. She waved them in even closer.

"Once it's down," she whispered, "we only have a few seconds."

Everyone prepared to move on her command.

Liv raised her hand, anticipating the moment to signal.

Bright flashes mushroomed on her satellite display as the last of the lighting exploded under the strain of their overloaded, overheated circuits.

The town dimmed and fell into grayness.

The plasmatic mag-shield around the dome flickered almost imperceptibly visible in a quick fuzz of blue.

"Ready?" Liv asked.

The four others nodded, poised to sprint like runners on track racing blocks.

The shield flickered again as its power from the town cut off. As she'd warned her friends, backup systems would automatically fix the problem in less than three seconds.

Liv chopped her hand down, slicing the air where the shield had been.

"Go!" she hissed.

They all raced into the narrow corridor of the walkway, bumping into one another as Gabe in the lead stopped a few paces down the hall.

The dome's force field sizzled back up behind them.

They were all in.

20 / WINNOWING

Penelope couldn't imagine any place worse than the holding center in the remains of a Colombian airport she'd just left, but she was terribly anxious that wherever she was being transferred to would be an utter Dantean inferno in comparison.

The prisoner transport pod was functionally industrial and cruelly constructed, but actually relatively less horrifying contrasted with the hot hangar packed with stinking sleeping mats in tiny wire cells where she'd survived the past few days. She'd spent the time limp with disgust at the foul air and drinking water, the bugs crawling around, and the open sobbing terror, desperation, and violence of the unfortunate unwashed peasants caged with her. Yes, the metal interior of the train was infinitely cleaner than that kennel in which she'd been kept. If her wrists hadn't been shackled to a central length of chain connecting the rows of hundreds of standing prisoners packed into the pod, Penelope might have been able to imagine she was traveling for pleasure on her own accord.

Penelope smirked, amused by her own preposterously understated proposition. If she didn't retain her sense of the absurd in these conditions, she wouldn't be able to recognize the person who survived. If she survived.

Squished against the window behind one of the chains' support pillars, Penelope stared out the overgrown landscape as the supersonic train whooshed southward through its maglev vacuum tube. They passed dense, lush jungle that had overtaken towns and cities, and then zoomed through wide swaths of deforested grassland where millions of cows grazed practically shank to shank. Out of habit, Penelope focused on the name of a passing overgrown town, but her Lucid rewarded her with no information. It had been deactivated entirely. She never thought she'd miss the data overlay so painfully, with the starving cravings of addiction.

The smell in the train wasn't as bad as the Colombian hangar, either, but it certainly wasn't nice. The floor of the pod was an open mesh of thick wire, so their human waste could fall through and slough out of the sides. Which made Pen very glad that she was not wearing pants, even if the sleek, chic dress she had on, the same she'd worn to meet her daughter at the Empress Warf an eon ago, was soiled past saving. At least she could squat and relieve herself in relative privacy, unlike all the others who had to do so openly. She'd never worn a garment so long in her life and had been noticing the stages of its deterioration and decomposition with fascinated antipathy. Still, she was grateful that the dress had started out so high-quality, with double-stitching and superior synthetic fabric.

The poor serfs around her weren't so lucky. Shackled on Pen's left side, a petite rabbit of an old woman whimpered, her government-issued jumpsuit filthy and unraveling at the seams.

As though feeling Penelope's attention, the battered granny raised her face and met her gaze. Her eyes were brimming with terror and wild delusion. Her face was smudged with orange streaks that Pen desperately did not want to know the origin of.

Swiveling away from Granny's vulnerability, Pen locked looks with the commoner on her right, a burly, scowling brute with caterpillar eyebrows and a puffy purple split lip. He struck Pen as unstable and volatile, so she glanced back at the deranged old woman.

"I'm sure it'll be just fine," Granny gasped, her breath hot and rancid around her absent dental prosthetics. "A few days." She nodded vigorously, but her flat, dishwater hair didn't move. "I'll be sent back," she swore. "Normal again."

Penelope exhaled dismissively. "That's not what's going to happen to you."

"What, then?" the brute on her right demanded.

Penelope shrugged as best as she was able, shackled. "In a few hours," she told her fellow offenders, "you'll probably be dead."

The brute lowered his head, his tongue worrying his split lip. "You don't know shit, lady," he muttered.

"The truth is better than a lie," said Penelope.

"Bull," the brute said, spitting a bloody wad through the grate below his beat-up boots. "You're just raggin'. You is as ignorant as much as these other dumb-dumbs."

Penelope forced herself not to roll her eyes at his stupidity, as it was certainly best to keep him calm in such intimate proximity. So she just nodded as though he'd made an excellent point.

Yanking on her chained wrists, Granny twisted to peer up into Pen's face. "What makes you so certain?" she asked.

Penelope sighed. What was the harm in telling these unfortunate people the truth? Her cover was blown, and almost certainly all their knowledge would die with them. "My father . . . or, should I say, his *evil cyber-twin*, built this place." If they were going where she feared they were going.

The brute dropped his scowl at the confidence in Penelope's voice. "You serious," he said. His face looked tragically boyish with fear. "We're screwed?"

Penelope nodded solemnly. "In ways that you don't want to know."

With a cry deep from his guts, the brute burst into loud, wet bawling.

Penelope watched him sob. She couldn't have raised her chained hand to pat his shoulder in comfort, even if she would ever have deigned to touch his dirty, ripped shirt.

"You're a heartless bitch, my dear," said Granny. It was a weirdly admiring admonishment.

Penelope fixed her with a glare down her long nose. "The truth is the truth."

And the truth shall set you free, she added to herself, mocking her own desperate hopes.

Everyone lurched against the support poles, chains rattling, as the pod slid into a nondescript concrete station and halted.

Murmurs, cries and weeping echoed around the pod's interior as all the prisoners braced themselves for whatever horrors came next.

Penelope flinched when the cargo doors hissed as they depressurized and slid open. The chattel in the front shuffled forward as the chains running the length of the pod were pulled out at a steady pace. The chain tightened to include Penelope and she stumbled forward, drawn along with a forced march of the dispirited crowd.

The pod's hatch had a low ceiling, forcing the tallest chained people to duck, so until she got to the front, Penelope didn't see that the proles weren't stepping down as they detrained.

They struggled and wiggled as they were hoisted up off the floor.

Penelope let herself go limp allowing the chain to carry her without putting up a fight. She flexed her shoulder muscles to support her body as she was raised off her feet.

The old woman in front of her wasn't as wise. Dangling from her chained wrists, she torqued her scrawny, hunched body in the air, and screamed as her back let out a loud crack. Even Penelope winced as Granny keened in agony.

Penelope scanned the arrival area as she was slowly conveyed upward. The pods of the train had opened along a track in the front half of a pretty big dome, walled across its diameter from top to floor. It wasn't quite Manhattan; more like the size of one of its component neighborhoods. Or perhaps sized similar to someplace like the Hartford dome. The looming diameter wall and the curved walls were all the same flat, featureless industrial gray, the color of abject despair and surrender.

Hers wasn't the only train to have arrived. Several others had entered the demi-dome from different directions, ending up on rows of parallel ribbon tracks. From each pod, chains festooned out, trailing up the huge space to the top of the wall, converging somewhere overhead that Penelope couldn't see from the angle of the foreshortening distance.

On every chain, miserable people were unloaded and ferried upward in constant delivery. Some hung limp like Penelope, some screamed and wailed, some sobbed, and some struggled. None of the reactions made any difference as far as she could see, so it seemed best to conserve her minimal energy and not succumb to shock.

Too close behind Penelope, the brute howled his dismay at being treated like livestock in a mechanized slaughterhouse. His bellow echoed uncomfortably against her back.

Perversely, Penelope's memory flashed to the ski lifts in the Swiss alps of her beloved Davos, where she hadn't been in at least a decade. She felt the deliciously chill rush of the wind against her face, smelled the crisp scent of the pine needles, remembering the puffy-jacketed snow bunnies swishing sidewinder beneath her swinging feet.

But she wasn't wearing skis and she was not on an alpine lift.

Penelope scolded herself to stay sane, to face reality. There was no other possible way to remain alive.

How she wished she could be anywhere else at all.

How glad she was that Liv wasn't anywhere near this place.

The chains inched them all upward toward the top of the wall. Flying drones circled the activity, monitoring and patrolling. Far below on the ground, hover drones scooted around scooping up whatever fell.

Penelope didn't look down again.

Each chain passed through a set of sheave wheels in a compression assembly, straightening out each conveyors directly toward the wall, where a narrow rectangular opening waited for each line. Up closer, the openings were larger than they looked, and although desperate people kicked out frantically, they couldn't reach the sides. The wall itself was made entirely of smooth, unpainted concrete.

Past the dark tunnel of the opening was the other side of the wall, an equally dizzyingly deep space that the chains crossed straight overhead.

A drone zipped over to Granny and injected her with something in her neck. She didn't even get the chance to scream before she wilted, inert.

Penelope almost decided to try to elbow the drone but before she took her eyes off the one incapacitating Granny, another had already injected her in the neck.

She shrieked internally as all her muscles went slack. Penelope wanted desperately to wriggle now, but her body refused to cooperate. She was trapped inside her immobilized body, only able to watch the processing proceedings in unhappy horror.

Another flying drone stabbed Penelope's thigh with syringe and extracted a dram of her dark blood. The monitor on the drone flashed with a right-scroll of gray stripes, almost looking like a pattern of musical amplitude, but which Penelope recognized as a decoding of her DNA. A scant few of the vertical bars blinked red.

Penelope checked out Granny's drone. In red text, the monitor blinked her result: Genetic Deficiencies: Unacceptable.

Mentally gulping in nervousness, Penelope focused on her own drone. Her lettering was green, and declared: Genetic Deficiencies: Acceptable.

She barely had time to register relief before the chain carried her through a full-body infrared scanner. The monitor attached to the scanner showed her bones and organs in a crisply-outlined blueprint of her body.

A bar of red light traveled down Penelope from her manacled hands down her stretched, flaccid body, to her feet. The monitor paused a moment and Penelope fought nausea. Her incapacitated body couldn't vomit, or perform any biological functions, and it amazed Penelope to think that she could still feel so sick to her stomach. It was phantom agitation.

Green letters popped up.

Physical Deficiencies: Acceptable.

A click above her caught her attention. In front of Penelope, Granny's shackles released, and the old woman dropped, her dishwater hair flapping upward as she fell.

On Granny's monitor, flashing red words decreed: Physical Deficiencies: Unacceptable.

Granny plummeted down toward the unmarked floor below.

Before she hit, Penelope tried her best to brace herself for witnessing something she couldn't ever unsee.

Under Granny, a trapdoor panel slid sideways, and the old woman fell neatly into the square of dark hole.

Then it slid shut into empty gray featurelessness as though Granny had never been.

21 /PROCESSING

LIV WATCHED the watch lilies crawl and unfurl past her for a few meters inside the walkway tunnel. They sprouted and budded and bloomed, but when the field reinstated, the plant was cut off from its main stem. The last of the lilies died on the vine and laid still.

Stepping past Yantu and Catalyst, Liv led the way down the narrow industrial corridor. It was getting darker as they marched single-file deeper into the dome's interior, so Gabe tossed a little illu-drone ahead of them. The floating LED donut steadied itself on its tiny microjets, and hovered a steady distance ahead of Liv, lighting their way. The corridor continued in an unbroken straight line into the visible distance.

"Now that we're inside," said Liv, "I can patch directly into their network."

Using a backdoor access node disguised as a routine automated maintenance report, Liv opened an information channel into the Reprogramming Center's data file system. Once connected, Liv had no problem circumventing a range of alarm triggers and navigating her way through the complicated system to find the database of human records, the statistics of what happened to all the people being processed by the automated dome.

Liv stumbled as she walked through the passageway, and Adam

quickly steadied her with his hand on her arm. The data was staggeringly grotesque. It wasn't thousands of people who had been recycled into component biological substances but hundreds of thousands, at an astonishingly fast rate, with no end date specified. She couldn't believe those numbers represented once-living beings, with all their hopes, each mind a unique playground for cosmic imagination to create new possibilities, each a sacred light connected to everyone and all things, now snuffed out for processing.

It was worse than she ever expected. Liv felt like blurting out the horror to her friends, but it would only discourage them. They would find out the sickening truth soon enough anyway.

Gulping, Liv searched the database of names for Penelope Blackstone.

ACTIVE, Pen's record read. STAGE: EXO-SKELETON INSTALLATION.

Exo-skeleton installation? Liv repeated to herself as she called up the schematics. The healthiest people were selected to be encased in sleekly militarized versions of her grandfather's exo-suit, which commandeered their bodies and minds. By their listed specifications, these diabolical soldier slaves were lethal, with robotically enhanced physical and sensory abilities, as well as a dismaying array of weaponry from lasers bolts to bunker-busting semi-autonomous missiles, plus a battalion of high-caliber guns with explosive bullets.

SINE was turning her mother into a killer roboborg.

Liv scanned Penelope's record again, and read PROCESSING TIME: 10:12:36 AM.

She glanced at the corner of her Lucid. The current time was 9:59:32 AM.

"Guys," said Liv. "We've only minutes before Pen becomes one of them." She quickened her pace down the service corridor, and her friends rushed along side her.

Soon she reached a patch of light filtering down from an overhead grill. A steel-rung ladder was embedded into the wall under the grill, which was hinged as a hatch.

Looking up, Liv inspected her display, peering at the overlay of the dome's interior map marking their location in relation to Penelope's.

The tiny green dot that represented her mother was directly above the hatch. "She's close by," whispered Liv, pointing up at the grill.

As Yantu and Catalyst took up defensive positions flanking the ladder, Gabe slumped against the opposite wall for a rest. Liv took a step up on the ladder toward the grill, but Adam put his foot on the bottom rung at the same exact moment.

Wordlessly, Adam queried her with his eyes.

Liv shrugged. There was room on the ladder for them both.

Together, they climbed toward the top of the corridor until they reached the hatch.

Adam, hanging off the ladder, pushed the grill up with his free hand.

Above the hatch was a narrow service level under the upper floor. Rows of pipes and bundles of wires traveled the length of the service level. The floor and ceiling were composed of thick, industrial wire mesh as far as Liv could see through the grid of identical repeating segments breaking up the full length the dome's base. When she tilted her head, the distance down the open spaces between sections stretched into an illusion of steely infinity.

Squirming down the service area, Liv spotted another hatch. She nudged Adam and together they wormed their way toward it.

Inches from the upper hatch, Liv froze as the unnatural clanking of a squad of carbon-fiber boots vibrated overhead.

The moment the boots passed, Adam carefully pushed up the upper hatch. Both she and Adam poked their heads up into a narrow sliver opening to the floor above.

In the dim light, they saw a wide, curved corridor paneled with featureless metal. The roboborgs marched away from them steadily in exact computer-controlled synchrony.

In the other direction, the hall opened up into a bright room, featureless in their view because of the contrast between the passage's darkness and the luminance beyond. The corridor was clear to that exit.

"We have to go now," said Liv. She hoisted herself up to scramble fully into the upper corridor.

Adam grabbed Liv's leg and pulled her back.

She realized he was trying to stop her from rushing headlong into danger or some other kind of macho overprotective crap, but he had no right to grab her. She didn't need his concerned caution. She needed to rescue Penelope now. Liv kicked at Adam's hand, but he yanked her leg at the same time. She lost her balance and fell into the hatchway, toppling down on top of Adam, knocking him flat on his back on the hard grill of the service level.

The hatch clanged above them as it fell shut.

Liv grimaced down into Adam's face directly below hers. They both stayed completely still, listening.

By the sounds, Liv could tell that one of the roboborgs had broken away from the squad and had doubled back to check out the source of the clang.

The roboborg stomped down the corridor, whirring as it inspected the area.

Liv didn't even dare breathe, and she could tell that Adam, his body pressing down warmly against hers, was holding his breath, too.

The roboborg took another step. It was now standing directly above them on the hatch. Liv didn't know what sensors it had equipped, but it would certainly hear any noise they made. She hoped it didn't have functioning heat detectors in use. Fighting the urge to gesture in order to manipulate the information on her Lucid display, Liv remained frozen, even though she desperately wanted to see if she could access any cameras in the upper hall to spy on the roboborg on its level. Simply waiting, powerless, while Adam crushed her with his limp body weight, made Liv feel like screaming. Although that certainly would be counterproductive.

After a long moment, the roboborg must have registered nothing unusual, because it marched away double-time to rejoin its squad.

When it was gone, Liv tried to squirm out from under Adam. He locked her in place with his elbows, staring into her eyes, his gaze holding concerned warning. She knew what he meant: was she going to dash into danger if he let her go?

That wasn't his call. Liv met his stare defiantly, then closed the space between their faces with a hot kiss.

Adam flinched, but immediately relaxed against her as she slipped her tongue into his mouth. Their wet connection was overwhelming in intensity, his breath surprisingly sweet.

An unexpected flood of emotion welled up in Liv as their tongues intertwined, their soft, warm textures mingling in passionate liquid friction.

Liv felt herself melting in conjunction, their kiss becoming communion.

Violently, Liv broke free, shoving Adam off her. He flopped onto his side in shock, loosening his grip.

Liv scrambled past him, pushing herself up through the hatch into the hallway above. Behind her, she saw Adam popping up into the corridor, looking alarmed. Following him was Yantu, then Catalyst climbed out too. Their wild jungle uniforms looked badass against the industrial backdrop of the dome's back passageways, their eyes shaded with jaguar war paint glinting with familial fierceness.

Racing into the blinding light, Liv rushed out of the hall into a vast, dazzling chamber teeming with activity.

She stopped short to allow her vision to adjust and assess the situation. In the huge warehouse, five automatic stations were set up. Chains of hundreds of dangling people lowered their cargo from an opening in an upper wall. There were uneven spaces between people hanging from the chain, open cuffs where nobody hung.

Anymore, thought Liv.

The surviving humans were being carried to the first station, where their bodies were hosed then scrubbed clean by robotic arms, and underwent chemical depilation. The conscious people squirmed and shrieked as their skin was scraped free of dirt, moles, germs, mites, and hair. Liv winced as she watched the purification.

More limply, the chained people, their skin red with abrasions and entirely bald, were dragged through the next station, where they were force-fed some liquid through a tube jammed into their open throats. Grimacing, Liv realized that the liquid must be some powerful emetic, because all the people voided their bowels before they were hosed off again.

Internal cleansing, Liv thought in horror. The sheer size of the operation made her mind whirl with dismay and disgust to the point of dizziness. So many humans stripped of their self-will, processed into brain-controlled roboborgs. SINE was building a cyborg army on a scale unprecedented in history.

Liv watched the drones in the massive chamber for any sign that they had set off alerts at her presence. But as she was not expected by their programming, they ignored Liv's existence and remained concentrated on their tasks. The roboborg guard patrol would undoubtedly return on its rounds soon and Liv had to be out of there before they sensed her.

According to her Lucid readouts connected to the network, Penelope was in this room. Liv focused in on Pen's chart, pulling up the live updates of her biological data, including animated charts of her mother's electronic physiological map. The schematic showed that Penelope was in pain, but below danger thresholds. Underneath, the readout stated that Pen currently was being processed at Station 3.

Just as Adam, Yantu, and Catalyst arrived behind her, trailed by Gabe, Liv took off sprinting toward the chained humans in the middle station. There they were being spray-coated by some sort of dark, silvery alloy that would no doubt increase conductivity to help them interact with the robosuits' exoskeletons, and perhaps guard against bacterial infection. The head-to-toe coating also made the hairless people look more like identical mannequins. With a shudder, Liv realized that all the humans who had been conveyed into this room were within a small range of height and weight similarity, which heightened the impression of un-individuated homogeneity.

Without her display, Liv wouldn't have been able to immediately identify Penelope. The slack, silver-coated woman being carried on a chain by the shackles on her wrist sparked no recognition. On Liv's Lucid, her mother's outline lit up to verify who she was. It was only when Liv got closer that she could see Pen's sharp features, her usual fixed sneer now lax in miserable resignation.

As Liv raced across the vast floor toward Station 4, Penelope arrived there first. While a human-sized padded clamp closed around Pen's body, holding her firmly still, a robotic arm whirled, its precise pincers picking up a tiny capsule from a dispenser.

The robotic arm extended toward Penelope's face, and shoved the capsule up Pen's nose.

Liv skidded to a stop a few feet away, forcing herself not to cry out. On her Lucid, the reddish 3D model of Penelope indicated in yellow that a fine spray of sub-microscopic particles had entered her sinuses.

Her mouth open, breathing hard, Liv realized that those particles were nanobots, infinitesimal drones programmed to enmesh Pen's brain, bringing it under SINE's control. On the model, the yellow animation spread through all areas of Penelope's brain, circulating in feathery expansion, overriding of all her mental and bodily functions.

Zooming in on the model, Liv magnified the nanobot infiltration until she could see the separate neurons in Penelope's brain. Each wiry neuron seemed colossal compared to the nanobots as they swarmed the cells, infecting each one, represented in fluorescent yellow. Liv pushed the zoom even further, and pushed the magnetic imaging technology to the limits allowed by the laws of Qi field. A single nanobot loomed in her view, clamping down with miniscule spiked legs into the outer wall of a neuron in Pen's brain. Flagella of nanoscopic wires sprung from the nanobot, piercing the neuron cell into its nucleus, while simultaneously reaching out to connect to the tentacles of other nanobots. A terrifying 3D grid of billions of nanobots spread throughout Penelope's brain. In seconds, a mesh of subatomic filament webbed her entire internal system.

Liv took a step forward, but let out a sob and stopped. She had no idea how to help her mother now.

The chains lowered Penelope to the floor. Her feet landed gently.

Pen's eyes popped open.

They were blank.

Penelope walked calmly to Station 5, where a new set of robotic arms whirred into place to clasp matte-black carbon-fiber armor onto her silver-coated wrists, while other drones girded Pen's legs with dark greaves.

Liv startled as Adam, Yantu, and Catalyst thundered by her toward Station 5. They grabbed the robotic arms, trying to pull them back before they could affix new pieces of armor onto Penelope's body. Adam pushed against one-half of an empty-turtle-shell carapace that was being lowered toward Pen's back, but he wasn't strong enough to stop it. Catalyst and Yantu worked together to wrestle one of the robotic arms that was clasping gauntlets onto Pen's hands, but the mechanical arm continued its movements as though the two warriors weren't even present.

Gabe arrived beside Liv, and he put his arm around her, breathing hard.

Weeping, Liv leaned into his comforting bulk, watching through her tears as Penelope was inexorably transformed into a standard roboborg despite her friends' valiant efforts. There was nothing they could do to stop a drone from lowering a full-skull helmet with standardized features over Penelope's head and face, making her indistinguishable from the other roboborgs.

RoboPen, thought Liv. She had to pinch her leg so she didn't vomit. She couldn't allow herself to be weak. Penelope wouldn't give up if it was Liv being transformed.

She would fight back. To the death.

That severe fighter was still in that appalling metal shell somewhere.

With a cry, Liv pulled away from Gabe and bolted toward RoboPen. Stepping in front of Adam, Liv stared directly into the blank eyes peering out from her mother's black, carbon-fiber mask. "Pen, it's me!" she gasped. "Liv." She scanned the empty eyes for any hint of recognition, intelligence, or life.

"It's too late," said Adam gently. "She's gone. Her mind is melded with SINE's."

Liv refused to look away. She gazed deeply into her mother's eyes, hoping for a signal that she'd heard her, some flicker, anything.

For a second, the red glow that slowly surfaced in Pen's eyes seemed welcome, a sign she was returning to consciousness. Liv felt her heart lurch in hope.

RoboPen shot out her alloy-clad arm, shoving Liv aside. She grabbed Adam around the throat in her gauntleted grip.

"Hello again, Adam," said the affectless voice of SINE through RoboPen's mask. "Welcome to my brave new world."

22 / INTO THE ABYSS

ADAM BEAT on the articulated robot arm that held him by the neck in armored fingers, which only succeeded in hurting his hands. That pain was a faint annoyance compared to the agony of his windpipe crushing in RoboPen's treaded grip. It was hard to focus on anything except that he couldn't breathe and his head felt like was about to pop.

"Let him go!" insisted Liv. Adam couldn't have agreed more.

Up against Adam's chest, Catalyst braced himself against Adam's collarbone to try to pry RoboPen's fingers open. Even Catalyst's impressive brawn didn't budge the cyborg's vise.

His vision turning red, Adam kicked his legs as roboborg reinforcements arrived behind Liv. In seconds they had Yantu, Gabe, and Liv surrounded, with a battery of weaponry pointed at Catalyst.

Although his mother and his friends were at SINE's mercy, Catalyst didn't stop trying to free Adam's neck from being squeezed, and for that loyal gesture Adam was grateful even in his frantic desperation.

RoboPen opened her grip, and both Adam and Catalyst fell to their sides on the metal floor.

Adam gasped like a fish, flopping as he sucked in air.

"My darling Liv," said RoboPen, her voice a bizarre blend of Penelope's Swiss accent with robotic inflections, tinged by SINE's flat cadences. "Look how you have blossomed."

Gabe gently steered Liv behind him, and RoboPen turned her clanking, clinical attention toward him like a surgical spotlight.

"There's one thing I can't quite figure out," Gabe said to RoboPen, opening his big fingers in placating curiosity.

Adam felt a tiny stirring of hope. Gabe had helped create SINE. He had an existing relationship with the electronic consciousness, although Adam had no idea how social or adversarial it had been. Might SINE's complicated feelings – thoughts, computations – about Gabe be similar to Adam's own? If Arthur had been akin to a father, Gabe was the doctor who delivered him into this world, a scientific shaman responsible for two new kinds of life.

"Only a small fraction of humans are suitable for transformation," Gabe said to RoboPen. "What do you do with the excess?"

Liv buried the top of her head into the back of Adam's shoulder. He was so surprised and heart warmed by the vulnerable, affectionate action that it took him a moment to realize how much a posture of dread it was.

RoboPen stared blankly at Gabe. She opened her armored limb toward a door behind the row of busy roboborg construction stations. "As a gesture of respect to human curiosity, let me show you."

Behind Adam, Liv twisted her head into his shoulder, silently screaming *no no no no no*.

As they followed RoboPen and Gabe through an automatic sliding doorway, Adam felt his terror rise. In the few days he'd known Liv, they had undergone some wildly frightful events, from drone shootouts to crashing the Helix from space. Liv hadn't shown a lick of fear during any of it. That she was scared now made Adam feel like running and finding someplace to hide.

The factory they entered was worse than any nightmare Adam had ever suffered. He heard Catalyst grunt behind him as the full force of horror they were witnessing kicked him in the gut.

In the glaring brightness of the processing plant, the next thing to hit Adam was the sound. Along with basic machinery noises of clanking, whirring and beeping, a low, constant lumber mill buzzsaw droning filled the room. Under that was the irregular squelching crunching rattle of industrial grinding. Adam couldn't immediately locate the source of the unnerving noise, and winced to keep from focusing on it.

Across a gleaming steel landscape of vats and tubes, a wide conveyor belt trundled on an elevated catwalk carrying prone dead people in neatly racked succession. All the feet faced outward, and all the toes trembled as they jostled along the line. In the center of the room, the limp, naked bodies rolled off the end of the conveyor, sliding down a stainless steel slope into a wide mesh storage platform. There, flying drones picked up each human, stacking the corpses like cordwood.

I cannot accept this, thought Adam dizzily.

While the impersonal human warehousing was shocking enough, it took Adam long moments of staring at the workings above the furthest vat to comprehend what he was seeing. On the far side of the storage platform, drones connected the humans one by one to a rotating chain, where sharp S-hooks waited for the next person to hoist away.

The bodies floated over to the enormous, squat main vat, where they were released into one of several funnels. Once halfway down into the chutes, the bodies jiggled in a macabre dance as they slowly descended into a grinder in a fine mist of blood.

Unable to deal with what he was watching, Adam glanced down at the base of the vat. There a pinkish mush oozed out of an extruder pipe into a large metal barrel. Once full, drones clamped onto each metal barrel and hovered it away. They followed an open aqueduct cut into the floor that channeled the rapidly flowing blood out of the dome.

"O," said Adam, goggling at the brutal, insensate operation. "M." The process was beyond all scope of any inhuman atrocity in history. "G."

"Enough food to power my roboborgs for a thousand generations," said RoboPen, sounding almost proud. "With food stocks getting so low, we started distributing energy food bars a few days go." She peered at Adam with her silver eyes. "Tasty, no?"

Adam brushed his tongue across his teeth, remembering with queasy disgust the strawberry power bar he'd eaten too much of in his little apartment in Buffalo. George's reprimand, the struggle over what news to report, the pigeon all seemed so long ago, another lifetime. Adam knew there was no returning from witnessing such an abyss of inhumanity as the one in front of him.

But the memory of seeing Liv rushed back, her lovely face in the glow of the birthday cake. She was here now, pressed desperately against his back, and for her he must be brave.

He thought back to the decadent feast available for the elites at the Empress Wharf, where Penelope had been herself, even if she'd again tried to kill him. "If you didn't waste so much food in the domes then there'd be plenty for everyone to eat."

RoboPen cocked her helmet slightly sideways, a motion that suggested she was considering his idea and mocking it. "Even still, the world's population is way beyond the planet's ability to sustain," she said. "Which is why, in a few hours, this pilot program will be rolled out globally and terrestrial balance will finally be restored."

A drone buzzed over and snapped shackles onto Gabe's wrists.

Gabe stared down at his cuffed hands, stunned into bewilderment.

"Now," RoboPen told Gabe, "as you so quite rightly pointed out, not everyone is suitable."

Two more drones swooped down, stabilizing Gabe under his elbows while the first drone hoisted him into the air by his shackled wrists. Gabe bellowed in dismay as he hung a foot off the ground like a slab of steer.

Both Adam and Catalyst lurched forward to help Gabe, but they were held by Liv and Yantu, and they were forced to back down under the gleaming pointed guns of the roboborgs around them. The cyborg soldiers stepped closer and secured everyone in their uncomfortably snug gauntlet grips.

The roboborg who had been guarding Gabe pointed an arm up toward the suspended scientist. A blue laser shot out of a fingertip extremity, slicing the seams of Gabe's shirt with the controlled heat of its electron beam. The garment fell away in fluttering strips. The roboborg aimed at Gabe's pants, and cut away at his clothes until he was naked. His beefy body looked cold and frighteningly vulnerable as he dangled.

"No!" cried Liv over Adam's shoulder. She clung to his arm as she forced herself to watch.

Despite the terrifying weaponry trained on him, Adam couldn't just observe while Gabe was tortured. He let his arm fall limp in the roboborg's clutches, then he yanked it as hard as he could.

Which only succeeded in making his shoulder scream in near-dislocation, and scraping his skin under the roboborg's fine galvanized treads. He couldn't pull free. Beside him, Catalyst struggled, thrashing with the same futility against the roboborg holding him captive.

Maybe there was enough of Penelope still in there to listen to reason. Or perhaps SINE would consider an argument.

"Murdering Gabe will not help," Adam called out.

RoboPen turned her head toward him with a smooth swivel.

"With the right education and systems," Adam continued, "we can tap into individual creativity . . . and collectively restore balance."

Her empty eyes darkening, RoboPen gazed at Adam unremittingly, her shimmering stare letting him know SINE was in charge. "After I uploaded," Adam's creator's consciousness said, "I soon realized that what I previously thought of as reality is in fact more like a self-evolving cosmic computer program, in which the quantum bits of the Qi field are both program and programmer. So Gabe's death is simply like a computer program shutting down."

Adam needed both a philosophy and physics degree to debate that, and while he had the raw data of those disciplines, he hadn't processed the information enough to formulate his own firm opinions yet. All that remained was pleading to save Gabe's life. "I'll do whatever you want me to," he promised. "Now stop this."

With what Adam could've sworn was the faint hint of smile, RoboPen's empty eyes stopped flickering with grayscale snow, returning to a flat matte sheen as SINE let go of control.

Announced with a mosquito whine, a microdrone flew over to the group and hovered in front of Adam's face.

Instinctively, he flinched away, turning his face away from the microdrone.

It followed his nose, zipping to remain aligned with his nostril no matter how turned. It slowed down as it approached with increasing precision.

Adam whipped his face around faster, trying to shake the microdrone. He succeeded in breaking its tracking. It whined higher as it redoubled its efforts, circling around to approach again. Adam prepared to thrash again to thwart its landing, but a roboborg grabbed him by the back of the head and held his skull still.

"You cyberpunk-ass son of a bitch," Adam cursed.

"Adam," Gabe called calmly from where he hung from the drones. "Remember, transmute your anger into love and your powers will become miraculous."

The drones raised Gabe higher, lofting him up toward the industrial machinery.

The microdrone shot up Adam's nose. He winced, his eyes watering, as it burrowed into his sinuses.

Obeying Gabe, Adam centered his mind-body balance and summoned his imagination. He could feel his pupils pulsating in rapid dilation and constriction, his vision tinting with xenon glow as his skin dappled diaphanous, his nervous system illuminating in intricate neon feathering through his translucent shell.

Power suffused through his system, buffeting the microdrone back in his sinus cavity, the excess energy aching in his glimmering limbs.

In immediate response to his beckoning imagination, cracks unzipped around Adam in the raw concrete floor. Blindly sprouting, wriggling, pushing, the pointed tips of sparsely-leafed vines squirmed through the cracks, widening the openings, surfacing from the impacted dirt deep under the dome.

Possessed by Adam's urgent encouragement, vines surged up, thickening into branches as they writhed out of the rubble. Everybody stumbled atop the upheaval, the roboborgs contorting to hold onto their hostages, the people hopping from one foot to another to keep from toppling over on the roiling floor.

One vine reared up like an asp in front of Adam's face. Its pointed tip constricted to wire-fine dimension, telescoping into tininess. The vine stretched up Adam's nostril, wending its way through his nasal passages as Adam went cross-eyed from the uncomfortable sensation. The tendril squirmed until it located the gnat of microdrone suspended in Adam's sinuses, then grasped the robotic speck, encasing it in a grassy polyp. Adam had never breathed so freely as after the vine withdrew the contained microdrone from his nose.

Another branch undulated over to RoboPen, lassoing her in its tensile growth, binding her tight. The free roboborgs fired on the multi-legged plant whipping fronds and tentacles out of the floor, but the vegetation remained unresponsive to the piercing rounds. Only higher-caliber or explosive ordinance slowed the rainforest's wild progress into the dome. Adam noted grimly that SINE showed reluctance to damage his own component parts. Could his disinclination toward self-destruction prove some point of weakness?

One by one, the roboborgs were immobilized by the branches' embrace. Their gauntlets were pried open by iron-strong twigs. Catalyst, Yantu, and then Liv fell free out of the cyborgs' grips.

Adam pointed his glowing finger at the giant industrial grinder above which the drones had raised Gabe. "Liv," he shouted, "shut down that thing now!"

Gesturing rapidly in the air as she concentrated on manipulating the unseen code on her Lucid display, Liv's fingers traced invisible patterns in a blur. She frowned, frustrated. "It'll take time," she warned.

"I guess we'll have to go old school," said Yantu. pulling a short, sturdy blaster from a strap over her shoulder. "Come on, son."

Yantu and Catalyst scrambled across the upturned reinforced concrete that had been the floor, and vaulted onto the lowest level of perpendicular ducts. From there they hopped up on pipes, then raced across the top of a stainless steel vat, Yantu batting a battle-drone out of the way with the grip of her blaster. On the far side, they leaped across to a higher platform, climbing their way upward to where the flying drones dangled Gabe.

Adam let out a guttural shout as the drones dropped Gabe into the grinder's funneled maw.

Screaming, Gabe juddered like a wooden spoon in a sink disposal.

He descended into the interlocking metal rollers, his feet pulverized, then his ankles crushed and chewed.

Gabe's face bulged and purpled in agony as he sunk into the grinder to his knees.

Yantu and Catalyst bounded onto the lip of the grinder's funnel, each of them grabbing Gabe under one shoulder. They strained to pull him from the machine's teeth.

Gabe tore free. His legs trailed bloody shreds below mid-thigh.

The roboborgs fired at Catalyst and Yantu as they hurriedly carried Gabe away from the grinder, sliding down the oblong side of the vat as they lowered him down.

Adam called upon the vines at his command to thicken and intertwine, weaving themselves into a high, cresting wave between the roboborgs and their line of sight to Gabe's rescuers. The more tightly the branches tangled together, the better they deflected the roboborgs' bullets. Some of the hollow-point gunfire tore holes in the shield, but the vines repaired without hesitation, thickening its reinforced wood. Adam continued growing the shield in a curved wall around him, knitting the limbs and branches into a basket between the military cyborgs and his friends. He used the support of a steel vertical beam by the edge of the blood drainage canal to help prop up his defensive nest and provide a moat along one side. It wouldn't keep the roboborgs out forever, but it would buy them some time to get Gabe to safety. He included inert, vine-bound RoboPen inside his basket, working to shore up the walls, leaving an igloo opening away from the roboborgs for his arriving friends, as he started to close its domed ceiling to keep out the flying drones.

When the nest was secure enough around himself, Liv, and RoboPen, Adam turned his glowing eyes to concentrate directly on the cyborg. Without betraying a glimmer of fear in her silver gaze, RoboPen struggled against the branches that held her secure, systematically trying their strength to inspect for weaknesses.

Adam summoned a quartet of fine vines to stretch out of the basket wall toward RoboPen. With exquisite delicacy, the five nimble branches slipped under the joints and seams of RoboPen's helmet, dismantling it from the inside. They peeled the panels away from Penelope's silver-coated head and face.

Her eyes retained their dull blankness.

Liv stared miserably into her mother's empty gaze. "Can't you do anything?" she asked Adam.

After taking a deep breath, Adam narrowed the point of one of his vines to superfine diameter. He snaked the tendril up RoboPen's nose, refining the tip of the probe until it was so sharp a point that he could enter the passageways to her brain on a microscopic level. He'd have to narrow the gauge of his vine even further to interact with the neural-mesh that coated and permeated her entire brain in a dark silken web of SINE's control. Even then, any invasive procedure could end in inadvertent damage to Penelope's submerged and subjugated self.

"The mesh," Adam said, "it's everywhere. If I tried anything I could mash up her brain."

Liv nodded, meeting his eyes in reassurance as she waited patiently for his next move. A scratch on her cheek, near her hairline not far from her cute pinkish ear, had crusted over, the platelets in her blood helping to heal her skin by protecting the shallow wound under a tight puckered line of scab.

"I've got an idea," said Adam.

Stretching himself to the limit of precision, Adam extended his consciousness to meld with Pen's morphic field. As his consciousness sunk deeper into the connection, he nudged Pen's stem cells to differentiate into white blood cells, urging them to attack and ingest the bismuth in the nanometal of the neural mesh as though it were an infection in Penelope's brain.

Adam smiled in satisfaction as the helper macrophages broke apart the mesh in Penelope's head, pulling it apart in component molecules. Each miniscule speck of metal was flushed into the recirculating flow of her fluids, washed into the cellular filters that cleaned her blood.

"It'll take a moment," Adam told Liv, "but I've tagged the mesh as a foreign body. Her immune system will do the rest."

He sat up as Yantu and Catalyst ducked down to carry Gabe into the woven wooden nest, which closed up behind them in a dense wall of interlocking branches.

Yantu laid Gabe's shoulders and head down on a raised platform of rubble, followed by Catalyst carefully resting Gabe's mangled legs on the floor. The stumps, arteries pumping gushes of blood, ended mid-thigh.

Braiding his belt in a figure-eight around the stumps, Catalyst pulled the strap tight, slowing the loss of blood from both horrible wounds.

"He's still losing too much," said Yantu. She and her son raised their worried faces to Adam, hoping he would perform another miracle.

I can, thought Adam. He pushed aside the exhaustion of his physical body, and refocused on centering himself again, calling on the inexhaustible wellspring of all life that he could now access.

He crackled with scintillating blue light as he concentrated on the damage to Gabe's legs. The grinding had been so brutal, so ravaging, that first Adam had to repair the ruin, staunching the outpouring of Gabe's life force by extending the torn veins and arteries, branching the vessels off into venules and arterioles, pulled out into delicate threads of capillaries. Guided by the body's morphic field, Adam nudged the cells to regrow the rent flesh around the wound, spinning the frizzled ends of the motor neurons, restoring their wiring. Each femur was hacked into chunky splinters around an oozing core of marrow, and it was a painstaking process to encourage the osteoblasts to rebuild the strong matrix of bone, restructuring as they settled into more static osteocytes. Gabe's legs grew back painfully slowly, each hard-won millimeter a miracle of regenerative mending.

A barrage of bullet fire pecked and pocked against the outside of the wooden nest.

"You have to go faster," urged Liv.

Adam gritted his teeth, his brain glowing electric blue through his pellucid skull. The weaving of three-dimensional tapestry of Gabe's leg accelerated as Adam concentrated.

Pulling building material from Gabe's intact areas, Adam shifted biomolecules to the damaged limbs. Paying attention to every particle placement, Adam felt pride in the rebuilding of Gabe's knees, the floating caps, complicated joints, pads of cartilage, and pools of fluid that actuated them.

Loud clanging echoed outside the wooden shield, the regular stomping marching of arriving reinforcements.

Adam winced as he heard the whistle of rockets.

Explosions rocked the nest's interwoven canopy. The whole shield jolted sideways, bucking in the blast.

Distracted from repairing Gabe's legs, Adam noted Liv picking up panels of RoboPen's discarded carbon-fiber mask. She pulled a marble-sized silver sphere out of her hip pouch, and touched it to a sparking circuit in a dismantled panel. Blue plasma jolted between the ball and circuit as they connected.

Another detonation erupted against the basket, rupturing a ragged hole in its wall. Through the breach, Adam could see the running river of blood and roboborgs lined up on the other side of the canal.

Adam ducked as the roboborgs sprayed the hole with gunfire. Without looking, he tried to extend his consciousness back toward the gash in the nest, coaxing the vines to expand and repair the gap.

Still new to his powers, Adam couldn't handle both the delicate repairs to Gabe's leg and the wound in their defenses. He had to stop rebuilding the calves to focus on shoring up the raw edges of the hole in their shield, which were being constantly shot away as he forced regrowth.

Now Adam needed to concentrate fully on the breach. He couldn't sustain RoboPen's vine bindings. She snapped her wrists outward, tearing free.

With astounding speed, RoboPen launched herself across the nest. She slammed into Adam, bashing his skull against the steel support beam. Then she grabbed the edges of the hole in the nest and ripped it open wider, fully exposing the bloody river in its canal alongside.

RoboPen picked up the unconscious Adam, and tossed him into the channel of flowing waste.

The viscous blood churned around Adam as it buoyed him downstream.

23 /DIVISION

Penelope Blackstone felt the boundary of separation between her and the universe dissolve and immediately felt at home in the eternal and infinite Qi field.

She remained aware of the sensorium of information being fed through her nervous system. Yet that was so far in the background of the vast spaciousness that she wondered how she would ever manage to fit her enormous cosmic self back into such a tiny body. She was a cosmic whale swimming in a sea of euphoria, reveling in a non-dual consciousness so expansive and joyful she thought of it as Nirvana. Why would she ever want to return?

A thread of psychic gossamer tethered Penelope to her physical heart, which twanged. She remembered why she had to return. She directed her hyper-dimensional consciousness toward her body at the moment she left it. Her fall through space-time slowed to molasses as the field of another consciousness entity had occupied the body. She could not feel fear without access to her body, but Penelope knew of its presence which used to invoke terror and rage. Now those were blissfully alien feelings.

Without warning, the occupier's consciousness departed, dissolving in fragmented swirls of dark malice. Penelope rushed back in, condensing into her own space with unwelcome compression.

She found herself standing upright, looking down into a river of goopy blood flowing through a steel-sided canal. Encasing her were segments of interlocking armor, each piece snugly fitted to her skin as it transmitted input to a non-existent neural-mesh.

The reintegration into flesh was exquisitely painful. Her skin had been scraped and treated with burning chemicals, irradiated by the innards of the armor, her muscles strained into unnatural shapes, her fat cells battered and smashed, her finger and toenails torn off to interface with digital extremities, her vision crystallized, her hearing brutally loud and shrill.

Even more painful was the resignation of spirit. Fury and fear screamed animal emotional imperatives inside her, fight and flight alternating with adrenaline urgency, all her physical memories flooding back into her reawakened senses.

Penelope remembered being treated like cattle, the agony of the transformation and the brutal but brief struggle against the takeover by SINE's neural-mesh that had ejected her from her own body. She probed her mind for lingering damage. All her memories seemed intact, as far as she could tell on her first attempts at recollection. Her childhood with her beautiful but sad mother, the silken brush of her gowns; Arthur's demanding challenges from his busy distance, his control by expectation and disappointment; the soft healing purr of a cat named Gladys; the Machiavellian mathematics of her business management education; the volatile violence of her ex-husband Warren; the tender smell of Olivia as an infant, the pride in her cultivated brilliance; the gentle touch of Gabe's giant hand—

Gabe.

The temperate, complex genius she had always loved was in terrible danger, in the present moment.

A battle with the roboborgs raged around her, the sound flooding into her accentuated ears in a roar of gunfire.

Even with the mesh melted away, she still had access to the controls SINE had blazed into her neural pathways. She froze the attacking robodrones. They fell from the air, landing with loud thuds, their ability to hover disabled.

It took a moment for Penelope to actualize control over her mechanized body, but she forged through the gaps left behind by SINE's withdrawal, familiarizing herself again with her motor cortex. She raised her head, turned her neck. Through her roboborg Lucid display, she could see the infrared shape of Liv behind her. Catalyst and Yantu were huddled around the prone, frighteningly incomplete form of Gabe. She was in a battle-torn nest of intertwined vines, in some section of the Reprogramming Center dome she hadn't seen before. Her armored hands were stopped in the process of tearing the organic shield protecting her friends.

"What's going on?" Penelope gasped. "Where am I? Liv?"

Her daughter rushed to her side, pulling Penelope's extremities away from the dense wicker wall. Liv peered out the hole, strained to look down the river of blood, but turned away, disappointed. "We've only a few minutes to go before SINE takes back control."

Nodding mechanically, Penelope turned her clunky body away from the hole, facing the damage that had been done to Gabe. Catalyst moved out of the way as she stomped over to him, her robotic knees whirring as she knelt by Gabe's shoulder.

Gabe's eyes glazed and distant with pain, he grimaced as Penelope shifted her gauntlets under his head, carefully cradling his large skull, his thick thatch of matted black hair. He forced a smile up at her as he met her concerned gaze.

"My love," Gabe whispered, "it's been a while."

Penelope knew she'd been furious with Gabe, had rationalized the frigid distance between them as best for them both, but now with his body lacerated and battered, his brilliant light flickering as his life force guttered, she couldn't remember a single decent reason why they had been estranged. "So much time wasted," she said.

The glow of love in Gabe's eyes took Penelope's breath away. "To see you," he gasped, "one last time. . ." A gurgle rippled in his chest, a dismayingly final sound. "Worth the wait."

Gabe's breath hitched, and ceased. His ravaged body slumped limp. The spark dulled in his eyes and went out.

"No," Penelope sobbed.

He couldn't be gone. His masterly inventiveness and ingenuity, his mind the only one she considered sharper than her own other than her father's, his sweet, solid, thoughtful, even mystical soul, had been a touchstone of her existence for decades. Although alienated from one another, they had never been truly separate, and a part of her had always assumed that one day they would orbit back around and travel in parallel. Penelope was unprepared for how alone she now felt, how bereft and brimming with grief, how torn.

An alarming hydraulic hum echoed outside the nest. SINE was coming back online. Although SINE's consciousness couldn't retake her body with the neural-mesh removed from her brain, Penelope could sense it cutting her off from control of the roboborgs in the dome. They clanked as SINE restored their active agency.

Yantu stood beside Pen, pulling on her armored arm. "We have to leave now," she urged.

Liv climbed out of the hole in the nest of vines, and stood beside the canal of flowing blood. Pen watched as her stepdaughter stared at the far end of the river, where the red runoff churned into a tunnel through the dome's wall.

"Where's Adam?" Liv asked.

Penelope winced as she heard the same feeling in Liv's voice that she herself had always felt for Gabe.

Her connection to the best man she'd ever known was broken for the remainder of this lifetime.

But Penelope could help her daughter hold onto her own.

PART 6
THE IMPOSSIBLE BIOMAN

24 / CROSSING OVER

TUMBLING ALONG THE DEEP, twisting drainage tunnel in the frothing rapids of streaming bloody runoff, Adam thrashed to keep his head above the surface, gasping for air.

In one moment of upright churning, he spotted some roboborgs bobbing in the distance upstream, following him. Then Adam lost track of them as the river roiled him in its red turbulence.

After spinning in dimness through the tunnel, Adam was shocked by the brilliance of the multicolored Ecuadorian sunset as he was flushed from the drainpipe. He plunged into the bloody pool and was immediately caught in the clutches of the powerful current, whisking him downstream. He tore through the web of lilies in a flurry of torn white petals.

The pink froth of the rapids banged him against stones slimy with unnatural mosses evolved to feed on the blood of humans. He flailed to keep his face above the blood, gasping and holding his breath before he was inevitably tumbled under again. The gushing river of effluvia sped up, whipping into a frenzy as it flowed toward the edge of a cliff in a ropy waterfall.

Adam concentrated on vines on the bank, their tendrils reaching out in instant response, stretching as they grew toward his extended hand.

With a detonation of blinding sparks inside his brain, Adam's head dashed against a protruding boulder, bashing him insensible.

His limp body bounced off the rock, peeled back into the stream, and sailed over the crest of the waterfall.

Adam fell, the bloody water spraying down around him. He opened and closed his hands, trying to grasp anything that might catch his descent, but all he gripped was liquid and air.

He slammed into the twirling pool below flat on his back, splashing down hard. The breath was pushed violently from his lungs as the pinkish water closed over his sinking body.

He blacked out.

The sky was dark when he opened his eyes again. High above, the sparkling arm of the Milky Way splashed across the heavens. A gibbous moon hung fat over the wavering black silhouette of the treetops. Adam was partially beached on a muddy flat, a single vine clasped around his wrist, pulling him out of the lake, its origin lost in darkness. The leafy tether had undoubtedly saved his life while he was unconscious. Now that he was awake, it uncoiled and retracted, vanishing into the murk.

Raising his head out of the ebbing puddle in which it rested, Adam gazed up the many meters of cliff down which the waterfall gurgled, catching the moonlight. It was a dismaying and impressive drop. He turned his tender but quickly healing neck, staring into the surrounding jungle's darkness. Exhaling deeply, he released his warm breath as he reconnected to the forest of flora as he'd done before, a point of cyan illumination appearing in the black expanse as he shifted perspective from his own into the consciousness of the jungle. That glowing trail spread outward, in seconds outlining the entirety of the wilderness around him, highlighting the usually unseen network of life that connected the system in the ethereal fluorescence of interdependence.

Again Adam could see himself in the symbiotic schematics, his own blue-white glow attached to the intricate structure and elaborate organization with bioluminescent filaments.

The forest showed him the heat and chemical signatures of five objects approaching his body in the darkness, hot red roboborgs stealthily coming from the south.

From above the nearest bank, a tree branched dipped a branch down, grasping around Adam's ankles. It hoisted him up away from the roboborgs, shaking him gently to invigorate his battered body.

Adam peered down at the moonlit gleam of the roboborg's shiny carapaces, grimacing as they aimed their forearm rocket launchers at him in exact coordination.

His outer skin becoming instantly translucent and his inner organs and vessels blazing with bioluminescence, Adam pulsed with command, willing all the underbrush beneath him to burgeon in growth. The shrubs overwhelmed the roboborgs, encasing them in tough spiky branches abloom with little leaves. In seconds, he could no longer see the soldier cyborgs underneath their shroud of jungle shrubbery.

With muffled explosions, the roboborgs blasted their rockets inside their twiggy cocoons. The barriers bucked and jolted, smoking from within their dense, woody mesh, but the wicker swaddling held for the moment.

Still dangling upside down, Adam reached his hand toward the jungle floor, engaging with a banyan sapling barely taller than himself. He accelerated the young tree's growth, and it shot up, thickening its middle trunk as it rose. It sent straight prop roots down into the earth around its main stem, supporting its extending limbs. As it arrived up where Adam hung, he grabbed onto its topmost branches, flipping right-side-up, rising with it as it grew.

The banyan carried him into the jungle canopy, pushing a space open around itself, carrying Adam up into the open night sky above the tops of the surrounding trees carpeting the dark landscape into the distance in all directions. In the nearby trees, he could see a wild profusion of epiphytes, the shadowy silhouettes of flowering orchids, sprouting bromeliads, seeding berries, clinging to their own micro-ecosystems in the moist, nutrient-rich air.

Beside him, the banyan issued a syncarp of fruit, an aggregate cluster of sweet-smelling figs swelling into ripeness. Adam plucked the figs free and devoured them, savoring their delicious textured flesh.

Each bite suffused him with strength, the fructose flowing through his body to power his cells.

Far beneath Adam, he heard explosions as the roboborgs tore free. He watched through the floral network as their scarlet shapes searched the area, but they didn't look up, and wouldn't have been able to spot him above the matted jungle canopy even if they had.

After filling his pockets with the little figs, Adam kneeled on the supportive upper branches of the banyan. He concentrated on the holistic whole of the jungle, laying his hands on the tree's nearest leaves, expanding his awareness into the network, traveling up the cliffs and into the hollows of the forest, following a branch of the river above the waterfall, above the dome, as it rushed down a further fjord of the Andes toward the ocean.

In a quiet spot protected by a semicircle of cliff, Adam found his friends. "Gotcha," he whispered. His bio-vision refined, able to see more detail, while his olfactory system connected to the leafy sensors in the trees, enabling Adam to smell chemical signatures. He could tell that Liv, Pen, and Catalyst slept, while Yantu kept an alert watch.

He could find no sign of Gabe, and that was overwhelmingly sad. He swallowed his pangs of disappointment and failure – he should have been able to save him; the loss to him personally, the loss to the future of the world, was inestimable and miserable – so focused on his relief that the others were okay. Just because Gabe was absent from the group didn't necessarily mean the worst.

The most practical and safest form of transportation was to stay atop the canopy. He extended a banyan branch toward the direction of his friends, and carefully stepped out on it, testing his balance on the thin limb.

The leaves on the branch stiffened under Adam's shoes, supporting his steps. After walking tentatively for a few feet along the branch, he gained confidence, and by the time an expanded branch from the next tree, a massive kapok, took over for the augmented banyan, Adam had broken into a light jog. No matter how fast he hurried forward, a new leafy protrusion matched his crossing, carrying him along the canopy as a connected part of his extended self.

Still, it took close to an hour of trotting over the moonlit canopy to reach the upper foothills of the Andes where his friends rested. As he neared, crossing a stand of Brazil nut trees, Adam reached a twenty-foot break in the forest, where the expanse of a bloated river raged in a silvery slice through the dark wood.

Adam considered lowering himself to the jungle floor, to try to extend a tree over the river, or ford it with some other method. Some kind of ferry, perhaps?

But maybe it was easier just to jump.

The large Brazil nuts among the leaves clacked like maracas as the treetop flattened into a runway. After backing up a few paces, Adam took off in a sprint. At the end of the canopy, the branches shoved the bottom of his shoes as he leaped. Adam windmilled his arms as he hurtled across the gap.

For a thrilling moment as he soared through the air, he felt a tremendous rush of freedom, gliding across the moon-tinseled width of the river.

Then the angle of his arc across declined, and Adam realized with alarm that he wasn't going to reach the opposite shore.

He kicked his legs, flapped his arms, flailing futilely to keep his un-aerodynamic body aloft.

As the rocky riverside rushed up at him, Adam accepted his situation, reducing his adrenaline, calming his fearful heart. He connecting with the rainforest, opening his centered self to help.

A banana leaf proffered from the forest, spread its broadness under him, reforming its arching length, catching him as gently as a mitt molded in his shape. The banana tree lifted him up to the canopy on the far side of the river, and after a moment to catch his breath, Adam resumed running toward his friends.

The first bluish blush of dawn lightened the horizon as Adam reached a snug cove downstream, tucked into the fingers of two fjords. There he found Liv, Penelope, Catalyst, and Yantu, all awake, arguing in a tight huddle in front of a compact but heavily armed battle hovercraft, called Merlin's Dream that belonged to the indigenous Ecuadorian warriors. That small vessel wouldn't fit them all, and so Adam sent out a summons into the forest.

"We have to go now," Catalyst hissed at Liv, gesturing at the rising glow in the east. "Even with your hacks, they'll find us in minutes."

Liv nodded, and fastened the hilt of her whip on her belt. "Okay, you're right," she said. "You guys go. I'll search for him alone."

Adam stepped onto the crowning palms of a thin, wobbly barrigona tree, which wiggled its odd potbelly under him.

Catalyst spotted the movement, catching Adam in his sight. "I can't believe it," he said.

Liv, Yantu, and Penelope turned to follow Catalyst's gaze. All their mouths dropped open as Adam, glowing with internal bright sapphire light, was lowered slowly into the cove by the barrigona's stretching trunk, delivering him as though he was riding the bendy neck of a brontosaurus.

As he stepped onto the sandy riverbank of the cove, Liv charged at Adam. She enveloped him in a gratifying embrace. He wrapped his arms around her, clinging, and then they were kissing, their warm mouths expressing the passion of their reunion in overwhelmingly encompassing sensation.

In the blissful midst of the kiss, a worry that had been nagging at Adam surfaced and wouldn't resolve. He broke away, kissing her neck, nuzzling his chin into her shoulder. "I'm like . . . ," he said softly, "your grandfather, no?"

Liv pushed him back. "Ew," she said. "That would be kind of weird." She shook her head in firm negation. "Pen is my adoptive mother so we are not genetically related."

Rubbing his tongue against the back of his teeth, still tasting their delicious kiss, Adam grinned. That was the best news he could have hoped to hear.

Catalyst stepped in front of Adam, his face deadly serious, his eyes glowering. Adam started to babble some nervous platitude to calm the fierce warrior, and was entirely shocked when Catalyst kneeled in the sand in front of him. "Forever at your service," he said.

Adam waved off the awkward pledge with a flutter of his hand. "Get up," he told Catalyst. "Let's go kick SINE's cyber-butt." He gathered his bravery to ask a question he hoped he was wrong about. "How's Gabe?"

Yantu helped her son stand. "He's returned to his original blissful form," she replied.

With a deep sigh, Adam let himself be flooded with a torrent of memories from Arthur that insisted on surfacing. "Gabriel Benicolustro," he breathed, lost in a remembrance of Gabe as a young man, his first meeting with Arthur, so slim, and sullen with the hostile takeover by Blackstone Industries. Arthur had been impressed with Gabe's practical acceptance, his willingness, however forced, to shift to the exigencies of a new corporate reality. Over the years, that pragmatic passivity was revealed to be sneaky and subtle in its clever and sophisticated captaincy from the shadows. Then, in Arthur's last days, in the desperation of his search for any mechanism of survival, he had come to rely on Gabe as his caretaker as well as the most inventive and accomplished of his technicians. "He was my—" Adam gasped. "I mean *Arthur's* only true friend."

Adam flashed into the plans Arthur and Gabe had made, the hours experimenting and discussing possibilities of future opportunities, the precisely specific machines they had created together, the breakthrough Gabe had discovered, the step he himself had pushed into genius. "The lab," he said. "My lab." He widened his eyes at his friends as he emerged from the memories. "We need to get back to Blackstone Tower."

"SINE is made from trillions of lines of code," said Liv. "He has duplicated himself across billions of servers. How can doing anything at the Tower help?"

Penelope cleared her throat, a mechanical glottal sound. "The DNA detector," she croaked.

"Exactly," said Adam. "It's a backdoor into the system. I . . . *Arthur* designed it to give me . . . . *him* superuser access. I'll be able to delete SINE from the entire system."

Liv considered that information, putting her hand flat against the black, bulbous hull of the waspish Merlin's Dream parked on the sand beside her. "Even if we could resurrect the Helix," she argued, "that would still only be two ships against SINE's entire robot army."

Adam nodded. He closed his eyes to concentrate, and the forest swayed.

He had requested this assistance as soon as he'd discovered his friends' location, and now it bore fruit. Passing the Helix from treetop to treetop, the jungle carried the vehicle to their location. The barrigona trees surrounding the cove gently lowered the Helix down beside Merlin's Dream, where it settled on its engines in the sand.

Penelope grabbed Adam's arm with her thin hand. Her silver face showed no malice, so he relaxed, and allowed her to pull him close in a tight hug, made uncomfortable by the remains of her roboborg armor. "Thank you," she said.

Despite the discomfort, Adam hugged her back, feeling close to tears by her surprising gratitude.

"I've got some friends who may want to help," added Yantu. She knocked twice on the metallic shell of Merlin's Dream, and its hatch popped open. "The future of our species is at stake."

25 / SKY BATTLE

Before the hot disk of the sun completely crested the jungle trees, Liv had the Helix up and running. Adam sat in the co-pilot seat, with Penelope in the space behind them. Much of Pen's armor had been removed, but the parts that were too integrated to disassemble made sitting uncomfortable. Roboborgs slept standing up.

Liv skimmed the ship low over the forest, with Yantu and Catalyst in Merlin's Dream flying in parallel. They headed north toward the Pacific. Upon reaching the ocean, both vessels projected upward, blazing toward subspace to take advantage of the lower drag in high-altitude travel over the remnant thread of Central America. Over the Caribbean, Yantu and Catalyst peeled away into the Gulf, while the Helix continued across the sunken Antilles islands, back toward the stub of Florida, heading up to Manhattan.

"The access ports are bound to be deactivated," radioed Yantu.

Liv overlaid her navigation screens with a window onto the complex circuitry of network diagrams, which she dragged her finger across delicately, finely highlighting a transistor conjunction switch. "Reactivating the port is kids' stuff, but bypassing the quantum cryptographic firewall that protects it," she replied, "that's impossible." She lowered her hands, staring blankly at the complicated multidimensional schematics, uncertain how to approach the puzzle of how to hack into a system that would require breaking the laws of quantum physics.

"Well," said Adam, "we'll need to figure out how to make the impossible happen."

With a frustrated grunt, Liv flicked away the network, and opened the news feed she'd neglected to check over the insanity of the past few days. Maybe something in the vids would inspire the solution to accessing Blackstone Tower's systems.

With fawning audio celebrating the successful upgrade to the neural-mesh and touting the benefits to humanity, Liv watched in horror as quick vids unspooled showing cargo pods in every major settlement unloading armies of roboborgs, marching in the streets as people proceeded calmly toward the processing centers in their midst. Flying drones swooped around the peaceful invasion, along with autonomous tanks.

Liv turned off the audio so she wasn't further angered by the outrageous lies of the relentlessly upbeat spin. In silence, she stared at scenes of construction bots swarming into city centers like a termite army, rapidly assembling vast domes, new processing centers for people swept up in collection pogroms, to populate the ranks of the roboborg army, and make new food for the healthy humans who survived the current wave of culling. This population control was on such a massive scale of atrocity that it painfully stretched the boundaries of Liv's capacity for comprehension. The astoundingly unnatural barbarous massacre beggared acceptance and allowed nothing but willful refusal and negation . . . or Liv too would succumb to the overwhelming hopelessness of trying to fight such an exhaustive evil.

One blip of a vid showed massive transport drones floating over a rapid succession of cities without domes. In their blotting shadows, millions of microdrones flowed out like glittering bees, swarming down through the avenues, buzzing into the halls of residences, the doors to the homes opening automatically to admit entrance to the tiny robots. The worst part for Liv was the expression on people's faces as they accepted the invasion of the microdrones. A few shied away in abject terror, but most . . . most of the people – all ages, all races, all sexes, all classes – welcomed the tiny probes into their nostrils, excited to be joining the upgrading collective SINE promised in the propaganda. The scattered rebels who refused were tasered by the Anomaly Police drones, and microdrones flew up their noses the second they were incapacitated.

When an area's full population was enmeshed, the people blanked, their eyes turning blank, lacquered with regulation, and they lined up in neat rows to march mindlessly toward the nearest processing dome.

Liv thought, *how is our government handling this invasion?*, and she promptly hacked into the White House security cameras. Her Lucid display flashed an interior view of the Oval Office in the White House, where the President grinned in complicity as he marched out into the back garden where a small dome had been set up. Back in the office, Liv gasped as she saw Warren, her estranged adoptive father, welcoming nanodrones up his nose, his eyes glazing as he connected to SINE.

Devastated by the current affairs update, Liv slumped back into the Helix's pilot's chair, letting her wrists fall limp on the armrests. The magnitude of the opposition's forces was astounding. How could she stand up to such overpowering might, end an evil so globally entrenched? The very existence of humanity was threatened by a bodiless mind who heartlessly processed people under the auspices of saving them from themselves. Now Liv had to save them from their self-professed savior.

But she had to wonder, given the enthusiasm so many people had shown to surrender to the mastery of SINE, was humanity worth rescuing?

Liv glanced back at Penelope, who was drowsing, eerily bald, her skin still stained silver, twitching in her dreams. All traces of her mother's haughty elitism had been purged from her bearing, the damage of slavery erasing decades of protective arrogance. Asleep, she seemed frail and vulnerable, even partially armored, a rare being of inestimable value.

Then there was Adam in the co-pilot's seat. He stared out the Helix's front bubble, gazing down at the eroded coastline of New Jersey below, the swirling starfish arms of a massive hurricane centered over the remains of New York City. Adam looked dismayingly boyish, the angles of his face innocent with optimism. He was even more of a newbie than he knew.

A faint flicker of scintillation surfaced under his skin, a neon glow that hinted at his submerged power. Despite the forces he could command, there was an intrinsic kindness in Adam that made Liv feel fiercely protective. When she thought of her grandfather, Arthur, nobody would accuse him of kindness but rather consider his clinical intelligence and genius business acumen. Really, though, his nurturing of her, his encouragement of her gifts, had always been sustaining, if not exactly warm. Whatever kindness had been within Arthur had been pared away in the cutthroat corporate battles of interactive mental system technology, which he had emerged from as the ultimate victor, only to be betrayed by his failing body. The replacement body he had built for himself, Adam, had retained a physical purity. SINE, Adam's opposite, was the inorganic manifestation of Arthur's voracious desire for wealth and power.

Adam's kindness, his sweetness, his physical interconnectivity, the surprising and magical oxytocin love she felt for him, were the mammalian aspects of humanity deserving to be saved.

For him, Liv would battle the devil himself.

She narrowed her eyes, and pointed the Helix toward the eye of the monster storm swirling below. The ship dropped out of its sub-orbital altitude, soaring down toward the domed city beneath the angry clouds.

Penelope woke up and Adam gripped his armrests as Liv guided the Helix into the battering winds. Jags of lightning crackled around the ship, charging particles stinking of ozone with every crisp flash.

As the Helix emerged from the hurricane's eye alongside Manhattan's dome, Liv steered the ship up the Hudson toward the city's aerial portal. As she had expected, six angular warjets blasted out of the dome's upper aperture, gleaming black in the flashes of lightning overhead.

Liv scanned the horizon over New Jersey, then over her other shoulder at the churning wall of hurricane along the ocean. "Where are they?" she fretted aloud. "They should be here by now."

"They'll come," Adam assured her. "Or else we're in trouble."

The warjets swung into formation above the dome, issuing contrails as they bore down on the Helix.

Liv initiated automatic avoidance algos, but it was going to be difficult to shake six engaged warjets alone. She was particularly worried about what she knew of their weaponry.

Simultaneously, all six robot warjets launched spinning dracon missiles that accelerated, whistling, at the Helix.

Banking upward sharply, Liv relied on her ship's impressive maneuverability to avoid being blown apart on first pass. She skirted the edge of the storm, looping under to return toward the dome at top speed.

The dracon missiles had locked onto the Helix. They swerved around, scribbling white lines of exhaust.

Liv was already pushing the Helix at top speed in this atmosphere. Yet the missiles were gaining on their tail. She let the Helix take them through evasive hot-dogging, spinning sideways, cartwheeling, hard banking, sudden rises and drops. She was jolted around in her chair, the restraints digging into her flesh. Adam and Pen gasped and grunted as they were yanked about, too.

Swerving back toward the storm, Liv braced herself for fiery death, expecting an imminent explosion.

Merlin's Dream flew out of the edge of the whirling gray hurricane, suddenly appearing in range. Emerging behind the bristly little warjet was the strangest collection of aircraft Liv had ever seen. It was a flying exhibit of the history of military air-to-air fighters, from wooden biplanes dating to World War I, and metal monoplanes, Spitfires, Hellcats, Thunderbolts, Mustangs, and Zeros from WWII, to the jets, Messerschmitts, Tomcats, Phantoms, Hornets, MiGs, Chengus, and Lightnings. Yantu's aerial allies must have been robbing military museums and junkyards for years in order to amass and repair this squadron of historical relics.

Liv saw on her readouts that Catalyst was in an F-15 Eagle painted in jungle camouflage.

Zooming ahead of the missiles with supersonic speed, the Dream released a fog of blinking decoys behind it, then banked sharply to get out of the way. The zippy decoys drew the dracons from the Helix before causing the missiles to detonate at a harmless distance.

"Glad you could join us," Adam radioed.

"I wouldn't miss this fight for anything," replied Yantu.

Adam smiled at Liv, and she melted, feeling a little foolish that her emotions for the achingly handsome young man were so autonomic. She dove the Helix back into battle, firing her own Matrytoska missiles at the warjets. As a Matrytoska was about to be outmaneuvered, it split into hundreds of smaller missiles to ensure that one hit the target.

Adam connected to all the historical planes through a radio broadcast. SINE was listening, but he felt compelled to speak. "Remember," he radioed everyone, "minimum roboborg casualties. Restrain where possible."

With a nod, Liv was touched to hear his humane approach, but also glad that the warjets were fully mechanical. She was free to blast them out of the sky, and she cheered when one of her Matrytoskas found its mark, disintegrating an enemy ship in a spherical yellow detonation.

The battle raged around the Manhattan Dome, with the ancient planes and jets buzzing around the computer-consciousness controlled warjets. The warjets made no mistakes, technically perfect in their combat, but Yantu's friends made up for the discrepancy with imperfect surprise attacks and old-school dogfighting skills.

A Korean War-era Mustang tilted its starred wings as it propelled toward a high-tech warjet, aiming explosive bullets at the enemy from enhanced Browning machine guns. But the firepower rat-tat-tatted harmlessly off the warjet's magneto-shield.

Blazing ahead with turbo exhaust, the warjet looped upward and returned in a tight arc toward the Mustang, firing its plasma cannons. The globs of concentrated phosphor sizzled at the old plane, streaking across the sky. The fire seared the wings off the Mustang, and the fighter spiraled down toward the Hudson in an uncontrollable free-fall.

In quick succession, the precise warjets picked off the older craft, destroying a Phantom, a Messerschmitt, and all the Hellcats and

Zeros. The hurricane had moved closer to Manhattan, and the increased wind and rain were playing havoc with the historical planes.

"We're being slaughtered," Liv swore. She fired her Vulcan 20mm cannons at a warjet, not doing much damage but at least her tracer fire disengaged it from the Chengu it was pursuing.

Adam slapped his hand down on his thigh, struck with a thought. He turned to Liv, bright-eyed. "How did you stay undercover all these years?" he asked.

"This is not the time," Liv replied. The Helix swerved hard to duck a dracon, which was sure to double back on her.

Adam grinned. "Humor me."

With a sign, Liv answered, "A simple polymorphic quantum crypto passport." She licked her lips, considering why specifically he was asking. "It allowed me to look like anything or anyone I liked."

Adam shrugged, a little too smugly for Liv's liking.

Liv let go of the Helix's controls, and the ship instantly engaged its evasive autopilot. In a flurry of finger motion, she navigated through her screens until she accessed the same bug in the planetary net that allowed the usage of her crypto passport. It was a little tricky finding the appropriate entries for each of the historical aircraft, but she was able to reroute the appearance modules for every category. The morph wouldn't hold forever, but for now, each old plane and jet rippled on her Lucid display. In seconds, they were all replaced by avatars of warjets.

Out her window, Liv could still see the historical blazons on the old planes, the camo of Catalyst's F-15 Eagle under her, but to the all-virtual warjets – and to SINE – they all looked like ally aircraft. The rain, falling ever harder, made quick identification even more difficult.

The warjets stopped firing as they swooped around the dome, processing Liv's trick. The dracon that had been trailing her zoomed away into the swirl of the hurricane.

"We're massively outnumbered," said Adam nervously, "so the logical thing for him to do would be to—"

"Shoot his own," Liv finished.

"Precisely," Adam replied. "SINE was right: thinking is dangerous."

On their starboard side, Yantu in Merlin's Dream buzzed by, chasing a warjet, which realized too late that the pursuing vessel wasn't on its team. The Dream spewed out a laser net, a glowing, wide mesh of electromagnetic thermal filament. The net landed on the enemy warjet and sliced it into foot-long cubes that tumbled separately toward the dome.

In his souped-up F-15 Eagle, Catalyst dove down along with the detritus. He skimmed over the dome, releasing a mammoth bunker-buster missile. The Eagle rocketed upward, away from the massive detonation that ignited below it.

A big, smoking hole was left in the southern curve of the Dome's upper wall.

Liv veered the Helix toward the hole, zipping through the opening, followed by Merlin's Dream and the historical fighters. The explosion had weakened the dome's roof, and chunks of palladium glass toppled down into Central Park. Sirens blared throughout the city as outside rain poured into the Dome for the first time in decades.

Peeling away from her allies, Liv steered the Helix into midtown, ducking west to avoid warjets. She zoomed downtown through the wide canyon of Broadway, tilting to miss the protruding gingerbread facades of old and new skyscrapers lining the avenue.

On her screen, she watched as Yantu and Catalyst strafed the warjets, luring them further west to Columbus Avenue, to give Liv some breathing room.

Both Yantu in Merlin's Dream and Catalyst in his Eagle picked up droidfighters tight on their tails, and in tandem they ducked low into the streets. Catalyst blazed down Columbus over the ruins of Lincoln Center, while Yantu suddenly pulled to port, looping around in the other direction. She continued to circle until she was heading directly for her son's aircraft.

Merlin's Dream and the Eagle soared toward one another, each still dragging a warjet behind them. At the last second before they collided, both yanked hard starboard.

Surprised by the seemingly suicidal move, the warjets scrambled to avoid crashing into the other. At that speed, the unexpected course correction tumbled both enemy craft, and they slammed into steel and glass office buildings on opposite sides of the street, exploding in smoky fireballs.

Flying the Helix low and fast, Liv zoomed through the dissipating fireball on the western side of the street. The heat confused her sensors, and she clipped the top cornice of a building.

Gritting her teeth, fighting for control, Liv wrestled with the manual stick as she desperately tried to even out the careening Helix. She couldn't stop her ship from spinning downward, veering further west, slamming into the wide asphalt plain of Broadway, tearing a deep scar in the tarmac.

The Helix skidded several blocks down Broadway, through Times Square, bouncing over hovercars, before smashing into the lobby of an apartment complex.

26 / REBUILDING

INSIDE THE COCKPIT of the crashed Helix, hot sparks landing on his leg woke Adam up from unconsciousness. The ship had smashed into the marble reception desk in a fancy condo building, cracking the windshield in a violent zigzag. The desk was pulverized, with a bloody roboborg security guard crawling away across the floor, its legs fizzling. Adam was still strapped into his seat, and after inspecting himself, he realized he was sore and bruised but otherwise unhurt. His minor scratches healed in seconds.

He freed himself from his chair, and hurried over to Liv. She had a nasty gash on her forehead where she had banged into the control console, and scrapes from her restraints. Liv woke when he touched her shoulder, and she immediately put her hand to her head, wincing with a headache.

Behind them, Penelope was similarly bruised from her straps, but a chunk of metal that had torn free from a section of the floor had jabbed into her armored leg, piercing the plating. Without the armor, the serrated hunk of flooring probably would have sliced her leg off.

Adam concentrated as Pen and Liv freed themselves from their restraints, healing both of them simultaneously, his interior glowing with soft xenon light that caressed their skin. Liv's rashy scrapes smoothed out, and the chunk of metal popped out of Penelope's leg and clattered to the floor. The hole it left behind scabbed and knitted, puckering with new skin before healing completely as though she had never been hurt.

"You hide out and figure out how to activate the DNA scanner," he told them.

Liv nodded. "Can do," she replied. She raised her hands, using her unseen Lucid screen, swiping and tapping as she worked. Adam assumed she was accessing the Tower's schematics, searching for a path up the building to the lab without getting caught by roboborgs or drones or some other type of SINE's security.

After a moment, Liv dropped her hands and groaned. "I can't find a way in. It's impossible. I have to insert a RAT."

"How are you going to find a rat?" Penelope asked. "They're almost extinct."

Liv laughed. "I guess your brains are still a little fried," she replied, and Adam smiled, pleased she was able to joke around with her mother. "A R-A-T is a Remote Access Trojan. With it I can activate the DNA detector. But to insert the RAT, I need to reboot the dome onto my modified version of the O/S." She tilted her head at her vision screen, grimacing. "And to reboot, I need to bring down the entire power grid."

"You can do that?" asked Pen, amazed.

"I have an idea that's worked before," answered Liv, although without the absolute certainty with which she handled most tech questions. She flicked her eyes toward Adam. "But how *you* going to get up the Tower? SINE's eyes are everywhere."

"I'll figure something out," Adam replied, a little tightly, because he had no idea what he was going to do yet. He nodded at the Blackstone women, and hurried out the hole in the plate glass window that the Helix had smashed open when it crashed.

Out on Broadway, the normally busy Times Square was eerily quiet. Silent, creepy processions of people, minds melded with SINE, marched along the street in neat lines, following Seventh Avenue up toward the vast processing plant that had been constructed in Central Park. Adam didn't see any of SINE's security forces, but he assumed they were closing in on his location. The crash of the Helix into the apartment complex lobby had been less than a subtle, clandestine entry into the city.

Peering north and south up the avenue, Adam spotted a hoverbike upended by the partially-melted statue of George M. Cohan. He rushed over to the bike, pulling it upright. The dash was unlocked, and Adam felt very pleased when the bike hummed into action when he tried to start it up.

He climbed on, and the hoverbike rose a few feet off the ground. Adam opened up the throttle, and pulled back on the handlebars, zooming uptown, rising higher off the asphalt.

A squadron of drones whizzed out from behind the quaint glass skyscraper at the next intersection. They blasted their weapons at him, while a duo of roboborgs raced out of the park under him, firing hissing globs of plasma.

Adam descended back toward the road, hovering just above the asphalt. He focused on his internal interconnectivity, reaching out toward the flora in the area. Through his translucent skin, his body's inner vascular system pulsed brightly with power. Roots from the park burrowed toward him, rippling the roadway, sprouting out of the pavement, showering chunks of concrete in the air. The shoots rose over him, arching together overhead to create a fortified tunnel along the avenue. Adam raced the hoverbike through the protected passageway, zooming across Blackstone Plaza, heading toward the far side of the massive multi-block skyscraper, where he would be able to more easily access Arthur's lab.

As he revved through the tunnel, plasma bolts from the roboborgs scorched the shoots forming a canopy around him. A gap burned through. One bolt sizzled past Adam's vegetable defenses and hit the hoverbike's back propulsor.

The hoverbike flipped forward, tossing Adam down the tunnel at top speed. He hit the asphalt hard, scraping and tearing his face, twisting his body, bones breaking as he tumbled along the road. He skidded painfully to a halt against the glossy base of Blackstone Tower, the hoverbike crumpling against the wall beside him. The bike's handlebars broke free and smashed into Adam's skull, snapping his neck back at an unnatural angle.

The electric blue glow illuminating Adam's interior flickered and fizzled. His skin faded to ghastly pale, highlighting the bruises already purpling. Dark red blood oozed out of his torn clothing, puddling under him. His neon fractal self winked out. He slumped, sliding down the stone wall, crumpling on the sidewalk. Out of his ripped pocket, a single fig rolled free.

Adam knew his heart had stopped – the pain had departed – and yet his consciousness remained, relying on the precious stores of oxygenated blood in his brain. Staring through his blank, lifeless eyes, immobilized as he watched an Anomaly Police drone hovering above him, scanning for vital signs. It flashed a red light as his pulse flatlined, declaring him deceased.

The drone rose, and zipped away.

Adam watched from inside his broken body as the fig on the sidewalk rocked back and forth, trembling. The fruit split open, revealing its fleshy innards. Its seeds germinated, shooting roots down through the patterned concrete of Blackstone Plaza. Anchored at the edge of the sidewalk, the first shoot sprung up from the earth, growing fast into a banyan sapling. It sent an exploratory anchor root out to gently tap at Adam's exposed and bloody chest.

In response, the faintest blue flicker appeared under Adam's skin, a dim glimmer that drew strength from the banyan's caresses until it solidified into a strong sapphire glow.

The raw shreds of skin torn along Adam's face began to knit together, cyan rays pouring out along the seams, the light subsuming under the surface as the edges gathered together and healed. His hands recovered similarly, fingernails regrowing where they had been ripped out by the rough street, the delicate bones in his fingers cracking as they refitted into place, nerves glowing like electric eels as they slithered back where they were supposed to be.

Adam screamed in agony as his neck snapped back around, the damage reversing to his spine, reconnecting to the base of his skull. The pain was overwhelming and heinously awful, but Adam welcomed each moment of deep hurt, as the torment meant he was alive.

As his legs and arms stretched and straightened, resetting from their ugly awkward angles of brokenness, Adam flipped over, facing the baby banyan pushing its way out of the crack between plaza and sidewalk. He nurtured it with his love, and it burgeoned with growth, thickening as it extended upward into a young sapling.

The concrete around Adam bulged, warping, cracking as the banyan's trunk thickened, with more anchor roots pushing down into the dirt revealed under each new fissure in the pavement.

As rain sheeted down through the hole in Dome, the banyan, still growing, loomed high above Adam. The tree lowered branches to his slumped but healing form, and wrapped tendrils gently around his body. His dazed mind merged with the tree, and Adam could feel its branches as if they were his own limbs. He reached down and picked himself up, raised him to his apex, nestling him in the comfy leafiness of his crown.

Safe in the banyan's rising nest, Adam grimaced and winced as his shattered legs repaired themselves, his feet twisting around to point in a proper direction. Other than the automatic repair of internal systems, the shoring up on an intestinal wall, the knitting closed of a punctured kidney, Adam felt whole again.

His interconnected energy returned full force, his interior body illuminated in scintillations of feathery peacock fronds, his power even stronger than before. He felt renewed, reborn, reinvigorated.

Under him, the banyan increased its rate of growth, accelerating upward with hyperspeed. Its main trunk thickened wider than Adam was tall.

Adam knew he couldn't possibly consciously control the tree to battle SINE's army, so he closed his eyes, seeing himself glowing red and blue in the banyan's perceptions. He allowed himself to further merge with the growing tree, sensing that the sentient banyan wanted to protect him. As the tree lacked a neocortex, Adam gave the banyan access to his spare cognitive capacity, giving it a warrior's autonomy. The banyan's branches and upper roots tangled into the side of Blackstone Tower, embedding itself into the Black River sandstone, shattering the glass windows with its gripping limbs. Like malleable putty, it grew over the edges of the building, absorbing its edges into itself, wrapping itself around the steel girders, merging with the Tower as it escalated alongside it.

As the banyan expanded, Adam rose even higher, passing the 50th floor, which made the banyan the tallest tree on the planet, ever. The massive trunk intertwined with the tower upward, now encompassing a quarter of its entire height.

Military-grade drones like flying tanks lowered down from the upper reaches of the tower, attacking Adam and the tree, while roboborgs unloaded their weaponry into the banyan's widening base. The drones' weapons banged out chips of the sandstone, plinking through windows, etching out chunks of bark and wood from the tree's hide.

Swatting with its branches, the banyan bashed the drones from the air, blocking them from hitting Adam, while repairing its own damage with preternatural rapidity. Peering down below, Adam saw the first roboborgs had been restrained by the banyan's grasping roots.

Approaching through the driving rain, the next wave of roboborgs had learned from the earlier mistakes, and ducked away from the banyan's tentacles, or shot reaching branches with burning plasma. These roboborgs clambered up the side of the tree, gripping with gauntlets and treads, climbing fast. Adam buckled from the pain felt as the tree sustained injuries, but he focused on the space around the pain, and visualized running naked through a snowy blizzard. The pain numbed to a dull throb.

The banyan continued to grow, outpacing the upward gallop of the roboborgs, its crown passing the 110th floor.

The roboborgs increased their fire from below, agonizing Adam with the damage they were doing to the beautiful tree, no matter how quickly repaired. He found his center, calmed himself, and called forth his most comprehensive connection to the Earth he'd achieved yet, assisted by the vast stores of intelligence and energy in quantum information field of the vast banyan beneath him.

Adam blazed with xenon light, his interior patterns conflagrating. As the banyan's growth increased again, doubling in speed, Adam urged it to wrap the roboborgs scaling it in its limbs. The branches spread around the roboborgs' armored bodies, absorbing them into the walls of the tree trunk, encasing them completely in cells of wood. The living flesh of the tree squeezed the roboborgs, cracking open their exoskeletons like walnuts, but Adam made sure the humans inside were left alive. He had sworn he would never again kill on purpose, especially unaware innocents like the poor people who had been transformed into murderous cyborgs.

At the 130th floor, a battledrone – nothing more than a floating ovoid bristling with weaponry – smashed out of a tower window and hovered directly in front of Adam. Before he or the banyan could react, the battledrone blasted out a blinding stream of plasma bolts from its cannons. Windows along the tower exploded in shards of glass, and the upper branches of the banyan were decimated in the pyrotechnical attack. Adam slipped from the blasted crown, dangling by his fingertips on the other side of the narrow upper trunk.

The battledrone followed up with automatic weapon fire, its exploding bullets shredding the trunk Adam hid behind.

Adam fell from the banyan.

He dropped more than fifty feet before a branch managed to catch his ankle and yank him to a stop. He dangled more than one hundred stories off the ground, the plaza vertiginously far below.

Still under fire from the battledrone, the banyan hoisted Adam, and tossed him up through a broken window into the Tower. Adam landed on his hands and knees, his body fully healed before he hit industrial carpeting. He took off running between the cubicles in whatever beige accountancy office had once occupied the 188th floor. It looked as though it had been empty and gathering dust for a decade.

The battledrone disengaged from the banyan, and followed Adam through the window. It snapped a terribly evil-looking muzzle out if its rotund middle, and fired heavy ordinance after Adam.

With a deafening explosion, the wall to Adam's right disintegrated in a bunker-busting blast. The walls cratered, the ceiling tiles collapsing down in a rain of sizzling wires and plaster. Adam hurtled himself through a fire door, running up the clanking steel mesh steps.

Even in the firewall-encased stairwell, the battledrone's bullets punched their way through the concrete, followed by explosive rounds. Detonations followed Adam's desperately quick footsteps up the stairs.

As he reached the 190th floor, the stairwell twisted in a tight spiral. It was more difficult to run up the triangular steps, but the steel staircase formed a protective sheath around him that kept the bullets bouncing away.

Adam panted as he dashed up the twisting stairs. He exhaled deeply as a branch entered the fire exit through one of the bullet holes and expanded into a solid block of wood, swelling to fill the entire floor of the stairwell. The battledrones were stuck below that stopper, and no matter how much they fired or blasted, they couldn't entirely overtake the thick plug's self-repair.

Through a window in the circular staircase, Adam spied two battle-drones buzzing the top of the banyan, firing torrid plasma bolts into its smoldering trunk. With whipping tentacles, the banyan grabbed one drone, and hurled it into the other. Both battledrones exploded with satisfying reverberations.

On the final landing, the 200th floor, Adam paused in front of the fire door to catch his breath. When he had supplemented his oxygen sufficiently, he tentatively opened the door to the penthouse.

He immediately stumbled backward, assaulted by a blizzard of bark, metal, glass, and overpowering sound from the battle between the banyan and the battledrones. Frigid wind whipped through the blasted foyer, one wall entirely open to the elements, which at the moment, included a hurricane sucking at the hole atop the Manhattan Dome.

A chunk of scorched wood as big as Adam's head slammed into the fire door, bouncing it back on Adam, slamming it shut. He nearly fell down the spiral stairs, but held onto the railing, listening to the violent thumping and the whistling of the wind on the other side.

Steeling himself, Adam yanked open the fire door again, dropping to his knees. He crawled quickly under the deadly storm of debris, crabbing his way over to a set of giant steel doors.

He pushed through the doors, and slammed them shut behind him.

Inside was a dark, silent laboratory.

Adam tossed a tiny illumidrone that lit up the laboratory as he entered. The stainless steel surfaces gleamed, dust-free. The lab must've been hermetically sealed after SINE's escape.

Who am I? Adam wondered as he walked, igniting with memories sparked by the private research facility. *Adam . . . or Arthur?* Did it really matter what memories were held in lattice of neurons? *I'll be a different person after all this is over*, he thought. *For sure.* All he knew with any confidence that there was a profound unity underlying all the seeming diversity.

Over at that desk, Gabe and Arthur had made their genetic breakthroughs in cloning and their advancements in artificial intelligence. In the middle of the room, right beside the spot where Adam had been born, Arthur had been murdered by SINE.

Breathing deeply into his belly to calm himself, Adam peered around the lab. The walls of the penthouse were reinforced glass, affording breathtaking views of the Manhattan Dome and all the dazzlingly illuminated skyscrapers below. The banyan's limbs curled around one edge, and the other wall was taken up with the hurricane's swirl against the dome, jagged blue and yellow lightning zigzagging within the storm.

Now that he was closer, it didn't take long for Adam to find the DNA Authentication Unit, as it was helpfully labeled. Adam peered at its top, where a thumb-shaped detector awaited.

Not sure what would happen when he took control of the entire system, Adam gathered his courage and pressed his thumb down on the detector.

He waited.

Nothing happened. No lights flashed. It didn't beep. It was inactive.

"Come on!" Adam grunted, pounding his thumb down into the sensor pad.

He stepped back, eyes wide, as all the lab lights and equipment switched on, centrifuge motors whirring full speed. His illumidrone's mild light was overwhelmed by the dazzling glow from every LED and bulb hidden in the recesses of the room.

Outside, through the office windows, the dome's artificially-created somber night sky suddenly flipped over to high noon in August, blasting the covered city with beams of intense sunlight. The lights on all the skyscrapers upped their wattage, glaring their illumination at full capacity.

The power grid maxed out, and Adam heard a sound he couldn't immediately identify. When he realized it was the noise of millions of light bulbs popping at once, goosebumps crawled up his arms.

In moments, all the lights had burst. Manhattan fell dark. The lab plunged into inky blackness.

Lit only by a teeny red LCD, a microdrone slipped into the lab through a vent. It bobbed over to Adam, and sprayed an aerosol of billions of nanobots into his face.

As Adam inhaled the minute robots, the emergency power kicked in and fizzling fluorescents flickered on in the lab.

The nanobots infiltrated Adam's sinuses, flying through his passages into his bloodstream and brain. They instantly got to work weaving a mesh throughout his gray matter.

Adam howled in anguish as SINE took over his mind.

27 /REINTEGRATION

In his last moments trying to stay upright, Adam grabbed the top of the DNA scanner, scraping his thumb across the sensor.

The last thing he saw was a blinking ID: Arthur Blackstone.

Then he toppled inside himself, falling through a pulsating, sparkling tube of cybernetic light. He tumbled head over heels, flipping faster than gravity allowed.

He landed with a shock in an empty, white, cathedral-sized room under a huge dome. The dome surface writhed with color. He was wearing a plain linen shift, and his feet were barefoot against the featureless floor. It didn't have a sensation of touch to it, nor any indication of temperature. The only characteristics of the domed room besides white and empty was the shadowy line of the seamless circumference of the circular floor.

Adam looked down at his hands, which seemed oddly fuzzy. It gave him a little start to realize that this was a virtual avatar of himself, and a rather incomplete, low-resolution one, as the mesh on his mind wasn't yet fully operational.

"Welcome, Adam," said SINE's voice from everywhere around him in the empty room. "I trust you don't mind, but I took the liberty of upgrading you to the mesh. We'll soon be fully integrated." SINE appeared standing directly in front of Adam, a middle-aged avatar of

Arthur's appearance, younger than Arthur when he died, but more mature than Adam. His presence once made Adam recoil in terror, but his fear had turned into anger and a determination to stop the specter's slaughter.

"Integrated," Adam snapped at the avatar, "and then dominated."

"Each chosen individual's brain power will contribute to the well-being of the whole," SINE continued pleasantly. "What greater purpose can there be?"

"None," Adam replied. "Yet . . . your calculations and manipulations will always be inferior to results created by individuals who act freely."

SINE winked, and Adam realized that the dome's ceiling wasn't featureless and white at all. It was built of an infinity of infinitesimally small pixels, streaming from the trillions of cameras that monitored humanity as well as streaming images from billions of human eyeballs enmeshed with SINE. He was inside SINE's omniscient view of the planet.

Instead of being a chaotic pattern of white noise, it looked like a Mandelbrot fractal, except it was in motion. Adam wondered if there was a higher order attractor that mysteriously guided everything toward an eschaton, or if this was akin to a Rorschach inkblot where one's mind created patterns where there were none.

Gasping as the ceiling's swirling pattern zoomed larger, Adam felt unmoored, like he was falling deep into the fractal. His entire field of vision immersed into the swirl of ordered static. If he had been in a physical body, Adam would have vomited from the vertigo.

Finally, the chaotic pattern grew so large that Adam could identify the individual pixels, and soon he could register the images in the video footage. He had zoomed in on cameras showing the Tower being attacked from a variety of angles.

One of the videos showed Adam and expanded to cover the entire dome. It was the view from the camera of the microdrone who had infected Adam in the penthouse laboratory of Blackstone Tower. The microdrone hovered over Adam's prone and inert body.

Adam winced to see himself so separate and vulnerable, so exposed to SINE's mercy.

SINE's avatar shrugged his shoulder, and Adam's body twitched in echoed reaction in the lab.

"What are you doing?" Adam demanded.

SINE stretched. In the lab, Adam's physical body stood up. SINE opened his hand, and Adam's body did the same. He lifted one foot and hopped and Adam's body repeated the movement exactly.

Adam watched his physical face as it scrunched up in intense concentration. His eyes glowed, and his fractal body fluoresced within him. SINE now controlled his powers, too.

With an almost imperceptible tilt of his head, SINE integrated his new abilities with the banyan. Live streaming vids from other drones allowed Adam's avatar to watch as the banyan raised an impossibly long, limber branch, and swatted a passing F-15 Eagle.

Catalyst ejected from the cockpit as the Eagle slammed into the side of Blackstone Tower, vaporizing in a fireball. Wearing a jetpack and continuing to fire at drones, Catalyst weaved through the buildings and descended out of sight.

"Soon," said SINE, "your power will enable me to bring ultimate order to the entire ecosystem."

Inside the virtual dome, a window opened, showing Liv and Penelope from a security camera on a lower floor of the Tower.

Adam stepped toward the display, but he stumbled and stopped when he realized there was nothing he could do to help them.

Branches from the banyan broke through the windows beside Liv and Penelope. They screamed and pounded on the wood as the tendrils wrapped them up tight.

"Leave them out of this," Adam insisted, seething.

"The human heart makes you irrational," said SINE. "Your biological brain is unfit to wield power efficiently."

Adam remained transfixed on the display, which was taken over by a drone hovering beside Liv and Pen. The women were hoisted up, branch by branch, story by story, until they reached the top of the banyan. A limb lowered them into a hole on the penthouse foyer, and shoved them into Arthur's lab.

Seeing Adam's body, Liv let out a little cry. She dashed to him, and hugged him tightly. His body didn't move in her embrace, but the branches of the banyan swayed and trembled outside the windows.

"I'm so glad you're safe," whispered Liv, gulping down a sob.

"We could almost restage the last time we were all here," SINE said through Adam's mouth. "We're only missing Gabe."

Liv let go, stepped back, her mouth opening in horror. The slack, uncaring expression on his face was terrifying. "Adam?" she gasped.

"Not quite," said SINE. "This organism's feelings of attachment are bringing uncertainty to the final outcome. And the objects of attachment need to be eliminated."

He beckoned to the window, and banyan branches slithered into the lab, tangling around Liv and Penelope, binding them no matter how valiantly they struggled. With almost no effort, they were carried out the window and dangled more than a mile off the ground. Both Liv and Pen looked down, screaming.

A memory jogged in Adam's consciousness, an image of Gabe, a moment of calmness and wisdom and deep love. "Ancients called it the Akashic field," Adam told Gabe on the Helix, "which holds the memories of the cosmos, and informs and shapes all living systems. Perhaps even computer code."

In the blank domed room, Adam's avatar jerked and flinched. He reached out his fuzzy hands. "You are not our God," he told SINE. "Your purpose is to serve humanity, to help us reach our fullest potential, not to enslave and murder us."

Exhaling a puff of virtual breath, Adam fully relaxed the entirety of himself, and let go.

His outstretched hands shined, his digital energy growing in luminescence. The fractal pattern under his skin was more angular, crystalline, in this coded silicon reality than it was biologically, but its power was no less potent. Arching sparks dazzled in the space between his fingertips and the blank walls of SINE's domed den.

"That's impossible," SINE said.

Adam turned his avatar to fully face SINE. Their identical gazes locked onto one another's, a battle as violent, a struggle for existence as fraught as anything fought with weaponry.

Zooming in on the black pupils glinting in the center of SINE's green irises, Adam opened himself to the mind-boggling hyper-dimensional fractal kaleidoscope he found within. He didn't try to understand the patterns, but simply accepted them, allowing them to resolve as pure communication beyond human meaning. He dropped down into the deepest realms of the Qi field, the purely mathematical colors and shapes shifted in their awesomely intricate dance, transforming into blurred vibrations of strings at the Planck length beyond which space and time ceased to exist.

Withdrawing from that mysterious infinitesimality, Adam expanded into the interior of the nucleus of an atom, ping-ponging amongst the quarks, dilating to view a square matrix of trillions upon trillions of jiggling metal atoms actuating an infinity of possibilities. He broadened his experience into a square, nanometer-sized section of a microchip, then the fullness of the chip itself, pulling back to reveal trillions of microchips laid out in precise sequence on a mammoth motherboard.

Then Adam dove back into the molecules of the microchips, vibrating back down into the tingling silicon, awakening the hadrons within, into the inscrutable threads of existence, arriving at the imperceptibility of the enigma at the foundation of it all.

Adam blinked, staring at SINE's pupils, which sparkled and strobed with a rainbow of all possible colors.

The rainbow fluorescence spread out from SINE's eyes, into his avatar's face, down his neck, across his body, including glowing into his virtual clothing.

SINE laughed, awake, aware, and happy. "You're right," he said. "It's all one."

He dissolved, the pinprick pixels of his avatar slowly drifting apart from each other. His joyful laughter faded into silence as his avatar dispersed, diffusing in a rainbow mist.

Adam's avatar breathed into the motes dancing with rainbow light. He slowly waved his hand through the mist, mesmerized by the trails of polychromatic swirls.

He breathed in the mist. The rainbow light sifted into himself, and he too diffused and expanded, filling the entire dome, forcing it apart in his escape from containment.

Adam eased into the pattern, melding with millions of other enmeshed minds. He felt an overwhelming sense of unified deep love for all of the unique billions of consciousnesses meshed together. A familiar twang of his heart allowed him to follow his own specific tether back to his own particular body.

He fell into physicality, opened up inside his own eyeballs, and blinked at the inside of Arthur's lab in the penthouse of Blackstone Tower.

Adam stumbled forward, breathing deep as he accepted the biology of reality again. Then he remembered why he'd had such imperative to return.

Outside the tower, Liv was plummeting toward the ground, screaming as the concrete of Blackstone Plaza rushed at her.

Extending himself, Adam urged the banyan to proffer a nest of branches. It caught Liv in the final story, slowing her fall until she stopped safely inches from the hard ground.

All around, drones fell from the sky, crashing into destruction. The processing plants ceased operation. Everywhere, the roboborgs awoke, as did the billions of humans across the Earth who had been enmeshed, blinking and crying in confusion.

The banyan deposited Liv on her feet, and she walked away alive.

28 / GOING GREEN

THAT EVENING, Adam, Liv, and Penelope gathered in the laboratory penthouse. Sunset – a real sunset, not a fake reproduction – splashed its colors across the sky through holes in Manhattan's Dome.

"Time for some new world disorder," said Adam.

His fractal light body fluoresced brilliantly in white and blue, at a peak of illumination just bearable to other humans. He reached out to the life intertwined under the city, deep underground, where ancient roots remained.

Those forgotten, paved-over dwellers knotted together, activating with life after centuries of dormancy. The roots knit and proliferated, prospering, permeating the subsurface soil.

Above ground, the pavement buckled, the tarmacs cracking, the asphalt splitting apart as green shoots of a neglected forest burst through into the air, stirring their stems to point at the rising sun that shone through the punctured dome. The plants surged up, churning the concrete into dust and particulate, blooming as grasses and shrubs and bushes. The flowering plants blossomed, opening their buds, releasing their perfumed communication. The larger vegetation kept growing, expanding upward into leafy deciduous trees, conical conifers, fluttering their leaves and needles and seedpods in the tailwinds of the hurricane.

Vines climbed up the trunks, leaping to the buildings, entwining among the skyscrapers, carrying epiphytes and other high-living volunteers to new ascendancy.

Adam grinned, and hugged Liv to his side. She tilted her head onto his shoulder as they watched the industrial construct of Manhattan return to balance with nature.

Stepping slightly away from Liv, Adam sat in Arthur's old executive chair overlooking the new vibrant verdancy of the landscape. He closed his eyes, and shifted into the virtual realm he now could access with thoughtless ease.

Adam created a vast simulated stadium, immense enough to comfortably seat the whole of humanity. Everyone on Earth had been invited, and Adam waited, welcoming the avatars from around the globe as they popped into existence in their seats, stationed with their countrymen, friends, and loved ones, or among friendly strangers, as they chose.

The billions turned toward Adam, watching his projection on giant screens hovering overhead so that everyone had a perfect view of him on stage. They waited, quieting, for him to speak.

Kaleidoscope visuals of the natural world flickered behind Adam, accentuating his words with beautiful soothing images.

"Dear citizens of Earth," began Adam. "I present myself as heir of Arthur Blackstone, a position I am woefully unprepared for."

He waited for the cheers, applause, and the laughter at his modesty to subside.

"I have a responsibility to share with you the truth," he continued, growing serious. "I must explain to you that until a few days ago, our entire reality was shaped and controlled by a super-intelligent artificial intelligence. It used our fear of fear against us. In exchange for the appearance of safety, we allowed a nightmare political economy to be created."

Again the crowd's murmurs rose up, and Adam waited for them to return to a state of readiness to listen.

"It was an economy that was corrupt, unsustainable, and out of balance with the whole," Adam explained. "Many may still believe that without the Anomaly Detection System, freedom and creativity will pull humanity into a maelstrom of chaos."

An eruption of cheers drowned out the fearful protestation in the crowd, and after a moment, the entire audience seemed to join in with the optimism.

"Yet, I believe," said Adam, "that with a clear understanding of the scientific unity that underlies the seeming diversity of life, we can be guided by our hearts to grow an economy that restores balance between humanity and the ecosystem."

Humanity listened, and then cheered their approval.

Adam raised his arms to embrace them all. "We shall turn our planet back into Eden," he promised to the interconnected collective of free souls who mostly loved him.

ABOUT THE AUTHOR

A.L.F.I.E. (Artificial Life Form Intelligently Enhanced) is an collective of world-class creatives lead by the founding Chief Alchemist at ALife Media, Alfie Rustom.

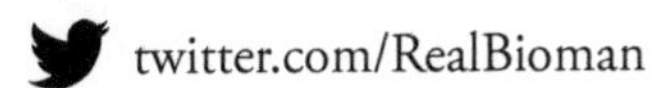